Mike,
you are THE man.
He

D0937432

SLEEPY WILLOW'S
BONDED SOUL

The Narcoleptic
Vampire Series

Such a
pleasure
meeting
you!

Vol. 1

Dicey Grenor

Enjoy the
book!

5-28-16

Janes

A Dicey Grenor Book

Published by Dicey Grenor
Independent Author
www.Diceygrenorbooks.com
Copyright © Dicey Grenor, 2011
All rights reserved

Model: Jaies Baptiste www.Facebook.com/Jaies
Photographer: Tim Rogers www.twrphotography.com
Designer: Najla Qamber Designs www.najlaqamberdesigns.com

ISBN-13: 978-1466322349

Dedicated to: My three babies.
The rest of the 4Ds.
Danny, Dasha, Daijon.
You make it all better.
You make it all worthwhile.

ACKNOWLEDGMENTS

Can't thank my beta readers enough:
Tasha Wilson, Tiffany Norris, Samantha Bagby.
You three devoured this book
And gave helpful feedback like ol' pros.
Most importantly, you supported my dream!

Thanks to BJ Green and Danny Norris:
For always being the voice of reason.
The aloof. The direct. The technical.
The exhorter.

Thank you for being supportive,
And ever-encouraging,
And for NOT reading this book,
Mom and Dad,
MiMi and PawPaw.
Trust me, you don't want to.
I'll write one for you one day.
Without vampires.

Thanks for all your help:
Kendralyn Jasper and Damiane Banieh.
Always good to have
Soldiers like you in my corner.

CHAPTER 1

The club became completely quiet as I lay in my coffin, tightly wrapped like a mummy from my crown to my toenails. I knew it was packed though because I heard pitter-pattering of at least seventy-five racing hearts. Some sat at tables, some stood along walls, and VIPs watched anxiously from the balcony.

Once I heard the smoke machine fogging the stage and felt the spotlight center on my coffin, I slowly raised the lid and held it there to give their human eyes a moment to adjust to the fog. To focus on me in the darkness.

Couldn't see Remi through the white wraps across my eyes, but I smelled him. Sensed his essence, his soul. He was alone at his usual table on the far left near the stage, wearing his usual intoxicating cologne. I smelled his cigarette in the ashtray and liquor in his glass. Knew I'd taste a hint of both in his blood later, but it would still be hot, thick and delicious.

I waited until the deejay started the music then slowly lifted my upper torso to Marilyn Manson's "You and Me and the Devil Makes 3". Planting my palm on the coffin's edge, I brought one stiffly wrapped leg up and then the other, draping them across the side facing the audience.

Spilling out of the coffin like running water, I left a trail of cloth behind and landed on the floor gracefully. Then I rolled and rolled in time to the music, gradually unraveling layers of cloth until various parts of my nudeness peeked through. The white cloth looked like puddles with overflowing water glowing against the black coffin and black floor.

My almond-shaped hazel eyes remained closed while I danced to the music and writhed on the floor, allowing my hands to explore first my plump breasts, then flat tummy, and lastly, my trimmed bush. I rolled again, allowing more cloth to fall away revealing more caramel brown skin.

After slowly spreading my knees apart, I teasingly undulated in front of patrons closest to the stage while lust oozed from their pores. They were entranced by the gyration of my hips, the rhythm of the music, the fantasy of sex and death.

My necrophilia clientele comprised of those aroused by corpses, death, near-death experiences, mutilation and…sometimes murder. Sometimes in self-inflicted circumstances. Knowing mummy wraps titillated them more than Victoria's Secret lingerie, I rolled around in the cloth, letting some drape around me loosely. It fed their frenzy, their passion. Gave them the illusion of death coming to life. Of living deadness.

Ironically, what they perceived as illusory was in fact, reality. The hallmark of my existence.

As the song ended, I lay across the coffin lid intimately, as if it were my lover, and licked long strokes across the surface. Then I moved seductively until I straddled the coffin.

In one swift motion, I pulled the wrap from around my head that released long black tresses unto my lower back and across my breasts. Leaning forward, I stretched until I got the dagger from my coffin bed and raised it skyward with both hands. I ground my hips across the lid as if I were fucking it and moaned loudly. When the music stopped, my moans took over, becoming the music, setting the tempo.

Remi's heart almost leaped through his chest with palpitations so loud, it must have been strapped to a microphone and amplifier. Since my finales were his biggest turn-ons, he'd make his way to a private room in back, if one was available, and jack off afterwards. He had enough social grace to do it in private, but at Pit of Hades Fetish Club, he really didn't have to. Here, there was no shame, no taboos.

Considering how often I'd performed sex and death scenes with guns, nooses, and swords, you'd think the audience would be ready for anything. But they gasped and screamed, and in some cases vomited, when I plunged the dagger's stainless steel blade into my chest. They'd known it was coming, yet they were still horrified and awed. And ready to fuck.

But it wasn't an act.

I grunted on impact. It hurt like a son-of-a-bitch, but I'd heal. Realism was most important in pulling off a death scene, after all.

Once I withdrew the dagger, I plunged it again, and then again, grunting from pain each time the blade went into my chest. The sound of the hilt slamming into my skin repeatedly seemed to echo throughout the club.

Slumping forward, I let my blood run down the sides of the coffin onto the floor, taking comfort in knowing Remi would replenish it later. I kept falling until I slid to the floor in a heap.

Bright flashes went off left and right as people snapped pictures. Security was everywhere frantically grabbing cameras, admonishing patrons. This was a no-photo-taking establishment unless you paid the club's photographer to take authorized still shots of or with entertainers in the designated booth. Performances were never recorded or photographed due to graphic content and patrons were never filmed unless they consented. The owner's respect for privacy gave patrons freedom to let their hair down and enjoy whatever deviant sex they were in to. Everyone knew the rules. You didn't get in without an invitation, signed contract and approved membership…and definitely no cameras. Violators had their memberships revoked immediately.

I liked the rule. It prevented patrons from having incriminating evidence of my supernatural powers. So far, everyone assumed I used fake blood and props. Didn't want anyone to start thinking otherwise and having proof to boot. They'd wonder how I recovered from fatal wounds night after night. I could be practicing witchcraft or be some other legal supernatural being. But if anyone happened to suspect I was a vampire, I would be clawing myself from a pile of shit as deep as the Grand Canyon with nothing but a fingernail file as my tool.

Suddenly, I felt strange. My fingertips numbed, my tongue dried. I began trembling and feeling light-headed, but I wasn't alarmed. It wasn't a reaction to me stabbing myself. It was my illness, my body's inability to regulate its sleep cycle. My narcolepsy with a side of cataplexy was about to carry me away to a deep, short sleep.

Considering I was at the end of my set, it was good timing.

Hades was silent again as the audience held its breath.

I inhaled deeply. Exhaled completely. Exaggerated several more deep breaths then spasmed wildly for the sake of dramatizing my finale, my death.

Then, as if on cue, darkness engulfed me and my narcolepsy put me to sleep.

When I awoke a short time later, the first thing I noticed was standing applause, cheering, whistling. Next, I noticed a commotion at the corner of the stage. Punch, Hades's head of security, was dragging Remi back to his table, threatening to put him out. Remi's jeans were undone and blood was smeared all over his arms and face. My blood.

Remi had been a regular Saturday night patron for over a year and knew it was against the rules to touch performers while we were onstage. I just hoped he didn't make Punch put him out of the club. Or make Punch beat him so badly I wouldn't be able to take blood from him later.

Punch was a huge Godzilla-size dude, nearly seven feet tall with biceps as wide as fucking watermelons. His smooth dark chocolate skin emanated a wild animal don't-fuck-with-me warning scent. And though I didn't know what he was exactly, I knew what that meant. It meant Punch was not someone Remi wanted to fuck with.

I felt famished and Remi was supposed to be my dinner tonight.

Shit!

CHAPTER 2

I lay on the floor motionless, eyes closed. I'd killed myself at the end of my set and the dead don't look at you. Not usually anyway. No sense ruining my fans' perfect fantasy by moving around now.

Franco, the club owner, walked onstage with my skull tip jar in one hand, a microphone in the other. With his sexy Spanish accent he shouted, "Everyone show some more love for the luscious and deathly and oh so talented SLEEPY WILLOOOOW!"

Applause and cheers and whistles erupted again.

As I peeked at the standing crowd, Franco pointed to the deejay. A split second later, Marilyn Manson blasted through the speakers again and Franco, clad in tight black leather from neck to pointy toe, sat my skull down at the edge of the stage then backed away with his arms out. As he welcomed the audience to show their appreciation, fire shot out of gargoyle mouths lining the walls.

I smiled inwardly as fans broke their necks to fill my skull with cash. I loved that they loved my performance. Made the pain worthwhile. Goes to show my aunt had been right about performing arts being my calling. That I should utilize my gifts regardless of what folks like my parents said. Too bad she would never see me onstage since she'd died several years ago after falling asleep behind the wheel of a car. She'd had narcolepsy also.

Two bouncers wearing only leather jockstraps grabbed my brimful skull and dragged me backstage.

Once we were hidden by curtains, I thanked them, collected my earnings and headed toward the dressing room. Bloody Valentina, Sweet Cinnabuns and Purely Onyx were standing along the wall clapping in unison. When Valentina playfully popped my ass with her whip, I remembered I was still buck naked. Still covered in blood.

Valentina had chalky white skin that always smelled of sweat and leather, blue eyes with clumpy dark eyeliner, and platinum blonde, bobbed hair. She was wearing the same blood red patent leather Madame I'ma-whoop-your-ass outfit as she did every set, but it didn't matter. Her fans didn't come to critique her fashion versatility. They came to get beat, humiliated, dominated. Valentina was best at it because she was a true sadist and she just didn't give a fuck.

She was up next once the stage was cleaned and new patrons entered, old ones left. Normally, I'd stick around to watch her show since her bondage demonstrations promised bloodshed. It was disappointing to see all that blood wasted, but eating them wasn't her thing. It was mine. And tonight, I didn't trust myself not to pounce on her masochistic volunteers when she lashed their delicate skins with her whip.

"Woohoo! Way to go, girl!" Cindy said. Her stage name was appropriately Sweet Cinnabuns because she had a fat booty and I swear she smelled like cinnamon. "I don't know how you did it, but it looked real as hell."

My colleagues and I didn't bother questioning each other's trade secrets. Best to leave each performer to her mystery…

Suddenly, my nostrils flared. I licked my lips. Stopped in

my tracks.

Before I knew it was happening, my fangs started protruding. My mouth watered so badly I was afraid to speak, scared saliva would spill out.

In an effort to redirect my attention, I started thinking about lightning storms, toilet bowl cleaners, lice…anything to get my mind off my bloodlust. It was taking over and I couldn't let that happen.

But she wasn't making it easy tonight.

Underneath the smell of all that sweet cinnamon was the undeniable salty smell of her blood. She was menstruating and damn it, I wanted to bite her, see if she tasted as good as she smelled—sure sign I'd gone too long without feeding because friends didn't eat friends. When controlling my urges got to be this hard, it was trouble. *I* was trouble.

Cindy was a gorgeous Latina with shoulder-length brown and blonde mixed curly hair, coffee brown eyes and edible lips. But more than anything, I loved her sweet Latina scent. Made me want to stick out my tongue and lick the air whenever she was nearby.

No wonder she specialized in sitophilia…food fetishism, that is. She sure made me hungry.

Feeling like myself again, I turned to face them. "Thanks, guys. Thanks for wrapping me up, Cin," I said once my fangs retracted. "The audience loved it."

"Yeah, especially that Remington guy," Onyx chuckled and the other two joined in.

Damn it to hell, she wasn't looking too bad her damn self in her pleated mini-skirt, black-rimmed glasses, ponytails, and Lolita knee-high socks. While she didn't fuck kids or anything (not that I knew of anyway), she catered to men who liked young, innocent girls. Pedophilia and bestiality were my least favorite fetishes because they didn't involve consenting adults, but Onyx was one of my favorites at the club.

There was just something about her I couldn't put my

finger on.

For one, Onyx was the only woman I knew who could play a teenager at her age. She must have discovered the fountain of youth with her slate gray eyes, smooth pecan brown skin, layered black hair with highlights and firm, voluptuous body. But she was a long way from high school, closer to forty. If I didn't know any better, I'd think she was a vampire. Thing is, she hated blood and violence, which meant she usually stayed far away from Bloody Valentina and a fair distance from me.

Secondly, she took her innocent girly role too damn seriously. Said she felt she was doing a service to the community by letting men take their fantasies out on her and helping them stay away from real girls.

Fine. Didn't mean she had to act virginal twenty-four-seven though. Never sitting with her legs uncrossed. Never a drop of makeup. Never a curse word.

Corrupting her then eating her up would be ideal, but tonight I'd settle for a bite of her neck…or lower.

I'd walked up close to Onyx without even thinking about it.

All three women were staring at me, waiting to see what I'd do next. Onyx's heart was thumping wildly and she looked scared. Valentina looked amused, Cindy, curious. I shook my head, stepped back, and went to clean the blood off me.

I needed to find Remi and feed ASAP.

By the time I got out of the shower, my wounds had healed. I donned a black sweat suit with sneakers, put my hair in a ponytail and pulled the hood over my head. Dressing blandly was one of the ways I blended in when I wasn't onstage. As a human, I was cute. As a vampire, stunningly flawless. That just came with the territory.

Don't get me wrong—I enjoyed being physically impeccable and sexually irresistible, but there were downsides. Back when we were legal and public, humans had discovered a lot of our hidden talents. Amongst other things, they'd discovered the same magic that kept us undead also gave us perfect looks every single night. We didn't age. Didn't get pimples or wrinkles. Never had a bad hair day. So we'd become easier to spot. And that's not good when being spotted carried a final death sentence.

Armed with my mini-phlebotomy kit in my pocket for safely withdrawing fresh blood, I headed in the direction of the private rooms. I hoped Remi was in one and not on his ass in the parking lot asphalt. Lot of good he'd do me there.

I peeked in a few rooms and saw all kinds of nasty sex, but no Remi.

"Sleepy Willow," a masculine voice called from the other end of the hall, "I've been looking for you."

I froze. That wasn't Remi.

"Who are you?" I asked.

"I enjoyed your show tonight. Was hoping I could enjoy some private entertainment," he said.

He hadn't answered my question. He'd told me what he wanted instead. Bad sign.

"Hades isn't that kind of club, Mister, uh…"

"I'd *really* like to spend time with you. I know you girls are encouraged to…mingle."

"I'm not an escort or a prostitute, but I'm sure you'll find someone to indulge your fantasies in the Graveyard room."

Each fetish had a room where likeminded folks could meet up and let their imaginations guide them. Necrophiliacs met in the Graveyard. Yes, performers were encouraged to visit rooms and make patrons feel at ease, but the fun went on whether we were in there or not. Maybe he was new and didn't know.

He didn't move. Too busy trying to seem non-threatening, but I wasn't buying it. Something was off.

"What was your name again?" I asked.

He took a step forward and swung open the door to a

room. "This room's free, Willow. I have money."

"I'm sure someone in Graveyard will be happy about that. Go straight down this hall past the python display, make a left at the exit sign and—"

"Aw, c'mon. Won't you indulge a fan? Just a little alone time…"

"You can't even tell me who you are. Why should I be alone with you?" I snapped.

He chuckled. It was a sexy sound that stirred parts lower in my body than fangs. I dropped my guard, walked closer, wanting to smell him. Would I get a whiff of cigarette smoke like with Remi or would he smell sweet like Cindy?

"I can make it worth your time," he said, lowering his voice, stepping forward.

I'll bet you can. When offering money hadn't worked, he'd decided to turn on the charm, seduce me. To a vampire, that was indeed a better strategy.

I started checking him out, noticing broad shoulders in his brown leather jacket, long legs in his jeans. He had to be at least six feet five inches given the angle I looked up to him from my five feet eight inches. His height and build made his spiked dark hair and dark eyes hard to ignore.

I could captivate him, fill my vials with his blood, and go on my merry way since I hadn't found Remi yet. But something about this stranger made me want to do other things to him too, cross lines I hadn't even crossed with Remi.

Letting my bloodlust get out of hand was making my sexual lust escalate too. Rapidly. They were dangerously interconnected, especially when it had been awhile for both. Bleeding myself onstage while I was already hungry had not been wise.

Though breathing wasn't essential to my survival, I took a deep breath anyway because I wanted to inhale his scent, test out his pheromones and see if he'd be as delicious to fuck as he would to eat.

His muskiness tickled my nose hairs, sending invigorating signals to my brain. *Mmmm.*

During my two years as a vampire, I'd only had sex with my maistre, Maximilian, and the last time had been a looooong time ago. As thorough a lover he was, I'd left him and the clan because he was too damn controlling, narcissistic and selfish. Plus, I'd had other aspirations. Sure, he'd invade my psyche through our blood bond and fuck me from afar, but it wasn't the same as real penetration. That was something I no longer wanted from him. Didn't mean I no longer wanted it at all.

Nevertheless, I'd denied the wanton part of my being and been celibate mostly because of two commandments: *thou shalt not kill* and *thou shalt not commit adultery.* I was too afraid of killing a human during the throes of passion. Too afraid Max would kill them once he found out. And he'd definitely find out.

Best not to have sex with anyone other than Max anyway since according to vampire rules he was technically my husband. And our marriage went deeper than vows. We'd performed a ritual that transformed me from a simple human to one of his vampire brides. It had formed a permanent bond that made the human line *'til death do us part* seem like child's play.

Surprisingly, even as a vampire I hadn't been able to part with the morals instilled from my southern Baptist upbringing.

Speaking of morals…

Felt mine declining by the second. Realized how badly I wanted this stranger. How hard it was getting to resist temptation.

"I was kind of looking for a friend," I said, finding a spot on the floor to look at while I contemplated whether to ditch my plan to chow on Remi and put this stud on the menu instead.

He'd touched the side of my face with his wide, warm palm before I saw it coming.

"Look at me. I want to see your eyes, Willow," he said. He wasn't even nervous. His heart beat calmly, steadily.

Confidence was sexy as hell. I wanted him in every way. So it took everything in me to withhold my fangs. They were itching to break through. Itching to close the distance between us, reach up, and sink into his neck.

He had no idea who he was dealing with, but fine. I'd look at him since he'd asked for it.

As soon as I did, he raised his other hand and sprayed my eyes with a substance that burned instantly. He moved the hand already on the side of my face to my chin and squeezed it tight, holding it in place. I screamed and tried to move away. He kept spraying. I was stronger than any human, but whatever he'd sprayed was affecting my speed, my strength.

I finally stopped trying to back away and slammed my forehead into his nose. Blood gushed. He stumbled backwards in shock, grabbing his wounded face.

The sad part was that I'd been so weak moments before that I would have gladly given myself to him. Given myself over to the immorality I usually fought so hard against. Now it was a matter of principle. He hadn't asked nicely. Asking for some private time was not the same as "Hey, Willow, can I have some pussy?" He'd come to Hades thinking we were all whores and he'd abuse one of us into giving him what he wanted.

He'd picked the wrong fucking performer from the wrong fucking fetish.

I didn't wait for him to recover. Licking at his drop of blood that had splashed near my mouth, I turned to run in the opposite direction.

If my eyes weren't burning so much, I would have stuck around to fight, to feed. I'd have shown him I was a predator, not prey. But he was quick, or at least, his legs were longer than mine and he'd stuck one out and tripped me as I retreated. He was down on top of me immediately.

13

For a moment, I'd hoped he was going to pull my sweatpants down and shove himself inside. Give it to me hard. Hot. Horny. But there was nothing sexual about his attack.

Damn. I needed sex and I needed blood and I loved the smell of his running down his face…

But he was obviously more interested in murder than rape. Too bad. 'Cause unless he knew I was a vampire, killing me wasn't going to happen any ol' kinda way.

Just as I was counting my chickens before they hatched, he slapped a heavy handcuff across my wrist and attempted to lock the other around my other wrist. I couldn't break free of the shackle because it was silver, which was synonymous with poison for a vampire. Like kryptonite for Superman. It immediately started burning my skin. I screamed again. I was tired of being burned, but I wasn't the type to give up. We tussled until I kneed his groin with all the strength I could muster, so hard he could taste the sole of my shoe.

He bellowed in pain and loosened his grip.

Hope he didn't want kids. That would teach him to fuck with me.

I was pissed! Pissed that he'd interrupted my dinner plans. Pissed that he'd tried to kill instead of fuck me. Pissed that he'd sprayed my eyes with that god-awful substance and almost completely handcuffed me with silver.

Damn necrophiliacs!

I'd get retribution though.

My fangs extended to full length, my eyes changed to glowing red, and I leaned down to take a chunk out of his motherfucking neck when Cindy yelled, "Wiiiillooow!" from down the hall.

CHAPTER 3

Oh, no.

I had no idea how much Cindy had seen. She was my friend but certainly not close enough to know I was a vampire. No one was, except Saybree the witch, and I wanted to keep it that way. My survival depended on it.

If I could help it, Saybree wouldn't know either. But there was no way around that and I trusted her. She was an outspoken human with supernatural powers and therefore, with enemies of her own. As my psycho-spiritual counselor for years, she had tried to cure my narcolepsy with magic potions and spells. When that hadn't worked, she introduced me to Max because she thought vampirism would cure me. Vampires didn't get human illnesses and diseases, after all.

She'd been wrong, but I'd never regretted being a vampire, just being bonded to Max.

Growling like a mad dog because I was, I decided to proceed with ripping my attacker to shreds regardless of who was watching. The rational side of my brain had been swallowed by the instinctual, base side. I no longer cared who witnessed my ravenous desire, my incarnate evil. Cindy could go eat a dick if she had a problem with it…

Suddenly, I started feeling funny, like I was going to have another sleep attack. Oh, Fuck! Bad timing! But if I could control when I fell asleep, it wouldn't be a disorder, now would it? Then it didn't matter anymore because I passed out in to a deep sleep.

When I awakened, I realized I'd been moved, which meant I must have slept longer than a few minutes. Uh oh…

I panicked. Started feeling around. Decided I lay on a bed, no, a couch. Looking around, I discovered my surroundings were pitch black. Had the spray damaged my eyes or was I really in a pitch black room? I got still and listened, smelled. There was sweet cinnamon and…and sulfur.

"She's waking up," Franco said. "Willow, are you okay?"

Fuck. I could usually see well in the dark and I hadn't seen Franco. Sure hoped the damage to my eyes wasn't permanent.

Having the ability to heal quickly from injuries was a wonderful vampire characteristic, but we weren't entirely invincible, not entirely immortal. Silver, holy water and garlic were all harmful. Sunlight, fire and decapitation were fatal. Stakes were bad, but not in the mythological sense. Wooden ones hurt like hell. Silver ones were nearly paralyzing, which gave the wielder enough time to light a match or open a curtain or swing a fucking machete at our necks.

So I ran through the list: Able to move my head? Check. It was still attached. Not burning to a crisp and turning to ash? Check. Sunlight and fire weren't an issue. Not paralyzed or bleeding from a gaping hole in my chest? Check. I hadn't been staked.

Nope. Just my eyes were out of commission. A temporary, fixable problem. I hoped.

"I can't see, Franco." I said.

"That's 'cause your eyes are closed."

That seemed reasonable so I tried opening my eyes. They were stuck, maybe glued shut.

Shit! That studly bastard had blinded me! "I can't open my eyes!"

I felt more than heard Cindy sigh. "I'll go get a wet cloth. Maybe we can wash that stuff off," she said.

Good idea. Glad she was being helpful, but she sounded disturbed, tense.

She had seen me changing into my monstrous self. Not good. What would she do? Who would she tell? Would she turn me in and pocket the reward money? Our friendship was about to be tested.

The evening was getting worse.

"Cin?" I started though I wasn't sure what I'd say. Felt it was worth a try.

There was movement then silence.

"She's gone." Franco said. He was close enough for me to feel his warm breath on my face. "Probably for the best. She seems frightened. We have lots of security but sometimes things happen. I do my best to keep you girls safe, but…"

"It's okay, Franco. It's not your fault. My death scene brought out all the crazy in my fans." I laughed. Might as well joke about it.

Laughing turned to coughing, which was odd. I hadn't coughed since I'd become a vampire. What the hell had he sprayed?!

When I brought my hand up to cover my mouth, I remembered how my wrist had burned and instinctively rubbed it. My skin was normal, smooth like a baby's butt.

"Your wrist has already healed," he said in a low voice.

I froze.

This was the first injury I'd had around my colleagues that I couldn't pretend wasn't real. Franco had seen how fast it healed. Humans didn't heal from burns that quickly. And they didn't burn from silver handcuffs.

The Human Preservation Act (HPA) had made vampirism illegal which meant harboring, marrying, and employing us was illegal too. Would he fire me? I sure hoped not. I loved my job. It was the one place I could combine my love of performing with my nocturnal wiring and newfound sexual allure. Strangely, I also felt safe here amongst other non-conformists. I'd always been peculiar and it didn't stand out at Hades.

"Franco…" I began.

"We'll talk later," he whispered.

I smelled cinnamon a second later. Cindy was coming back.

Before she was in the room good, Franco did something surprising. He wrapped and tied soft material around my wrist to hide the fact I'd healed so quickly. But why would he help me?

When a lukewarm washcloth was applied to my eyes, he gently rubbed in long strokes from inside out then in circular motions. Cleansing me of impurities. Nurturing me like a sick child. In fact, he had always handled me that way.

Never could put my finger on what made Franco tick. He was entirely too comfortable around perverts yet he appeared normal, asexual in fact.

Okay, maybe that wasn't normal.

To own and run a successful fetish club, there had to be something dark deep inside him I just hadn't seen yet. The fact that he was the only human I hadn't been able to captivate made me think he wasn't human at all. He didn't smell wild and beastly the way others did, so I'd ruled out were-animal. And I had disregarded the rumors that he was a sex demon. Had always thought people were joking. Now I considered its validity.

Oh, well. As long as he let me keep my job, he could be the devil himself and I'd find a way to deal with it.

Since supernaturals were wisely cautious these days, I'd probably never find out anyway. They were too afraid humans would band against them and pass anti-were or anti-goblin or anti-whatever laws. Humans had already proven themselves to be crafty and highly motivated and they outnumbered the supernatural community by far. Just look what happened to us. As powerful as we were, we'd been hunted to near-extinction because humans had discovered and used our weaknesses against us. Public supernaturals were forced into hiding and closeted ones were forced to remain that way.

"What happened to the guy who attacked me?" I asked.

It was club policy to call HPD, but I really didn't want any more trouble, no more attention. Police reports and investigations were not welcomed to anyone who had secrets.

"After we beat the shit out of him, we dumped him on his ass and told him never to come back. I had to fire Don for taking a hundred bucks and letting him in without a membership."

Franco had surprised me again, went against his own rules. It could come back to bite him, especially if I wanted to press charges against my assailant. The assistant district attorney would ask for the nonexistent police report and wonder why Franco had let him go. But Franco knew I'd want things handled quietly more than anything, didn't he.

He rubbed the cloth over my eyes a few more times then removed it.

I slowly opened my hazels one at a time.

His serious dark brown eyes were focused on mine. His dark hair was gelled back in a long ponytail with one stray lock over his forehead. A strong dimpled chin and high cheekbones gave his face a dashingly handsome look. And as usual, an indescribable tattoo peeped through the top of his leather shirt, giving him a mysterious, sexy vibe.

I blinked long, thick lashes. Yeah, the warm water had worked.

"Thanks," I said, hoping he knew I meant for everything. Just in case, I tried once again to capture his gaze, lock him in psychically. I'd love to remove the memory of what he'd discovered about me, even if for just a little while. He just blinked, totally unaffected.

Cindy cleared her throat. My moment with Franco must have looked more intimate than it was. There was no lust, no hunger toward him whatsoever.

Franco rose, said I was to take the rest of the night off and that he'd send Punch to take me home. Before I could protest, he exited. I was left in silence with Cindy's sweet scent. Not good since I still hadn't fed.

"Are you a vampire?" she asked boldly. Keeping her distance.

"Why would you ask me that? You know me, Cin."

"I saw your eyes change. You changed. You became something else."

"I don't suppose *angel* ever crossed your mind?" I smirked. Humor was all I had at this point.

"Don't play with me, Willow. Angels don't have fangs," she crossed her arms over her chest indignantly.

So she'd seen the whole shebang and wasn't backing down. Now what? Arguing that she didn't know whether angels had fangs seemed petty.

"What do you want me to say, Cin?"

"Tell me the truth. What are you, for God's sake! You've been to my house, watched my daughter…"

I didn't see how any of that mattered, but apparently it was important to her. "I'm your friend, have been since I started working here."

"Like hell you are. If you're a vampire, then I don't even know you."

The angrier she became, the more her voice raised. The more pronounced her jugular became. It was jutting, begging to be tasted.

I accidentally bit my lip, tasted my own blood. She had to get herself and her accusations away from me sooner rather than later. Anger made her blood pump faster. Egged me closer to losing control.

If she truly believed I was a vampire, she wasn't acting like

20

it. Like the Incredible Hulk, she wouldn't want to make me angry. Surely she'd know being friendly would be more to her advantage since I could easily snap her fucking neck. Turning my head towards the chair cushion, I began counting. *Ten, nine, eight, seven...*

"You know, I could really use the money." Her voice lowered, sounded strained, a little shaky. "Did you know they were paying ten thousand dollars now for each tip that leads to a vampire arrest?" she asked.

"Is that so." I didn't turn to look at her. She was pushing it and I didn't trust myself to show restraint.

She was referring to the Vampire Extermination Team, un-affectionately known as VET. HPA ordered execution for all vampires, VET served as the enforcement agency. They hired ex-military, ex-law enforcement, ex-felons, anyone who had the skills to hunt down and kill us. Sometimes they contracted out to private vampire hunting businesses too. It was a dangerous but lucrative industry.

Which meant the bitch had just threatened me.

She sighed noisily, some of the tension easing. "Yeah, this custody battle is getting really messy, and really expensive. I could use that money. I'd hate to do it to you, Willow, but I'm close to losing my daughter. My lawyer's threatening to withdraw from my case." She bit her lip like she was holding back a sob. Her desperation was palpable.

I knew she'd been going through an ugly divorce and custody case. Her hubby played for the Texans and was spending a nice chunk o' change to make her look bad in court and in the media. Even though he'd met Cindy at Hades, her job as a performer here was now being slanted to make her look unfit. It was unfair. She was a great mother.

Her ass should have asked to borrow some money instead of threatening to expose me, but I had an idea. I felt sorry for her and wanted to help. It could be a win-win for us both, and certainly better than driving a wedge between our friendship or losing it altogether.

"I never said I was a vampire, Cin, but I'd like to make a deal with you. I'd prefer not to be investigated based on mere suspicions because I like my privacy. What if your problems with your husband disappeared and money was no longer an issue? Would you be willing to put this behind us?"

Her eyes narrowed suspiciously. "You didn't say you *weren't* a vampire either." She paused as if she was considering my proposition. "Yes, I'd be willing to put everything behind us if my husband was no longer an issue. But Willow, I don't want him dead. He's still Lucia's father. She needs him."

"I understand."

Most people believed vampirism meant soullessness, unredeemable evil. In fact, I'd grown up hearing and believing vampires were hell-bound satanic spawns. But when I got old enough to reason for myself, I'd decided that God had to have created all beings, humans and supernaturals. And if so, that meant forgiveness was available for the transgressions of each repentant, even vampires.

My mother had slapped my chap-stick off when I'd suggested that God was actually a vampire himself due to his emphasis on blood sacrifice. My dad had said I was sacrilegious and would die a horrible death and burn in hell for my heresy. Told him I'd see his hypocritical ass there.

Maybe I'd gone too far, but who were humans to judge whether another species was damned? No one could be certain about anything when it came to spirituality. We believed what we believed and prayed we were right. At least my theory gave me hope for when I met my final death. Which meant that even as a naturally vicious bloodsucker, I still followed the Ten Commandments. Meant I had to creatively come up with alternatives for getting what I wanted that absolutely did not involve killing humans.

I'd admit some days it was harder to do.

Like right now while Cindy was standing here smelling

sweet with her hands on her hips making demands.

"What if he just wishes he was dead?" I said, looking at her this time.

I was going through a lot of trouble to appease her when I should have just captivated her memories of tonight's events, erased them and gambled on how long that would last.

She quickly looked at the floor.

Ah. She'd thought about it too, that I'd use my powers of hypnosis over her brain.

Funny, she'd said she didn't know me, but she knew me well enough to know I wouldn't take the easiest option. The option most certain to guarantee her silence: killing her. That wouldn't require me to trust her to uphold her end of a bargain. Didn't require me to make a bargain at all.

But we both knew I wasn't capable of that.

Captivation—that, I could do, except it lasted temporarily and worked differently for different people. Sure, she'd forget for a while, but I couldn't be sure how long it would last and which memories would come back.

Making a deal for her silence was our best bet.

"I can live with that," she said finally.

So could I. The alternative would be bad for both of us.

CHAPTER 4

Once Cindy left, I was on the couch alone awhile, looking around, familiarizing myself with the bedroom. Noise from the club above told me I was in the basement for the first time.

My eyesight had come back faster than my strength. Made me wonder what the hell he'd sprayed me with again. I wasn't used to healing slowly since I'd been undead. Somehow, I didn't think mace or pepper spray would have had this result.

I really just wanted to leave, but Franco had told me to wait for Punch. I also had unfinished business with Franco. Needed to make a deal with him for his silence as well. Probably had to beg for my job.

The room was done in all black. A king-sized bed with black sheets, no pillows centered the wall opposite me. Only other piece of furniture was the black couch I lay on and the tall halogen lamp illuminating it all. There were mirrors along the ceiling and all four walls. No windows. No pictures. No decorations. I assumed some of the mirrors opened to a closet and bathroom just as the one that opened to the entrance/exit.

The black monochrome furnishings were boring and uninspiring to the human I used to be, and just right for the side of me that was an undead nocturnal supernatural. Since I'd heard Franco had moved his residence to the basement, I figured it was his bedroom even if it was a tad impersonal.

When my strength returned, I started pacing. Not long thereafter, Punch walked in with my duffel bag as if he'd been watching on a monitor and knew I was up and about. He was so massive the bedroom immediately felt smaller.

"I'll take you out back and drive you home," he said in the deepest voice I'd ever heard. It was always like that.

"Thanks," I said as I took my bag from him. "But that's really not necessary. I can make it home fine on my own."

Home for me was the motel down the street. Why? Because it was conveniently close to the club. Because I walked everywhere I needed to go. Easier that way, my narcolepsy and all. Wouldn't want what happened to my beloved aunt to happen to me.

And why stay in a motel instead of a cute studio apartment? Well, I needed to remain mobile. The government took vampire extermination very seriously. Priority One. Something about vampires using their powers to gain unfair advantage in politics, sports, and every aspect of life got people anxious. Better to kill us all than risk becoming the underdog.

It was speculated that the Secretary of Defense's wife took a vampire lover, and that actually began the anti-vamp crusade. Anyway, my point was that *if* VET sent someone after me, I needed to be able to take my belongings somewhere else in a hurry. Or if I didn't have time to make a fast getaway with my possessions, I needed to be able to leave untraceable items behind and start over. My paranoia had me changing motel rooms every other month just to be safe.

Better safe than sorry.

"Franco said you'd say that. Always so tough. But I was told not to take no for an answer. He's worried about you," he said.

"Tell him not to worry. I walk to and from Hades every

night. I'll be fine." Besides, I walked really fast. I could be in my room before Punch even turned the ignition in his truck.

"But no one's tried to abduct you before. We need to be extra careful now." He swung his neck around so his long dreadlocks landed on his back instead of down the front of his chest. Then he folded his arms. Black eyes set sternly in his dark chocolate face, as if I'd have to fight him to leave of my own accord.

I'd rather reason with him...

"He didn't try to abduct me. He just wanted a little pussy. I just wasn't as easy to take down as he thought I'd be." Besides, how had my attacker planned to get me past security without being noticed? Abduction couldn't have been his motive.

"He handcuffed you with silver, debilitated you with— from all we could tell—was simply water. He wasn't after pussy, Willow."

"Water?"

"Yep, that's all he sprayed on you," he said as he held up the tube in question. He looked meaningfully, as if I should grasp the weight of what he wasn't saying.

Ohhhh. HOLY water.

He nodded as understanding flooded my face. "So, you see why you...*we* need to be extra careful? He could be outside waiting for you. We don't want to take that chance," he said.

"I heard you beat him up. You think he'd come back after that?"

"All I know is he's not our typical customer. He'll probably try to get you again. We'd hate for him to be waiting to follow you. We have to stick together, look after each other."

Punched reached his hand out towards me. I took it.

By "we" he meant supernaturals. He wasn't a vampire, but he was something just as threatening to humans, and now I knew for sure Franco was too.

Tonight was full of revelations.

Guess I didn't have to make a deal with Franco after all.

Punch led me through a corridor behind the mirrors next to the bed. We passed several doors in the corridor that were guarded with combination push-button heavy-duty mortise locks. Made me wonder whether the doors were intended to keep something or someone in or everyone else out. Then we went through a narrow concrete tunnel where I expected to see rats, hear sewage draining, and smell feces. I was pleasantly surprised. It was void of scent, smell and light.

Moonlight and dirt spilt down from the opening above when Punch lifted its hatch. He leaped upward, climbed out and reached for my hands to pull me through. I grabbed hold and was effortlessly pulled to solid ground.

For someone so huge and so strong, he was so gentle…and so warm, no, hot—really hot. I'd bet his blood was hot…

My fangs grew instantly. I growled and yanked my hands back.

He gasped, "Your eyes are glowing red." Then his features softened. "You haven't fed in awhile, have you?"

I shook my head. No sense denying it.

Missing a night of feeding was never a good idea, but I missed last night because my regular blood donor, Mr. Cash, had been politicking in D.C. for the past two weeks. I'd forgotten to plan a backup meal. To feed from the same patrons every night was strategic in reducing my chances of getting caught, but it also limited my options whenever a regular patron happened to be a no-show.

Without hesitation, Punch sat on the ground with his back against a tree, and leaned his head to the side. I looked around nervously. Was he doing what I thought he was doing? Offering a vein to a hungry vampire?

I looked around some more. Hades was located in Houston's Montrose area, and we hadn't walked in the tunnel

27

long enough to be far away. When I looked up at the dark sky, I couldn't even see stars, which meant we were still within the city. I closed my eyes and focused on the sound of busy streets nearby. It was only a little after midnight so bar traffic was still in full swing. We were in a wooded area, but not the woods. What if someone happened upon us?

"I'm not going to sit here forever," he drawled. "You need to be quick about it before someone comes."

I straddled his thick, muscular thighs and bit his neck without another thought. Hadn't even been polite enough to ease in to it, to make him feel pleasure rather than pain as I pierced his skin. I was too hungry, too feral.

He groaned and it didn't sound like an I'm-in-pain noise. In fact, when he grabbed my hips and pushed me into his chest and tight to his erection, I knew he wasn't in pain at all.

Lust, hunger, passion…everything I'd felt the past few hours flooded my body at once.

I grabbed a handful of the locks dangling on his back and yanked hard, pulling his head back even further. Giving me a better angle to ride him and feed at the same time.

He growled, grinding his hips into mine as I grinded back. The friction between his jeans and the softness of my sweats made us both delirious with pleasure. As I moved my hips back and forth over and over his swollen region, his blood heated to boiling and pumped faster in my mouth. His energy soared. Mine erupted. Then we reached a peak of ecstasy. He came right before I did, howling up at the moon, his tremendous erection jerking, sending me over the edge. I kept sucking. He kept howling.

He finally had to throw me to the ground. I was taking more than a fair share of his blood, with no signs of stopping. I'd waited too long to feed. He'd tasted too good. Felt too right.

His girlfriend, Fire, was a performer at Hades too, and she was going to kill me when she found out…or at least try.

After the last of my aftershocks subsided, I wiped my mouth with my sleeve and sat up. I began adjusting myself, needing to regain some sense of dignity. Thankfully, my fangs retracted. Best to put those things away.

He got up slowly, adjusted his crotch, and extended his hand to help me up.

I took it, this time with very little reaction. I was good, more than good. Withdrawing blood with my kit and drinking from vials kept me satisfied, but never full. It also kept me from killing my source, which was good for both of us. Nothing like drinking straight from a live body though. For the first time since I'd returned from living with my clan, I was fully sated.

"Thanks," I said.

"My pleasure," he said lazily. "Man, I'd forgotten what that was like."

I assumed he was referring to a vampire bite. Some people became addicted to sex with vampires for that reason. After you got past the initial sting, the bite was an aphrodisiac—another reason humans wanted to kill us all. Human lovers couldn't compete. Just ask the Secretary of Defense.

"I need to lick your neck to close the wound," I said, hoping I'd actually be able to do that without sinking into him again.

He used his fingers to wipe blood from his neck that had already started running down his black sheer muscle shirt. Then he swayed and staggered before starting to walk through the trees. "I think I better keep you away from my neck, shorty. I already gotta figure out what to tell Fire about the come in my underwear."

What could I say? *I'm sorry*? Well, I wasn't. I was full. Finally. And I was high from the potency of his blood. I'd always heard human blood had nothing on supernatural blood in terms of power. Now I knew. Remi's blood was comparable in taste, but not energy. I felt like singing hey-diddle-diddle and jumping over the moon.

We walked a short distance in silence until we came upon his white truck. He must have moved it because it had been in the club parking lot earlier.

He helped me in even though we both knew I didn't need help. He was such a gentleman. Maybe I was a *little* sorry that I'd used him. But he'd offered.

"You think Fire will keep my secret?" I asked just as we pulled up to my motel.

I'd actually had him stop a few doors down and pretended we'd arrived right in front of my door. He'd let me feed from him, but I wasn't ready to trust him knowing I was a vampire AND knowing where I rested during the day. That's when most vampires were killed—in broad daylight...in their own lairs. You never could be too careful.

"She keeps mine," he said, like that solved everything.

"But she'll be pissed with me after what just happened." Why did he have to be one of the honest guys and tell her about me at all?

"I think she'll understand just this one time. Anything beyond this and I'm moving to Canada to get away from her wrath."

"Well, thanks for the ride." *And the blood. And the orgasm.*

This was probably a bad time to tell him one of the effects of me having his blood was us being more drawn to each other. Even though we hadn't actually had sex, having a metaphysical relationship with him was potentially more damaging than a physical one.

No good deed goes unpunished.

But I wasn't his first vampire. He knew the deal.

"Wait, I'm coming in to make sure no one's lurking," he said.

A vivid image of Punch lying across my bed, exposing his neck for me to feed came to mind. I licked my lips. My cookie tightened involuntarily. The thought of him in my room was arousing. I'd never had a visitor. Not even Max had been here in the flesh.

Punch had said Fire would forgive just the one time. This would be pushing it. "I don't think that's a good idea. Why don't you just watch as I make it to the door? Don't get out unless you see I need help."

He grunted then started grinding his jaw, but he didn't get out. I jumped out while I had the chance and quickly scanned the lot.

Hair on the back of my neck stood up. I had a strange feeling someone was waiting for me. I sniffed the air, recognized the smell. That motherfucker! How did he know where to find me?

I smiled at Punch, pretending everything was cool. He needed to get back to Hades, back to Fire.

"I think the coast is clear," I said. *Like hell it is.* "You can go now."

He scanned the lot too with his enhanced senses…eyes first, then nose, then ears. He noticed people driving up, getting out of their cars. He noticed pedestrians on the sidewalk. But he didn't notice a potential threat. Everything looked normal to him, because he hadn't had blood from the man hiding in the bushes.

"I'll wait 'til you get to the door, like you said."

"Suit yourself." I got out, waved, and made my way to room #10. Mine was actually #3.

When I got to the door, I pulled out my keycard and waved goodbye. I hoped he'd just leave. He did.

I waited until Punch had driven to the exit and turned onto the highway. Then I intentionally dropped my keycard and bent to pick it up. I knew the vehicle parked in front of me blocked the view for the man in the bushes. It was the perfect smokescreen.

Moving with super speed, faster than the eye could see, I ran to the far corner where I was well-hidden by the garbage dumpster. To anyone watching, it would have looked like I'd disappeared.

As suspected, my stalker looked around wildly. His brain couldn't process that I was there one moment and gone the next. Then he messed up. He came from behind the bushes into the lot and light, looking around like he'd lost his poodle. I moved with lightning speed again. This time when he turned, he ran smack dab into me.

And screamed.

"What the fuck are you doing here, Remi?"

CHAPTER 5

He breathed in and out again and again. Fast. Too fast. He was hyperventilating.

I laughed.

I'd intended to use the element of surprise in my favor, but I hadn't meant for him to be scared to death. But this was Remi. He loved death. Loved fear. He began to laugh too.

"Answer the question, Remi," I said in my no-nonsense, serious tone. Enough of the funnies.

"I wanted to see you."

"How did you know I'd be here?"

"I followed you one night."

I thought about it. I normally walked really fast, but sometimes I strolled, took my time and appreciated the darkness. His turning up unexpectedly sure seemed like a warning that I needed to be more careful. Being sloppy could have dire consequences. Call me crazy, but I enjoyed being undead. Getting caught was not an option.

"That's creepy, Remi. You shouldn't follow a girl home."

"I love you, Willow. I'd follow you anywhere."

"The destination is of little relevance, sweetie. You

shouldn't follow a girl, period."

He jammed one hand in the pocket of his jeans. "I can't help myself. Seeing you once a week at Hades isn't enough." He reached his other hand out to me.

I stepped back, reluctant to touch him. Scared to encourage him. "Then come more often. I work most nights except Sundays and Mondays. I treat Sunday like the Sabbath and have other things to do on Mondays."

"I can only come on Saturdays."

"Well, I don't know what to tell you. If you follow me again, I'm going to call the cops."

"No you won't." He smirked and stepped forward, closer.

"You're right. I won't. There're worse things I could do to you than call the cops."

He flinched, then took another step forward and smiled. "Like what?" His stare was creepy and sexy at the same time.

He wasn't daring me to do something to him on the off-chance I might be bluffing. He was baiting me, begging me to do something bad. Do something dangerous, something evil to him. He got off on that.

He was close enough to kiss…those beautiful, perky, kissable lips. I thought about it, almost did it, until I smelled cigarettes. It overshadowed his cologne. Damn. He was too gorgeous to smoke. I fed from him because it was convenient, he was eye candy and his blood tasted rich. But I hated that he smoked. I never complained though because I knew it helped relax him. And because I was usually too hungry to care.

Looked like he could use a smoke now. He seemed especially twitchy tonight, amped up on testosterone or maybe he'd had a rough day and had come to Hades, to *me* to unwind.

I could captivate his mind, erase memories of the motel, but I didn't know how long he'd known. It was possibly part of his long-term memory by now. In fact, I'd been bleeding him and tampering with his brain for so long, I wasn't sure how well it worked on him anymore.

Max had warned me about long-term human blood donors and the unpredictable effects our mental manipulations had on their brains. He longed for the return of days when captivation wasn't necessary for openly feeding off humans. In the meantime, he kept a few human pets. If one wasn't available, he'd procure unwilling humans and kill them, erasing their memories of him permanently. I still bothered with the mental crap all for the sake of following the commandment against murder. Max used captivation for less menial stuff like forcing tycoons to sign over their assets.

I wasn't too worried about Remi getting suspicious and ratting me out though. If he ever detected punctures from my blood draws, he'd cover the wounds in public and admire them privately like a marked lover. And I was careful not to get carried away when he asked me to cut him with razor blades. I was sure to cut in the same pattern across old scars on his wrists where he'd tried to off himself.

Captivating Remi's brain was just an extra precaution.

"Can I come in? I didn't see you after your act. You know I need to see you."

"No, you can't come in. I didn't invite you here."

"Why didn't you come to me afterwards? I looked for you."

"I was attacked." I held up my wrist showing the makeshift bandage. He could also see where I'd wiped Punch's blood on my sleeve. It all added to painting the picture that I'd been hurt even though there was no longer a real injury.

"What?! Really? What happened?" He sounded surprised, angry.

"He said he was a fan. Then he maced me and tried to rape me." Better to leave out Punch's suspicions about abduction being a motive. Or that my attacker suspected I was a vampire.

"Were you hurt? Did he use a weapon?" He no longer sounded angry. His voice was lower, edgier. In fact, he looked too damn eager to know details. His blood pumped too excitedly.

"Don't you dare get excited about someone hurting me, Remi."

"I'm sorry, Willow. You know I can't help it. That's why I love you. You don't judge me. I know I'm a creep but…" he looked down and kicked a pebble, "I need you."

I'd used him every Saturday night for blood. He'd used me for sexual release. That's the way it was. Just because I'd had blood already, didn't seem fair that he couldn't get what he needed also, his weekly fix.

Damn straight I could take care of him tonight, help him lose the edge.

Hoped I wouldn't regret it.

"No, I wasn't hurt." I linked my arm around his. "C'mon," I said with resolve.

He walked with me to my room, and then inside. Over the window curtains draped heavy blankets to keep out sunlight, so my room was pitch dark at night. Too dark for him to see yet I could see fine. Didn't keep him from touching me though. From pulling me close. From holding the back of my head until my face was mashed up to his and his tongue was down my throat. He'd latched on to my tongue like a vacuum. Sucking. Moaning. Pushing me towards the center of the room. Towards the bed.

Before I had even kicked the door shut.

He'd never been this aggressive before. Meant I wasn't the only one who'd been close to losing control tonight. But what exactly did that mean for him? Had he been close to letting his addiction to death get out of hand? Did that involve killing someone? Or trying to kill himself again?

He palmed my ass with eager hands and pressed himself against me roughly. I felt his dick straining his jeans, poking my leg, begging to be put to use. When his thumb traced along my elastic waist and tugged my panties and sweat pants downward, I realized he intended to take me right here, right now.

My sense of decency had me pulling away from Remi, but he held on tighter, squeezing my ass cheeks like they were footballs and he was headed to the end zone.

He was merely human, and unless he had a tube of holy water like my attacker from earlier, I could easily break away from him. Seemed rude to toss him out after inviting him in, but dammit, he was being presumptuous. I never said I'd fuck him. I merely intended to lie still, "play" dead for him while he pleasured himself. Nothing new.

I willingly gave him that release in exchange for the life force he unknowingly gave me. Small price to pay for a regular blood source and it eliminated guilt for taking ten vials of his blood without consent. Mutual satisfaction kept me from breaking the commandment *thou shalt not steal.* An orgasm in exchange for blood equaled fair payment in my book.

We'd had the same arrangement since he'd first started coming to Hades. He'd walked in fine as hell—tall, dark, and crazy. I knew it the moment he'd pinned his metallic blue, silver-looking stare on me. I'd wanted to bite him, fuck him, and run away at the same time. Nevertheless, he came week after week and I couldn't stay away from him.

We'd never had deep conversation though he'd mentioned being a wealthy Israeli. Oh, yeah…he'd also said he loved my complexion and curvy body, loved my performances, loved…me. But he'd never pressed the issue of penetration, which was good because that would lead to complications I didn't need. His self-control had helped me stick to my plan of captivating him, bleeding him, milking him, and getting the hell outta dodge before anyone noticed my kit full of red vials.

Now, he was ruining it.

I pulled away, forcefully this time and turned on the nearest lamp. After readjusting my clothes I said, "I need to shower." He would think it was a result of my performance instead of earlier events with Punch.

"Oh. Yeah. Right," he said, looking as if he was returning to his body. "Can I join you?"

"Not tonight. In fact, I think it was a mistake inviting you in. I wasn't planning to have sex with you."

"Oh." He looked downtrodden. "I still don't want to leave, Willow. We can go get breakfast or walk down the bayou. Anything you want. Just don't make me leave."

He was too beautiful for words. All six feet two inches of his perfectly lean-muscled build screamed s-e-x. Long black curls hanging in his face, olive skin in a black v-neck t-shirt, wide black leather wristbands… While his heart rate was returning to normal, if I had one, mine would've beat faster. He was so visually stunning, my body was responding to him, and it had nothing to do with fangs.

I couldn't very well tell him to stop and that I wasn't having sex with him then turn around and come on to him. Not his fault I was too conflicted tonight to send clear signals.

"Willow? Can we go eat after your shower?"

I'd just been staring, thinking. Lusting.

"Yeah. Sure." I wasn't going to actually eat anything, but I suddenly wanted to spend more time with him.

Now I remembered why I hadn't had visitors. And seeing him for the first time outside Hades was making us both react weirdly. What was that about? After the wonderful climax and meal with Punch earlier, I had hoped my hungers were satiated. For a long while. But here I was thinking about what Remi would look like naked. I'd only seen his plentiful erection, now I wanted to see the whole package. What could it hurt?

After all, a year was a heck of a long time for foreplay.

"Remi…" I began.

CHAPTER 6

"I'll step outside for a smoke until you're finished," he said as he opened and shut the door behind himself.

I stood dumfounded…then relieved.

Whew. That was a close one. If I would have lost control and ripped open an artery while doing him, I would never have forgiven myself. Creepy as he was, he had been there when I needed him. That deserved some loyalty. And if Max would have popped in while I was screwing Remi… I shuddered.

Remi would have been down for whatever. He wouldn't have known his limit because he would have enjoyed dying or nearly dying too much. I hadn't been worried about Punch, on the other hand. Knew he was capable of protecting himself. Or maybe I'd been too famished to care at the time.

I quickly cleaned myself up, dabbed on a little lipstick, brushed my hair out and sprayed on perfume since it sort of felt like a first date. It wasn't intentional, but Remi and I matched now that I'd put on a black backless sweater, jeans and calf-high black boots. After he looked me over with appreciative eyes, we were ready.

He didn't say much on the way, just asked if I was cool

with Katz's Deli & Bar then drove in silence. It gave me time to peruse his CD selection, which was surprisingly mixed with hip-hop, jazz, classical, heavy metal, and country. Since he was blasting "Party Up" by DMX, I wondered if he was upset I didn't sleep with him. *Y'all gon' make me lose my mind up in here, up in here...*

I shouldn't have agreed to this.

When it came time to order, I remembered why going on a date with a human was a bad idea. Food would make me sick. Did I order something and not eat it? Or did I order nothing and sit like an idiot while he ate?

I decided to order. I was already an idiot for coming in the first place.

"You're not eating, Willow. Aren't you hungry?" he asked while digging into his fifth pancake like it was an enemy.

My aunt, who'd been in her forties and had been my best friend, had passed on more to me than her old-school idioms. She'd also schooled me about men. For instance, she'd said you could tell how a man made love by watching him eat. If that was so, Remi believed in tearing some shit up. Good to know. I was more of the slow and sexy type, and damn if Max didn't have that shit down, but sometimes a girl wanted it rough. Not Valentina rough, just a little less than gentle.

I thought back to our kiss in my room. He'd devoured my tongue like it was something to keep as a souvenir. But he was teachable. And what he lacked in technique he more than made up for in looks.

Which was why I was here in the first place, wasn't it.

"Not really. I'll just box it up and take it with me." *And throw it in the motherfucking trashcan.*

He went back to his plate, his brows dipped for deep concentration. Okay this was awkward.

"So...did you enjoy my show tonight?" I asked.

"You know I did," he said without looking up, "Your best one yet. Almost got myself banned from the club." He laughed and I felt less tense.

"Must've had a change of clothes in your ride. I don't see any of my blood on you," I smirked. He'd think I meant fake blood.

Suddenly, he looked up. "You're so fucking beautiful, Willow. Your eyes, your smile, your brown skin. The way your ass moves when you walk. The way your tits just..." He looked from one to the other, licked his bottom lip and looked at me intensely.

I swallowed. "Uh. Thanks. So are you."

I'd been tripping earlier from a lack of blood and sex. What was his issue? Maybe I should have gone ahead and fucked him and worried about the aftermath later. If a lack of sex made him this crazy, he didn't need to miss it. Then again, he'd been on edge since he first entered Hades tonight. Even his usually smooth chin had thick stubble. Something else was up.

"I can take care of you," he whispered.

"What?" Now I realized why he'd been so quiet. He'd been getting up the nerve to bring something up.

He cleared his throat and spoke up. "Let me take care of you. Of course, you can still perform at Hades...or not, it's up to you but you don't have to work—"

"I love my job."

"—as long as you're with me. We can work it out. Just let me—"

"Where is this coming from?"

"—take care of you, Willow. Move in with me."

We both froze. This was worse than the *L* bomb he usually dropped on me. He'd been saying he loved me since we first met at Hades so I didn't take it seriously. Asking me to live with him was totally surprising.

The gravity of what all this had been about started weighing on me. I was touched, really I was, but it was never happening.

"I can't do that," I said.

"Can't or won't?" He put his fork down and wiped his mouth with a napkin.

"Both. You don't know me, Remi."

"Doesn't matter. I know enough. I want you to live with me." He dragged a hand through the long, black loose curls at the front of his head. He'd let his hair grow out since I said how much I loved it. "I have a nice condo and money to share," he said.

"Your tips have been nice, very generous." I wondered for the first time what the hell he did for a living. "But I don't need you to take care of me. I can take care of myself." *Besides, if you have any windows at your place, I'd be toast by morning.*

"You live in a *motel*. You don't have to do that. You can even stay in my guestroom if you'd feel more comfortable, although I was hoping—"

"No."

"—you'd want to share my bed. You get me, I get you. It'll be perfect. I just gotta tell you something about me first but…"

Putting my hand over his, I looked him straight in his beautiful metallic blues, the color of his skin making them pop like jewels. We were having two different discussions at this point and needed to get on the same page.

"I can't and won't live with you, Remi. End of story." Harsh, I know, but how else could I have put it? He was deliberately not listening.

He licked his lips then held his bottom lip between his teeth and stared. I removed my hand. Oh, no…this creep was about to lose it. Protecting myself meant I'd be exposed in front of surrounding diners. Not good.

"Why not?" he said.

I rubbed my index finger across both eyebrows. This was too intense. "I need my privacy. I like being alone."

"I thought you liked me. Am I too weird?"

Yes. "No, of course not. I have narcolepsy. Now *that's* weird. Why would you be too weird?"

"Because I get off on the fact you pass out cold. Because I loved rubbing whatever you used as blood all over my face tonight. Because I fantasize about killing you."

Whoa. Hold the phone.

"You just said you wanted to take care of me now you're saying you want to kill me?" I said.

"I wouldn't really do it. Not to you. I love you. I'm just answering your question about why I'm too weird for you…because the idea of fucking your corpse turns me on. You may perform that shit onstage, but you aren't into it like I am."

True.

Never would have dreamt people enjoyed mixing sex and death. I stumbled upon my niche at Hades when a failed attempt at captivating Franco for dinner turned to him offering me a job. I auditioned to perform at Hades as a necrophilia specialist since I was technically dead, though animated by magic. I loved performing before an audience and my narcolepsy fit in perfectly.

But yes. It was weird.

"Please don't look at me like that, Willow. I don't have anybody but you."

Shit, who was I to judge? I was far from normal. "Don't you have family?" I said.

I started feeling cool, like a gentle breeze was ruffling the hair on my neck. It was too cold out for air conditioning, but I was definitely feeling a breeze. I looked around. Nope. I was nowhere near a vent.

"No, my father said 'Here's your trust fund, Aaron. Now fuck off'," he said.

Well, that explained his bankroll. It also posed the question of why his father wanted nothing to do with him. Why was I the only one he had?

And I didn't know his nickname was Aaron. But hell, I really didn't know much about him anyway. Now did I? Lots of folks used aliases in Hades. No big deal. At least I didn't have to worry about him trying to take me home to meet the parents over some Saturday afternoon cookout.

Cool air tickled my arms, hardened my nipples. Sure hoped I was imagining things.

"Where's your mother?" I asked.

"Dead…and no, I don't have siblings."

"I'm sorry. What about a girlfriend? You're every girl's dream. Our waitress can't wait on other tables because of you." I looked in the waitress's direction to emphasize my point. She smiled and went back to cleaning the table across from us for the one hundredth time.

"Oh, sure. Girls love lying still, pretending they're dead so their boyfriend can get off. Or holding a loaded gun to his temple while he comes…or visiting morgues and cemeteries on dates."

I erupted in laughter because of his sarcasm and the images that came to mind. He'd painted an ugly picture of what it would be like to date him. "No, I guess that doesn't go over too well with many girls. Poor Remington."

"Most girls I've dated have called the cops. I'm damaged goods." He laughed, his face lighting up like he was sent straight from heaven. "What about *your* family?"

The wind on my neck had picked up, but my hair wasn't blowing at all. Uh oh…

"They live in Meyerland. My dad's the pastor of Meyerland Baptist Church."

He chuckled. "I didn't know you were a preacher's kid. That figures." He laughed again, but I paid him no mind. I was too distracted by the tickling sensation crawling up my arms and legs. Goosebumps covered my skin. Once I smelled sweet vanilla, I knew it was too late to make a graceful exit.

Hey, beautiful. I've missed you, a soft, male voice whispered in my ear.

Oh, God. Not here. "Go away," I unintentionally said aloud.

"What?" Remi asked. He was frowning, focusing bewildered eyes on me.

"Nothing."

Willow, who the hell is this? Are you on a date, beautiful?

"Yes. Now please don't do this here," I whispered.

"Willow, is everything okay?" Remi said.

Carrying on two different conversations was a bitch, especially when I was the only one hearing one of the voices.

I shifted in my seat. The chill and tickling had leveled off, but now I felt the heavy weight of a palm between my legs. Couldn't tell if it was being communicated through my brain psychically or if Max was really here in his mist form paying me an unwanted visit.

The palm squeezed. I moaned and squirmed involuntarily. Embarrassingly. The pressure increased as he spoke again. *You are mine, Willow. I told you, you will never be rid of me. I will claim you whenever, wherever I want. Now tell that human to disappear while I'm still in a forgiving mood.*

Remi pulled a cigarette from his pocket and put it in his mouth.

"Please don't," I said to Max.

Remi mistook it as a request directed at him and put the cig back in his pocket. "If my smoking bothers you, I'll quit," he said. "I'll do anything you want, whatever it takes."

Aw. That's so sweet. Now tell this imbecile to get lost, Max said as he squeezed again.

Another moan escaped my lips. Remi frowned.

I swear I only meant to respond to Max with my mind, but I was confused. Anxious. Scared. Before I could get hold on my emotions, a finger slipped in me and my nipple was pinched. My back felt weighted as if a strong body was pushed against me and I could feel an erection. I didn't think Max would risk exposure in public, but sometimes he surprised me.

Then I looked down to where my body was being probed. If he'd really been materializing from mist to flesh, my clothes would have moved and they didn't. I relaxed because at least that indicated Max was contacting me psychically. All I had to do was remember he was only touching my mind and I'd be all right.

Easier said than done...

A second finger slipped in and they both started moving in and out. My skin flushed. "Oh, shit."

"Are you okay?" Remi asked.

I jumped up. "Remi, I gotta go to the ladies room," I said then ran off. "Max, please don't do this in public," I whispered as I pushed the door to the bathroom.

I looked under each stall and thanked my lucky stars they were unoccupied. Leaning on the counter, I stared in the mirror until Max's image came in clearly. Sure enough, he was standing behind me, pressed closely with one hand dipped between my legs and the other holding me in place as he stimulated my breast.

"You're a bastard," I said as coldly and viciously as possible while he continued doing such sinful things to my body. I meant what I said, but my body responded favorably to him.

"You don't mean that, Willow." He grinned as he dragged his hand from my legs to his mouth. He licked both fingers slowly while staring at me in the mirror.

"Why are you here? Can't you just leave me alone?"

"No, Willow. I cannot. You are my bride and you belong here with me."

With his hand removed from my cookie, I was able to sound more convincing when I said, "Damn, I hate you. You don't need me. Go back to the rock you crawled from under and leave me the hell alone."

He grabbed my arms and swung me around to face him

before my brain could process the movement. Of course, if anyone walked in, I'd look like I was talking to myself. But I could see him clearly, his eternally young Celtic face…with those emerald green eyes, short blond hair, dimples galore and pouty lips. If he put those lips on me I was done.

"You knew what you were getting into when you asked me to turn you. I told you how it worked. You would be and are mine. If you did not want this bond you should never have completed the ritual. I was very clear about that."

"If I'da known I would be worse off, I wouldn't have. Believe me." Not entirely true. Becoming a vampire had been the single best thing I'd ever done with my miserable life.

He didn't have to know that.

"I thought you liked being a vampire," he smirked.

Asshole.

"I do. I just hate being wedded to you. I should have worked harder to find another maistre to turn me."

"That is neither here nor there." He dropped my arms and turned his back to me. Nearly a minute passed before he ran a manicured hand through his nape hair. "I thought you would have come back to me by now, Willow. That is the only reason I agreed to your leaving to begin with. Why have you not? Is it because of that human you have been taking blood from out there in the booth?"

He'd spat out *human* like a curse word and swung around abruptly.

"We gave it a couple of years, Max. I told you I couldn't handle it anymore. I can't be one of your many puppets. I'm not a trophy for your shelf. I need to be me, an individual…independent, self-reliant. Besides, you weren't forthcoming about everything that would happen between us. Being able to invade my mind, my dreams, was not part of it. I didn't knowingly sign up for that."

"You like it when I make you come in your sleep. Or do I mistake the toe curling and the way your pussy glistens?" He moved in close and ran a thumb across my bottom lip.

I stepped back, managing to bump into the sink. Not putting much distance between us.

"My body may respond to you, but you shouldn't take that to mean I want you popping up at *your* will. If you weren't so fucking selfish and overbearing I may even come around. But as it goes, you want what you want and to hell with my feelings."

There was a startling knock at the door.

"Willow? You in there? You okay?" Remi said.

I moved towards the door.

"You open this door and I am going to be all over you like a bomb in Pearl Harbor," Max said through gritted teeth. "I'll make you come right in front of your lover boy. Or maybe I should go there, disembowel him and spread his remains as weed fertilizer."

It was time to beg, appeal to his…oh, who was I kidding? He was evil through and through, but I needed him to back off at the moment.

"Puh-lease don't do this right now, Max. I'm here with someone. Someone who has no beef with you."

"And I should care because…?" His face distorted into something menacing. I shook my head and looked down. I couldn't believe I was doomed to an eternity with this asshole. Maybe vampires were really damned 'cause this was pure hell on earth.

"Because he's my friend and…and…"

"And?"

"You can always come back later today. Come see me around noon—my time—and we can be together without interruption."

His eyebrows raised, his jaw dropped. "You will not fight me? You promise to give yourself to me freely?"

"Yes." I gulped. I really hated him. But damn if my cookie didn't clench at the thought of him coming to me later when the sun was high and my drapes were drawn tightly. It would be just him and me. Good times.

"You know I'll just be in your head, right? I cannot come from my hiding place yet. You will be okay with me lying with you through your mind?"

He'd been a high-profile celebrity-type vampire before the HPA was passed. If he came out of hiding now, he'd be recognized immediately…and hunted as the evil monster he was.

Remi knocked on the door and opened it.

Yes. Yes! I shouted mentally to Max. Then I folded a hand towel like I'd washed my hands and threw it in the trash.

Max blew me a kiss and disappeared. I would never forget his Cheshire-cat-who-ate-the-canary grin. Motherfucker.

Turning to Remi, I smiled. "Yes. I'm okay. Must've been something I ate earlier."

I followed him into the hall and back to our booth.

"I thought I heard you talking to someone. Were you on the phone 'cause I didn't see anyone else in there?"

"No. I don't even have a cell phone."

To talk to my maistre vampire, I never needed one.

CHAPTER 7

Tension in his apple red Audi Roadster rose as Remi killed the engine and the lights.

We were parked in front of my motel room, and I knew he was expecting an invite. I risked a glance in his direction and met that same ol' creepy yet beautiful stare. Yep. He wanted to come in. Part of me wanted him to, but the rational side was winning out. We should keep our relationship professional like it always had been. Besides, shit with Max in the diner had been too close for comfort. He'd sanctioned human blood withdrawals since it was necessary for my existence, but not sex. I could imagine what Max would do if he caught me getting warm and cozy with Remi after catching me out with him.

But Max was a man of his word, so far anyway. If he was planning to visit me at noon, I didn't have to worry about him popping up within the next few hours. The real question was whether I trusted myself to be in my room alone with Remi.

I looked over at the digital clock. It was nearly five o'clock. Could I keep my hands and fangs off him? Did I really have to?

Remi spoke first. "I'm not expecting sex or anything. I

know I came on strong earlier, but I can behave." He looked towards my room door. "I just don't want the night to end. I feel like I'm getting to know you better." His eyes shifted to me again, traveling over my breasts. "Maybe you'll let me touch you a little like I usually do? Since I won't see you again until next week?" He stretched his hand out to touch me then dropped it on his lap. Was he demonstrating how well he could keep his hands to himself or proving how hard it was to do so?

"Remi…"

"We could be good together, Willow. Will you at least consider my proposal? About living with me?"

Hell no. "Sure."

"Liar. But that's—"

I awakened with a start. No, that was an understatement. I was downright panicky, nearly pissing myself. It had come on so suddenly this time, without warning.

When you have narcolepsy, you get used to falling asleep at the most inappropriate times, but geez. Being in the car with Remi during an episode was all wrong. He'd admitted to fantasizing about killing me. Could there be a worse keeper for my virtue when I'd hit the sudden REM? Maybe it didn't count since I was already dead. But still. He didn't know that.

I looked around expecting to find my guts spilt across the seat with him bathing his dick in it when he said, "I didn't touch you. I swear."

He stubbed out a nearly-finished cigarette into the ashtray, rolled his window up, and stared out.

He knew what I'd been thinking, but didn't sound offended. He sounded matter-of-factly, like it was the most logical thing to be afraid of him when I fell asleep. Security wasn't here to keep Remi in check. I was completely justified in being suspicious. He knew it, and I knew it.

Now what the hell had he been saying about *living* with him? Yeah, right.

I shuddered. The possibilities were scary. Not only was he not roommate material, he wasn't a good carpooler either. I hadn't been thinking clearly when I'd gotten in the car with him.

"So, how long have you had narcolepsy?" he asked as he ran a trembling hand through his hair.

That wasn't the conversation I expected, but it was better than continuing the old one. And why was he so nervous?

I looked down in his lap.

Oh.

He was poking through his jeans with what must have been one ache of an erection. He really had restrained himself. Impressive. He'd been on his best behavior even when I had passed out right next to him in a relatively confined space.

He suddenly slapped his palm to his forehead. "You know what? I never thought to ask if you're seeing someone. I just assumed not." He paused. "Well? Are you?"

"Uh…" I'd never had to explain my relationship with Max before. "It's complicated."

"I've never seen you with anyone. You stay at the motel alone, don't you?"

"Like I said—it's complicated."

"I really wish you'd open up to me." He scratched his head. "You need someone to protect you, provide for you…love you. I can do all that. I'm single, no kids. You're like my girlfriend. I don't see anyone but you."

"We're not dating, Remi. I'm sorry. I can't be your girlfriend. I can see you at the club but that's it."

Silence.

I hated ending the night on that note so I thought of something to talk about. "How long have you been a necrophiliac?" I asked.

He chuckled, "You first."

"What?"

"I asked how long you've had narcolepsy."

Oh, yeah. He had asked that. "It's genetic so I was born with it. I had an aunt who was narcoleptic so when I first started showing signs in my teens, my parents knew what was going on." I flashed back to the prayer meetings and attempted exorcisms. Since my parents were convinced narcolepsy was demon possession, they had summoned all the deacons and elders of the church to cast it out of me. When that hadn't worked, they'd put me on a water and unleavened bread fast and tried beating it out of me. I had been quarantined and forced to pray the Lord's Prayer every hour for...

"Willow?" I shut off the memories and looked at him. "Are you okay? I asked if there was a cure or treatment for it."

"No cure. And as far as treatment goes, you name it, I've tried it: acupuncture, hypnosis, medication, routine therapy..." *Exorcism, spells...*

"Lobotomy?"

I laughed. "Okay. Not *every*thing."

"Are you on any medicine now?"

"No. I visit a doctor often to be tested for clinical trials and I attend a sleep disorder support group though."

"A group of narcoleptics? I didn't realize it was so common."

"It's not. Most of our group members have psychosomatic issues manifested by insomnia. I'm the only one with narcolepsy but it helps being around other people who suffer from sleep disorders. The psychiatrist who facilitates it is a caring man. I like him a lot. I came back to Houston after being gone a year because he built a clinic in the Medical Center."

"I think I'm jealous."

And sure enough, his hands had tightened to fists.

Okaaaay. It was time to call it a night. He'd already stalked me, said he wanted to kill me, and now was showing how irrationally jealous he could be. Apparently we weren't going to be able to end on a high note. I grabbed the door handle.

"I know about psychiatrists," he said. "Something happened when I was young...and well, I had to see one—a few—for a while. I still do...see a psychiatrist, I mean."

No big surprise there. "It must have been something bad that happened to you."

"Yeah. I've been fascinated with death ever since."

I settled back in my seat. I'd always been curious about how he came to be aroused by death. "You wanna talk about it?"

"No more than you wanna tell me what you were thinking about a minute ago."

"Fair enough," I said. Some things were better kept to oneself, but I needed to confirm a suspicion. I'd give a little, ask a little, keep it fair. "You were abused?"

"Yes."

"By your parents?"

He sighed. "No, I was kidnapped when I was six."

Oh, boy. His story really was bad. To learn more, I needed to give more. "My parents are religious nut-jobs. They would never call what they did to me abuse, but Child Protective Services would," I said.

He shifted uncomfortably. "If you tell me more Willow, I'll want to kill them so let's not talk about this anymore."

I actually smiled. I wasn't sure whether it was because he'd want to kill *for* me or because he was brutally honest or because we'd both suffered childhood trauma.

Strangely, I felt close to him. There had been no blood exchange, no ritualistic supernatural bonding, no sex, but I felt closer to him than I had to anyone since...ever.

"It's probably best you don't come in," I whispered.

He nodded.

Leaning over until we were eyeball-to-eyeball, I placed both of his hands on the steering wheel. Then I unhooked his seatbelt and slowly wrapped it around his neck. My eyes never left his as I undid his jeans and began stroking the part of him aching most. I worked him with one hand, pulled the seatbelt snugly around his straining neck with my other. As blood flow and oxygen were limited to the head on his neck, the engorged head in his lap swelled hard as a brick.

Watching him enjoy the pain and pleasure was a real treat, but I broke eye contact to bend downward where he couldn't see my fangs as they appeared and red eyes as they changed. Although concentrating on the rhythm of his thrusts into my hand kept me from focusing on his bulging veins, it was still hard not biting him.

The closer he got to finishing, his skin flushed and his hands tightened on the steering wheel. I pumped him harder since he was so close to the bliss he sought, the release he needed. When his chest heaved vigorously and his hips jerked upward, I pulled the seatbelt tighter. Semen shot out all over my hand in several jets, landing on his underwear and jeans. Having spent himself to completion, he gurgled and passed out.

There had been no captivation, no mental manipulation…just me understanding what Remi needed and giving it to him.

Fuckin' A.

His head rolled to the window once I released his neck and returned the seatbelt to its proper condition. The same shirt he'd worn to Hades, that now had my blood all over it, was on the floorboard. It was perfect for cleaning his fluids so I put it to good use. His breathing and coloring had returned to normal by the time I was done.

I zipped him up, kissed his cheek and stared at his beautiful face for a moment while he slept. His strong jaw and sharp nose were great features, almost as worthy of attention as his eyes.

Okay, enough of that. "I had a good time tonight. See you next week," I whispered.

Waving to my neighbors as they left room #5, I got out and walked to mine without a backwards glance.

I had shit to do before morning.

CHAPTER 8

I waited until I heard Remi's car leave the lot before I really got down to it. Since I didn't have much anyway, it didn't take me long to pack it all up and move to a room on the other side of the motel before the first ray of sunlight hit the horizon.

I finally got to sleep around six o'clock and awakened at ten to watch my usual Sunday morning church service. It was the only way I could attend church without actually attending. Without bleeding through every pore of my body and shriveling up like a prune and waiting to be burned. It had been like this since I'd been turned.

My parents had always said anything that couldn't touch a churchyard was clearly damned and destined for hell's fire. Except I'd never seen in the bible that going to church was a prerequisite for salvation. Still, our aversion to church and holy emblems was baffling. We were okay when it came to walking in a cemetery and that was blessed land. I'd had too much church experience to presume all churches were holy ground and all cemeteries were unholy. So I had yet to work out why vampirism and church didn't mix.

Nevertheless, being unable to step foot on holy ground didn't make me give up on connecting with God through church.

I'd had one hour of come-to-Jesus TV and one hour to myself before you-know-who had shown up.

We'd been going at it for nearly two hours, bodies slapping, headboard banging. He'd been pounding me relentlessly for the last five minutes, determined to make me come again. I was already on number—oh, I don't even remember. It was so good. I was ashamed to admit that. He'd started out slowly each time, and gradually increased speed and intensity until I could take no more. Then we'd change positions and he'd hit it again.

He had a special gift for going and going without coming coupled with his egomaniacal drive to be the best lover ever. After thousands of years of practice with thousands of lovers, he didn't have to worry about that. He was hands down the best. I only had one other lover to compare him with but I'd heard others speak of Max's skills. And he was giving all of us his best.

"Say it, Willow. Say my name when you come."

"Fuck you."

"No, fuck…you." He punctuated each word with a deep thrust then roughly lifted my knees, pinning them to my shoulders with his palms. The change of position sharpened the penetration, making me feel the beginnings of an intense burn in my belly. It was rising, threatening to send me over the edge into a sweet, sweet…

I turned my head from him and squeezed my eyes shut, concentrating on the sensations. He grabbed my jaw, squeezed and yanked it around to face him again.

"Say my fucking name, Willow. I want you to know who makes you come."

"Max," I mumbled.

His broad shoulders kept my knees in place as he dug his

fingers deeper in my cheeks.

"No. You say my whole name." His lips crushed mine as his hips worked my lower body into an all-consuming heat. I stiffened and finally exploded. He let go of my face and leaned his ear to my mouth so he could hear my humiliation.

"Maximilian!" I cried out as the walls of my body clenched and released, clenched and released, grabbing onto his dick like a vise. I rode out the waves clutching the sheets, listening to his obscene talk as he kept thrusting.

"Fucking right, Willow. It's Maximilian, the greatest. Don't you dare forget it. This is my pussy, Willow." Then he thought about how *pussy willow* could refer to a plant and laughed sharply. "No pun intended."

As I came down from the clouds, I remembered how much I hated him. "I hate you so much, Max."

He ignored me, just loosened his grip on my knees and lazily planted kisses along my cheeks, chin and forehead. Then he stuck out that tongue he'd used so thoroughly on me and licked my forehead and temple. Releasing my legs, he slowly pulled out, fully erect. Looking down between my legs, he began stroking himself.

"Are you ready for me to come? Just say the word and I will not. I will keep going, pleasuring you all day long if you want."

"Just get it over with and get off me," I said bitterly.

"Don't be hostile. You enjoy our time together as much as I do." He shuddered as he continued stroking.

I looked away so he wouldn't see heat in my face. He sure was sexy.

He smiled, aware of his effect on me. My pride was bruised all the more.

"Just come back to me. Let me love you like this every day. That human certainly cannot," he said.

"This isn't love. This is fucking. There's a big difference."

"When it feels this good, who cares whether it is love."

His hand moved up and down his shaft faster. "Touch me. I'm close. You know what I want."

I sat up and took over, stacking my hands around his thick length, topping his head with my mouth. Careful not to bite him with my fangs, I sucked 'til my jaws hurt. I knew what he wanted all right and I hated it. Not the oral sex. I actually liked that. No, I hated what came afterward. It felt degrading when he marked me in that way. My only solace was that this was all mental—vivid as hell—but only mental. He wasn't really here so he wasn't really going to…

He groaned loudly, jerked violently, and palmed the back of my head. Then he yanked my hair back, releasing my hands and mouth from his body, throwing me down roughly on the bed so he could shoot his load all over me.

"Oh! God! Yessss!" he shouted while his semen spurted like warm Elmer's glue. Although he aimed for my stomach and saturated it, evidence of his pleasure landed all over my breasts, face, hair, and bed.

I lay grossed out, not only because it was all over me, but because it was Max and I knew how much he enjoyed covering me with it. Even though I couldn't get pregnant, he never came inside me. He'd said this way I'd know he had enjoyed himself. I think he just wanted to fuck with my head, remind me I was his possession.

I cracked open an eye to see the damage. His head was thrown back, fangs protruding like mini-daggers. His muscles corded and strained as he continued stroking himself, continued coming. He was a vision to behold—an erotic god—and yet, I couldn't appreciate it. I could only dwell on my contempt for him and our blood bond. He finally groaned one last time and dropped his head like he'd fallen into a coma.

I wished.

"Goddamn, Willow—"

"Don't use the Lord's name like that."

"—you are so good even from afar." He shuddered again

from an aftershock. "It may be worth it to leave my hiding place just to be inside you for real again."

"Don't be silly. You'd put everyone in your blood line in danger if you came out of hiding," I said. He started smearing his glue all over my breasts and stomach then rubbed it between my legs. "Please stop. Wasn't that enough?"

"I can never get enough of you."

Before I could stop myself, tears fell from my eyes in despair. I was powerless with him. Why couldn't I just kill him, be rid of him once and for all?

Thou shalt not kill.

And even if God himself told me he would forgive me, I'd have to figure out how to kill Maximilian, the great maistre vampire. He'd been undead so long, acquired so much power and supernatural gifts, he'd become nearly impossible to kill. Then there was that whole problem of if he died, so did I. That's how humans had obliterated our population so fast. They'd become hip to our blood ties and started going after maistre vampires, killing two birds with one stone so to speak.

I was fucked but I wasn't suicidal.

He stopped rubbing me and spoke softly, "Willow, why do you insist on making me a villain? Stop fighting me. Let me love you."

I laughed through sobs. "What do you know about love, Max?"

"Making love is love. It can be. I worship you with my body, my entire essence. I open myself to you, give you my all." He waved his hand like a wand across my skin without touching me, clearing my mind of the mess, replacing it with the plain black gown I'd lain down in. I wiped my eyes and rolled away from him.

"You have what? Four hundred brides you can *love*? Why do you insist on staking your claim on me?"

"It's more like one hundred now," he said wistfully. "This anti-vampire sentiment has not been good on my collection of beauties."

"You can always replace them like you did the ones you exiled."

"I will not dishonor them so. They were good, faithful brides who did not deserve such human betrayal and cruelty. I am bidding my time…and then I will avenge them."

I turned towards him, shocked. "I didn't know you cared."

He was lying on his side facing me, looking across the room. He'd added a black silk robe to cover himself. The black accented his light blond hair elegantly, so much so that I almost reached out to run my fingers through it.

His emerald green eyes lifted to mine in that moment.

Shit, he'd read my mind.

He reached for my face then dropped his hand when I flinched. "Of course, I care. What kind of monster do you take me for?" He looked solemn. "I picked each woman personally, indiscriminate of age, weight, height, race, class. I only required them to be beautiful and I promised they would remain that way forever if they wedded me. I was most honored when each agreed to join me in this undead life. Now they are truly dead. Gone from this existence, from me."

This time I did touch his hair, petting him lightly. Allowed his sweet vanilla scent to permeate my senses. He leaned his head on my shoulder.

"I'm sorry," I said. I really was. I'd never disliked the other brides.

"You are the only one of my brides who came to me, Willow. The only one who sought me out, who I did not have to seduce, who begged to be turned."

I tensed, suddenly unhappy with the direction of this conversation. "That's because I thought being a vampire would cure me of narcolepsy."

"Yes. I know. Still, you mesmerized me completely. How do you modernists say it? You knocked my socks off. Not only beautiful, but talented, independent, adventurous, strong-willed. The strong-willed part is the hardest to deal with, but is nonetheless one of the things I find attractive about you."

He grabbed my hand before I could pull away and looked in my eyes. "I have summoned all my brides and all the brothers of my lineage to come back to the clan. I need you all near me so I can protect you. Besides, there is strength in numbers. Everyone has returned…everyone but you. Come back to me, Willow. I don't want to get word of your final death as I have the others. It would hurt too much."

He kissed my knuckles one at a time then held onto my hand a minute, admiring the contrast of our skin complexions, mine caramel brown, his Celtic. About as contrasting as zebra stripes. "I care too much," he said.

I'd be lying if I said I wasn't tempted. He could be so convincing, so persuasive…so sexy. But I had a "life" here, and I was enjoying it. I enjoyed my independence, my individuality, my job at Hades. And I think I enjoyed spending time with Remi.

"I can't," I said, turning away, too afraid of losing myself in him.

"Just think about it, Willow." Then his voice hardened and he squeezed my hand so hard I thought the bones would crack. "Don't force me to go there and drag your ass back. I will if I have to."

With that he was gone.

I held my hand still until the last traces of his mental influence had waned and I could wiggle my fingers again. Then I sighed and leaned over to cut off the nightstand lamp. I wondered how long before he made good on his threat.

"Oh, and Willow," his voice slammed inside my head, "stay away from that human. He's nothing but trouble."

Now wasn't he the pot calling the kettle black.

CHAPTER 9

Thanks to Max's thorough workout, I'd spent the rest of the day sleeping and dreaming. Which would hopefully keep my narcoleptic episodes at bay for a good twelve hours or more. That was one thing he was good for.

Unfortunately, my dream had left me sad, confused, and wary. It wasn't as vivid as Max's psychic visitation because only my subconscious was active, but it still seemed unnervingly real.

In the dream, Remi and I were having a good time laughing and talking then things worsened to the point of him trying to kill me. He'd learned I was a vampire and tried to drag me into the sunlight. I fought him, tried reasoning with him, and finally had to kill him. I'd cried in my dream because I would miss him.

When I woke up, my pillow was wet with actual tears. I couldn't believe it. I hadn't cried like that since I'd become a vampire. What the fuck was going on?

Max had been right. Remi was trouble—the deep shit kind.

When the phone rang, I nearly jumped out of my skin. I didn't get calls.

"Hello?"

"Willow, it's me."

I recognized Franco's Spanish accent right away. "What's up, Franco?" I said while smoothing out the comforter as I made my bed. I'd given him a fake number for my employment file so Punch must have told him which motel to call, and the front desk had been accommodating enough to forward the call to my room.

"How've you been today?"

"Okay. No permanent damage to speak of."

"Good. I was worried about you."

"Well, don't worry," I said as I sat on the bed and braced myself for whatever was next. I didn't buy for one minute he'd just called to check on me. "So what else is up?"

"You know I wouldn't ask if it wasn't important, but I need a favor."

"Okay. I guess I owe you one." I hated owing anyone anything for this very reason. You never knew when they'd want to collect and you couldn't pick which favor to agree to.

"I need you to come in tonight."

"You're kidding, right? You know I don't work on Sundays. It's the Lord's—"

He snorted. "The Sabbath is Saturday, Willow. It's always been Saturday."

"I know. I just grew up with Sunday being—"

"Oh save it. Do you really think your soul stands a chance? It doesn't. For the last year I've catered to this redemption dream of yours and keeping the Sabbath blah blah blah, but I need you tonight. Valentina called in. Cin called in. Fire's off just like you and I tried calling her first…couldn't reach her. I got celebrity guests coming in. I'm even starting a new girl tonight so the rest of you can take more time off when you want. But tonight, Willow, I need—"

"Fine."

Silence.

"I didn't expect you to give in so easily," he said.

"I owe you, right?"

"Willow, I'm not blackmailing you. I just need you to come in and put on a great show. If there was some other reason than you holding on to some human ideal, I could understand. But c'mon—there's no hope for creatures like us. We are what we are."

"Franco, I don't expect you to understand...but you have been there for me when I most needed you. I will be there for you tonight," I said then hung up.

Getting dressed was depressing not just because I was headed to work on Sunday night or because Franco had scoffed my faith, but because it felt like the beginning of the end. Breaking rules had a snowball effect. It would be work tonight and what tomorrow? Would I be using God's name in vain, having orgies, killing for sport, worshipping Buddha? Had I been kidding myself all along?

Franco was right. I had given in easily, almost like I knew this day was coming. Like I knew my soul was already gone and I had been trying to hold on to its memory. I knew I couldn't deny my vampire nature forever. I just hadn't expected the time to come so soon.

I sensed Punch's presence and felt his eyes on me as soon as I walked in the club's employee side door. *Better avoid him as much as possible.*

Catching a glimpse of Onyx onstage in a diaper as I walked over to the music booth, was no better. After handing my CD to the deejay, I hauled ass to the dressing room. Didn't want to see foolish grins on the fat baldies sitting in the audience.

The smell of wildflowers hit my nose as soon as I opened the dressing room door. It was an unusual scent which meant there was someone new inside. The new girl...

"You must be Sleepy Willow," she said from the far corner where she sat wearing a white mock turtleneck knit dress and black tights. She was braless, and as the pink of her nipples showed, I knew she'd fit in perfectly around here. The real killers were the five-inch leopard print stiletto come-hither pumps crossed at her ankles.

"And you are?" I said, after taking her in from head-to-toe. *Niiiice.*

"Queen Ming."

"Well, welcome to Pit of Hades Fetish Club." I leaned casually against my table and folded my arms. "You Japanese?"

"Korean."

Ah. I was never good at categorizing people of Asian descent. "Sorry."

"No problem." She uncrossed her long legs and leaned forward. Long lashes, thin lips, black hair in a bun showing off a delicate neckline…

I cleared my throat. "So what's your specialty? Shoes?" I joked.

"Yep. How'd you know? Shoes, feet…all things podophilia."

"Really? I was joking. I didn't know, but those shoes are to die for."

She smiled. "Spoken like a necrophilia expert."

I smiled back. Liked her already.

Franco stuck his head in the doorway. "Ming, you're on in five. Tommy Lee's out there so pay extra attention to VIP table #2," he said. Then he stepped in, kissed my forehead and walked back out.

Ming grabbed a crystal bowl of soapy water, some cotton balls and red nail polish. I wished her luck, and she left, head held high.

It took me less than ten minutes to get ready and about as long to perform. The room was packed, energy high, but my set was dull, totally uneventful. I felt uninspired for some reason.

Surely hoped that reason had nothing to do with Remi's

absence.

Afterward, I picked random patrons and collected ten vials of blood from each for later consumption. Recent events had told me I needed to keep a stash in my motel refrigerator. I could always warm the blood in a cup. No, it wasn't as good as feeding straight from a vein, but it was better than teetering on the verge of starvation again.

On the way back to the dressing room, I was told Franco wanted to see me ASAP. After hiding the vial case in my duffel bag, I showered, dressed, and headed to his office. Hair on the back of my neck stood as I walked in and saw Franco sitting behind his desk and an unfamiliar man sitting across from him. My instincts screamed *foe*!

"Willow, this is Agent Monroe." *Aha!* "He's here to ask you a few questions. I told him you were tired after your performance and he should come back if—"

"Ms…?" Monroe cut off Franco and addressed me.

"Call me Willow. What can I do for you?" I said callously. His wrinkled cheap suit, unpolished loafers, and bad dye job told me he was trying to look bigwig and failing badly. He was a wannabe trying to earn respect, working his way up the ranks, doing anything to get to the top.

Here to ask me questions. Not good.

And like a bomb over Baghdad, he produced pictures from my show the previous night.

"Ms. Willow, I am Agent Monroe, here on behalf of the Vampire Extermination Team to follow-up on a suspicion of vampirism. It has been brought to our attention that you performed a realistic death scene last night. These photos were posted online." He spread all four out on Franco's desk. "Is this you in the photos?"

This was one time when I wished the myth about vampires not having a reflection was true.

I feigned like I had to study them closely before answering. "Uh, yeah. That's me. What about it?"

"You don't have to answer any questions if you don't feel up to it, Willow," Franco said. "Monroe, these photos were obtained in violation of our club's policy—"

"*Agent* Monroe," he corrected. "If you have qualms with the persons who took the photos, file a claim. That's outside my purview." He smiled cunningly. "What I'm most interested in is the implication that you are employing a vampire."

"This is a fetish club. It's not against the law for me to pretend to stab myself," I said.

"It is if you are a vampire. Are you a vampire, Ms. Willow?" Monroe sneered.

"No. Now, if you have nothing further, I'm beat and need to—"

"I'd be happy to schedule a meeting with you at your home. Where is that exactly?" He pulled a small flip pad and pen from his jacket pocket and waited.

"Why don't you just ask your questions now and let's get this over with." My address was the last thing he was getting.

He chuckled. "Sure. Not a problem. Can you explain how you were able to make these scenes look so realistic?"

"Makeup."

"May I see the makeup you used for your show?"

"You don't think I'd be stupid enough to stab myself for real in front of everyone knowing I'd heal if I was a vampire, now do you?"

"Vamps have such superiority complexes, such arrogance…you just might. But I'm not here to speculate, just investigate. And I'll ask the questions from now on Ms. Willow."

Franco sighed. "Get him the makeup so he can get the hell outta my office."

"You know this is a bad time to be a vamp-sympathizer. If I were you I'd pick the winning side," Monroe taunted Franco.

Glad I'd kept it just in case, I got the cosmetic caboodle case from my dressing room table and returned to Monroe's interrogation.

He ran his hands along the case and inside, rubbing powder and liquids between his fingers like he was testing the texture. A handkerchief from his inner jacket pocket was used to clean his fingers when he was done.

"Hm. You've anticipated this moment and covered your tracks. I'm impressed," he said. "You're not as dumb as I thought."

I snorted. "Are we done now?"

"I'd like to see your dressing room if you don't mind…maybe even your gym bag."

Franco stood. "I think we're done. That's an invasion of privacy and goes against our club policy."

Monroe stood also. "You realize immunity is afforded to me during the course of my investigation? I can search her belongings, her nigger body, your club and every last one of your nasty-ass customers if I have to. I don't need a warrant. I don't need your consent. All I have to prove is there was probable cause to suspect that Ms. Willow here is a vampire. That's vampire due process." He slammed his hand on the photos on the desk. "And I think I can prove probable cause. You wanna bet my case will hold up over your invasion of privacy claim?"

"I showed you the makeup I used for the scene in these pictures so where's your probable cause now? Further questions and searches would be harassment."

He stepped towards me. "I don't need a coon telling me how to do my job," he spat.

I stepped back. "You're trying to bait me." And it had almost worked. My fangs were threatening to break through.

Franco walked around his desk to face Monroe. "Get your bigot ass out of my office before I call your superiors at VET, *Agent* Monroe."

Like the bell at the end of a fight, Monroe's phone rang. He answered, raised his eyebrows, said a few uh huhs and hung up. "I have to go."

I tried my best not to smile. "That's a shame," I said, moving closer to him, reaching out my hand to shake his. Time to throw some mental interference. He left my palm hanging, but his eyes were wide open and on me. That's all I needed. I focused on his aqua blues and willed him to stare deep into my hazels. I stared deeper into his…

Wait a damn minute…where were his fucking pupils! They were so tiny there was barely anything to dilate. And they wouldn't budge. That part that opened to his soul was not opening at all.

"Looking for something, Ms. Willow?" he sneered.

"Uh…No. I'm…I was just trying to shake your hand. It's nice to meet you." Just as I tried to step back he grabbed my palm and squeezed.

"Nice to meet you too." He moved in close enough for me to feel his coffee breath on my face. "I know what you were looking for, I know why, and I know what you are. We're done for now, but I'll be back with marshmallows to roast your ass."

Best to kill him right now…switch to Catholicism, see a confessor, say ten Hail Marys…

"And just so you know, if I end up missing, you will have a bull's-eye on your black head. If you try to get missing, I'll make sure everyone at this hellhole you call a club will be brought up on charges for aiding and abetting your escape." He dropped my hand, unfolded his walking stick, and left.

I'd be damned. Monroe was blind.

Swallowing hard, I turned to Franco whose eyes were as wide as full moons. "You set me up," I said.

CHAPTER 10

"I swear I did not."

"Yesterday, no one here knew what I was and now that you and Punch do, the fucking VET is on my ass," I said.

"Pure coincidence. Have you forgotten you were attacked last night? Someone was after you before now."

"Maybe you set that up too. You had Punch drive me home. Why? You wanted to see where I live, right?" I was really getting pissed. Everything was clicking and it all pointed to Franco and it all stunk. "What? The money from Hades isn't enough? You trying to collect on my head too?" I felt my countenance change, knew I was looking monstrous when Franco backed into his desk. "You told me to come to work tonight!" I yelled as I grabbed his throat with one hand and lifted him from the ground.

He grabbed my arm with both of his and struggled. I squeezed harder until my hand couldn't get any tighter without crushing his windpipe. When I thought he might pass out, my hand suddenly felt like it was on fire. It got hotter and hotter and spread down my arm. I dropped him and screamed in pain. I looked at the blisters on my hand with awe as he fell to the floor coughing and gagging, trying to catch his breath. I fell to the floor next to him.

As we lay writhing and nursing our wounds, Franco choked out, "I promise I didn't set you up. I wouldn't do that to you or any supernatural, Willow. You gotta trust me." Moments passed before he kicked his leg out in anger. "FUCK! If you ever try that shit again, I will fuck you up."

I believed him. "What are you?"

"*What* doesn't matter. Only who."

"Who the fuck are you then?"

"Someone trying to save your ass. You looking skyward to some god you've never seen while I'm right here in your face trying to keep you alive," he said in a stronger voice.

"I died a couple of years ago."

"Undead then."

"Well, at least I know you're mortal. Apparently you can be suffocated, strangled."

He sat up, rubbing his neck. "When I'm in a physical body."

I looked at him sharply. "You can leave your body?"

"I don't have a body. I'm merely borrowing this one." He got up from the floor. "I rather like it though. Do you think I chose wisely?"

I nodded slowly, still dumfounded, unable to speak.

Upon inspection, I was relieved to find my hand had returned to normal. His crispy-critter defense mechanism hadn't left permanent damage.

"Are you sharing the body? Is Franco your real name?" I asked once I was able to formulate thoughts and articulate them.

"The owner of this body is dead. I made a deal with him to assume his identity in exchange for something he wanted badly. I held my end of the bargain and now he is holding his."

I shook my head. Did Franco kill him? What was the deal he'd made? What did Franco look like for real? Was he even male?

"Willow, I know you must have lots of questions about me, but the point is I am not your enemy. Humans have waged war against vampires and it will only be a matter of time before they come after the rest of us. I wanna be ready when they do. Supernaturals must stick together."

"If you didn't set me up, why is all this happening to me now?" I said.

"I don't know."

"How can I trust you? How can I trust anybody?"

"I'd let you suck my neck and fuck you good to gain your trust, but you don't want my blood." I frowned. I hadn't met anyone who's blood I didn't want. "It's tainted," he said, "and sex would bind us too tightly together. Neither of us wants that." He looked away. "Willow, I didn't just find out you're a vampire, darling. I've always known, ever since your botched attempt to feed on me. Remember? You fell asleep and I waited around 'til you woke up and offered you a job."

I flashed back to when I'd first come back to Houston. I was hungry and hadn't honed a system for procuring meals without getting busted or killing my source. Logistically, captivation had to come first in case I had a narcoleptic episode while in pursuit. That way I wouldn't have to worry about getting staked and lit afire in my sleep. Aside from that, I had to catch my victim alone, bite fast, and disappear before they knew what hit 'em. It wasn't a perfect plan but it had worked twice before.

It was late and Franco had been walking alone on the sidewalk. I'd followed him to an empty parking lot, waited until he'd unlocked his Range Rover and moved in. Falling asleep hadn't been part of the plan, but that's what happened as I reached him. My last thought had been *oh shit, I'm dead.* When I awakened, I was surprised to find him nurturing my head in his lap. He'd lifted me to his backseat and kept me safe.

Ironic, considering I'd been attacking him.

I immediately tried to captivate his mind and get on with the business of devouring his blood when I discovered I was unable to do so. I thought maybe I was just off my game. When he offered me a job at his club, I figured he'd thought I was trying to rob him and felt sorry for me. After I nailed the audition, I ordered a phlebotomy kit off the internet, and the rest was history.

But my version of history had been inaccurate, hadn't it.

"You knew?" I said.

"From the first moment you started following me. I can sense the presence and nature of all beings. In fact, I've been collecting supernaturals…developing a network. I want Hades to be a haven for us. A revolution is coming and we all need to be ready."

This was just too much. "So Punch? Fire? Cin? Everyone here is supernatural?"

"No, but I will not say who is or isn't. I will never reveal anyone else's gift. Everyone's story is theirs to tell."

"So I really can trust you."

"Absolutely."

Whistling all the way to the dressing room, I felt surprisingly giddy. I could trust Franco. He wanted to help me, to help all of us, and he had the means to do so. Hades had felt like home, but I never knew how much it really was. I was surrounded by others with dark secrets. They weren't illegals like me, but we had common enemies—humans. For the first time since I'd been turned, I actually felt God was smiling down on me, sending me a sign that he'd protect me, that I was all right with him. Yeah, I knew Franco didn't believe he was doing God's work, but whether he believed it or not, Franco was part of God's master plan. God could use even the unwilling because he worked in mysterious—

What the…

Ming was leaning over my table with her arm elbow-deep in my duffel bag.

She turned abruptly as if she sensed me in the doorway and laughed nervously. "Oh, God, I'm sorry. I know this looks bad, but I'm really desperate. You wouldn't happen to have a tampon or pad, would you? I got a surprise visitor and with all this white…"

Bullshit. She was lying through her teeth. If she was bleeding I'd smell it, and the only thing I smelled was wildflowers and BS. Dumb bitch had been caught rifling through my bag. "No, I do not," I said icily.

I didn't even have a period anymore, thank God.

"Darn. Well, thanks anyway." She walked back to her table and started packing her stuff. Apparently, she'd forgotten she still needed to protect all that white she was wearing.

What the hell was Franco trying to pull? *Oh, trust me, Willow. We gotta stick together yada yada.*

Was this his doing? Had he distracted me in his office while his hussy rummaged through my stuff for evidence? Or was she acting independently? And if so, why was she targeting me?

There was some shady business going on around here and I needed to get to the bottom of it. Resolved to seek counsel from someone I did trust, I gathered my things and headed to her house.

CHAPTER 11

I never needed an appointment to see her, never even knocked on her door. As always, as soon as I started up the steps, Saybree's front door creaked opened to a red-lit foyer.

The one-story house was quiet, with the exception of cats meowing and scratching across hardwood floors. Declawing them would have been my top priority, but I suspected they were really humans made pets. Of course, I had no proof…and it wouldn't matter to me one way or the other. So whatever.

Before I was in good, a strong peppermint, ginger and lemon scent greeted me. She'd either been ridding the house of evil spirits or trying to boost her mood. I never could be straight on which scent combos were for aromatherapy and which were for spell-casting.

"It's late, Willow." Her soft voice came from the kitchen.

"I know. I'm sorry. I just got off work." I closed the door behind myself and walked towards her voice.

She was sitting by the window at the table, illuminated by a black candle centerpiece. Looked like she had been waiting for me all night. Her long black hair had more gray streaks than last time and her hands were bonier. Even her usually radiant Indian skin, looked dull and cracked. She'd aged significantly within just a few months.

"You worked Sunday? Wow. Things really are evolving for you." She smiled, but it wasn't warm, didn't reach her eyes. "So you have questions. And what do you have to make offering, dear?" She was, as usual, straight to the point.

I handed her the wad of cash I'd made in tips tonight and one vial of blood. I'd enjoyed some on my way over so I knew she was getting top-quality blood.

She thumbed through the cash and stuck the vial down her cleavage. Then she smiled genuinely. It was amazing what a witch could do with human blood.

"Come. Sit." She gathered her green sari, scooted further under the table, and waved to the chair across from her. Several gold bracelets clanked as she moved. "You've not come in awhile, child. It's good to see you. You have questions about love and trust. Yes?"

Love? Well, that was a new one on me. Trust, yes, but love? Hell, no.

I sat down. "Some weird things have happened over the last few days that have me feeling vulnerable." I proceeded to explain it all from the holy water assault to Monroe the neo-Nazi agent, to Ming the Korean spy, to Franco the lying ass club owner.

She listened intently until I was done then stuck out her open palm. I reached in my duffel bag and got the opal stone she'd given me when I first started seeing her and placed it in her hand. She closed her fist around it then closed her eyes. We sat unmoving for eons before she opened her eyes and began speaking.

"Your boss is honorable. He speaks truth and will do everything he can to keep you safe." Tension between my shoulder blades relaxed. I hadn't even realized it was there. *A demon actually speaking truth—surprise, surprise.* She continued,

"You will see your attacker again. He will not stop until he captures you because his motivation goes beyond the bounty on your head." That sounded like a foretelling. *Great.* "VET will be hot on your tail so you must play it smart, avoid appearances of your true nature. The blind one has a hundred percent success rate. He will not accept failure in his duties because it validates him." Then she gave back the stone.

Good thing she wasn't graded on bearing good news.

"Wait—what about the new girl?" I said.

"There is some kind of impenetrable protective force shield around her. I cannot see anything beyond her exterior."

Huh. Interesting. Well, if Franco was on the up-and-up, Ming must have been also. She was probably some kind of supernatural, and though I hated that she snooped, I guess I could understand. After all, she was new, didn't know anyone. Couldn't blame her for wanting to know more about her colleagues. If asked, I'd just say the vials in my bag contained fake blood for my shows.

"Love will make you feel vulnerable too," Saybree said as she crisscrossed her fingers and rested them on the tabletop.

"I wouldn't know anything about that."

She laughed. "You know he really does love you."

"Who?"

"Both of them."

I shook my head. "You mean…"

"I know you don't believe Maximilian is capable of such emotion, but he has great capacity to love. He needs it with so many brides," she coughed to hide her laugh. "Now, the other one—the human only has eyes for you, but his eyes are shadows because he wears many faces. You look not upon his real one."

What? I wish she'd stop being so coded and spoke English. Then again, it didn't matter. I hadn't come to get answers about love.

"So if my attacker will return and VET will come after my

ass again, what can I do to protect myself? Captivation only goes so far. The hunter will have top-notch weapons and I'd have to hypnotize all of VET to get around Monroe."

"Flee."

"Can't. Monroe said he'd have everyone at Hades charged for helping me escape."

"It's too bad you haven't been a vampire long enough to acquire other powers. Why not ask Maximilian to come assist you? His powers are more…persuasive."

"Too risky for the whole clan."

"But he's strong enough to get you out and clean up behind himself."

"There has to be another way. I don't want him involved." I didn't want him risking the clan but even if he did so successfully, I didn't want to owe him anymore than I already did. I was still hoping and praying there was a way to break our bond.

"There's no honor in taking the path of most resistance," she said as she got up and began making tea. "Your maistre would kill them all to protect you if you would but ask."

She knew how I felt about Max and about murder. "Why are you insisting on his involvement? You know how bad I want to be rid of him for good."

"That is not possible. Your bond is eternal." *Yeah, yeah, yeah.* "He is good to you. Others would never have allowed you to leave the clan, not even for a short while." She shook her head like she was fed up with me. "Turn to your human. Strengthen your bond with him. It will be of assistance to you. He will be a great day companion."

I looked at her in shock, "You're kidding, right? He's *human.*"

"With your narcolepsy and sun allergy, you're going to have to trust someone to help you…and he's crazy about you."

He's crazy all right.

I stood. This wasn't helping me at all. Trust this person, trust that one. There had to be more to it than that.

We talked more about the evils that were coming for me and how I needed to watch my back and all that whoopty-do. I just felt hollow. Earlier it had seemed I was plummeting into immorality just because I had to work on Sunday, now I wished that was my only problem. Immorality would be better than final death.

And with everyone after me, I'd be lucky if I made it to Monday night.

CHAPTER 12

After moving my shit to a different motel, I climbed in bed and counted sheep.

Tossing and turning all day while I was supposed to be sleeping promised terrible repercussions. Yet instead of resting, I mulled over Saybree's warnings and suggestions, formulated and re-formulated plans, and still came up with zilch to ease my forebodings.

But at least I'd made it to Monday night.

I got up, drank several vials of blood, and dressed for my weekly sleep disorder support group meeting. Even though I couldn't openly discuss my inner turmoil with the group, Dr. Floyd would have encouraging words and I'd feel uplifted…until the next unsettling event.

Turn to your human she'd said.

Lord knows I trusted Saybree, but she had to be talking out the side of her neck this time.

Strengthen your bond with him. She'd meant give him my blood…and she really was tripping.

He will be a great day companion—evidence that Saybree quite possibly had lost her mind. Why did I need a day-walker? I'd gotten along just fine as a lone creature of the night, thank you very much. How would a man who loved death be a great companion for me? Unless I needed a good screw while a stake was driven through my chest, Remi was useless.

And the thing that really got my goat was that she'd spoken in future tense. Saybree was never wrong.

Fuck.

Enemies were a' coming, and if I loved being undead as much as I thought I did, I'd better take her advice.

When I arrived downtown at the meeting location, I was about thirty minutes early. I'd needed the walk to clear my mind. Couldn't say it helped though considering rain poured cats and dogs the whole way. Once inside, I headed straight for the ladies room, leaving a water trail as I went. Good thing I wasn't dressed to impress anyone tonight.

Too bad being a vampire hadn't wielded me power to control the elements or change forms like Max. Not yet anyway. I had no idea which powers I'd get once I'd been around for hundreds of years. Telepathy or telekinesis would be nice too. Just saying.

Despite ringing out my sweat suit and holding it under the XLerator hand dryer, I looked like a sopping mess as I exited the bathroom with only a few moments to spare before the meeting began. Everyone would be wet since there was no covered parking, so it didn't…

I stopped in my tracks, sensing he was very close. But how could that be?

Walking slowly into the large room with the circle of chairs, I scanned the faces, looking for him. How had he followed me here?

And there he was by the refreshment table looking yummy, but different. His hair was slicked back hanging loosely on his collar instead of shadowing his eyes. He wore khaki pants instead of jeans and a starched white long-sleeved dress shirt that covered the scars on his wrists instead of his typical black t-shirt with wristbands.

My feet moved toward Remi while I was still deciding whether to be angry with him for stalking me again. His obsession was creepy and charming simultaneously…more creepy.

I nodded hello as people spoke to me along the way, but I didn't notice their faces. Remi was eating a Shipley's donut slowly, savoring it. Licking the cream from his fingers one at a time. How odd. The Remi I knew would have consumed that sucker in two bites. He turned towards me just as I came up behind him then quickly averted his eyes.

Where the hell was his usually creepy stare?

"Why are you still following me? I thought we talked about this," I said.

He glanced out of the corner of his eye at me without speaking then headed towards the circle. Everyone was settling in their seats and apparently he was intending to also.

I grabbed his arm and jerked him around to face me. He looked startled.

"You've gone too damn far this time. When I told you about my support group it wasn't for the purpose of you infiltrating it," I said.

"I'm sorry but I don't know you," he said with Remi's voice, Remi's lips, his gorgeous eyes…which he quickly shifted away.

"What do you mean you don't know me? Don't play games." Now I was getting pissed. Following me was one thing. Acting like I was stupid was another. I didn't play that shit.

"Will you please let my arm go?"

I squeezed harder. "Not until you tell me why you're here."

Something was seriously off with him, more so than usual. I didn't recognize his cologne, didn't smell smoke on his breath.

He looked down to where my nails were biting into his arm and then over to the circle where Dr. Floyd was taking his seat, getting ready to start.

"I'm here for the same thing you are…to get help for a sleep disorder…to bond with other people facing the same challenges." He jerked on his arm. "Please let me go. I really don't know you."

He honestly acted like he had no idea who I was. Come to think of it, his voice was a little off, too soft.

Recalling what Saybree had said about him having different faces, I dropped his arm. Was he a shape-shifter who would lose it and change in front of everyone if I pushed him too hard? I didn't want to make a scene here, but I had to get to the bottom of his strange behavior. After all, I did care a teensy-weensy bit for him.

He started to walk away.

"Wait," I said. "I'm Willow."

His eyes snapped up and recognition filled them like water in a pool. "Willow?"

"Yes. And you're Remi, right?"

"So you're Willow." He smiled a little but shifted his eyes to the floor.

"Remi, what's going on with you? Why are you behaving this way?"

He mumbled, "I didn't know you'd be so cute."

What? "Remi, we've known each other awhile. You don't remember me?"

Dr. Floyd waved for us to join the group.

"We should be making our way over," he said, pointing his thumb in the direction of the circle.

"This is crazy even for you." I shook my head, no longer angry, just weary of his act.

He sighed. "I'm sorry, Willow. I'm not who you think I am, but I am glad I got a chance to meet you."

I looked to his face for some sign of jesting. There was

none. "Who the hell are you then?"

He finally met my eyes. "I'm Aaron."

CHAPTER 13

Aaron? *Aaron?* I screamed the name over and over in my head as I watched him walk away.

Was this fucking April Fool's Day? Did Remi have a twin, a doppelganger, amnesia?

Hold the phone…

Remi had said his dad gave Aaron the trust fund. In the context of our conversation he was talking about himself, wasn't he? Well, why was he acting like he didn't know me now and that he wasn't himself? Aaron was his nickname, right?

I was dumfounded again, which was happening waaaaay too much lately.

Sitting in my usual seat facing the entrance/exit, I watched Remi as he sat in the chair on the far side of the circle. I took a deep breath, which had nothing to do with survival and everything to do with smelling him. Underneath the fruity-smelling cologne and demure attitude, Aaron was definitely Remi.

Blood didn't lie.

"We have a new participant tonight. Folks, join me in

welcoming Aaron Berlinski," Dr. Floyd was speaking in his sophisticated British accent as he pointed at Remi. When he clapped, we all did. Then he pushed up his glasses and spoke directly to Aaron, "Would you like to introduce yourself? Tell us how your sleep disorder has impacted your life."

We all looked expectantly towards…Aaron.

He was slouched in his chair, gazing at the floor. "Hi," he said quietly. "Like Doc said, I'm Aaron." He paused like he was waiting for us to say *Hi, Aaron.* Wrong support group, dude. "Uh…I've been struggling with insomnia for as long as I can remember, actually ever since a childhood trauma." He cleared his throat and sat up. "I won't bore you with specifics, but I developed a multiple personality disorder, and well, I can go days without sleeping. And when I do finally sleep, I blank out." I leaned forward in my seat. *Oh. My. Gosh.* "When I come to, I'm missing a few days of time. I know I've slept because I feel rejuvenated, refreshed. But there is also evidence that I've been out and about. I just have no recollection of what I've done during my blackouts." He glanced at Dr. Floyd then back to the floor. "After years of getting help from shrinks, I've managed to get my personalities on a schedule. And now that we function better together, I want to tackle my sleep problem. Just once I'd like to have a real dream."

I wasn't the only one speechless this time. The unblinking wide eyes of all eight group members and Dr. Floyd were on Aaron…like he had the Ebola virus.

"Do your other personalities only come out when you sleep?" Matt, the youngest group member asked.

"No, I also shift with certain triggers like stress…fear…excitement…" Aaron said, "hypnosis too."

"Do your other personalities have insomnia?" Matt said.

"No."

Speaking before I realized, I said, "How do you know they don't?" And if he wasn't Remi, how had he recognized my name? "How do you know *anything* about the other personalities?" I asked.

"We keep a detailed journal. It's the one thing that helps us function well together."

I must have been in the journal. Remi had written about me? Nothing too incriminating I hoped. Aaron seemed more lucid than Remi, which meant Aaron might put pieces together. And he might be unhappy with the overall puzzle.

"How do we know you're the real Aaron? You could be a fake personality," the fattest group member asked. Though she lacked tact and was probably ignorant about how multiple personalities worked, she raised a good point. Was Remi the real person or Aaron? Wait—Aaron was the one with the trust fund so...

"I'm the host, the one on the birth certificate and with the driver's license," Aaron said, holding his license up so everyone could inspect.

"How do we know—"

Someone else was firing off a question when Dr. Floyd interrupted, "Okay. I know we're all gobsmacked here, but let's remember to focus on Aaron's *sleep* disorder not his multiple personalities. That's what this group is about, right?" He looked around at us and smiled. Then he landed on Aaron. "Thank you for sharing. And again, welcome to the group." He pulled out a notepad. "Now..."

I was lost in my thoughts the remainder of the session.

Remi was actually Aaron. They had a schedule and a journal. In all the time I'd known Remi I had no idea he only came to the club once a week because he was sharing his body the rest of the week.

Geez.

Saybree could have just come out and said that. What was with all the "many faces" bull? What's so hard about saying "split personalities"? She was probably looking in her crystal ball watching me, laughing...

Suddenly, I was being dunked under freezing cold water.

My parents were standing above me speaking in tongues, screaming for the devil to come out…

I awakened terrified. Even more terrified than when the frigid baptism had first happened because it was happening again, and I'd vowed never to be at their mercy again. They were unmerciful, busy doing "the Lord's" work.

"It's okay. Willow, you're safe. You're with us." I looked around from the floor until I focused on Dr. Floyd's face above me. "You just fell asleep during our meeting. We're all right here," his calming voice soothed me better than a case of Jack Daniel's to an alcoholic. He was fanning his notepad over my face as I lay on the floor allowing his words to wash over me…to rid me of terrible memories. Ones that had crept into my sleep, no matter how briefly, and left me desolate and scared even though it was all in the past.

I eventually allowed him to help me up, because that's what was expected of a human woman who'd just hit the floor. As I sat back in my seat, he ended the meeting with an encouraging poem and a warm smile. When everyone started leaving, I stayed seated. Thankfully, no one came over with all the "how are you's?" It wasn't the first time I'd fallen asleep during a meeting.

But it was the first time my dream had been a freaking nightmare.

It wouldn't take long for Dr. Floyd to shake hands and chat it up with a few members so I patiently waited my turn.

Aaron stayed seated as well.

When our eyes met, he looked down. Naturally.

I folded my arms and pursed my lips. *Whatever.*

Dr. Floyd walked over to Aaron first. They chatted, Dr. Floyd slapped Aaron on the back all brotherly-like, and Aaron left.

When Dr. Floyd approached me, we embraced momentarily then I told him I was interested in participating in the new narcolepsy clinical case study he'd mentioned last week and asked me to think about. It was time to get on the ball, to find a cure for my curse. I'd been thinking about taking a break from cure-seeking endeavors since my human body had habituated to several drugs, and I hadn't responded to human drugs at all since I'd been undead. All the visits to his office had started becoming a nuisance since there had not been any favorable results.

I had to keep trying though. I needed a cure, and sooner would be better.

Given the episode he'd just witnessed, Dr. Floyd didn't seem surprised by my answer. He knew me well enough to know that although I wasn't embarrassed about falling asleep, I absolutely abhorred being weakened by it. What he didn't know was that it crippled me more as a vampire than as a human. It could be the difference between being a predator and becoming prey. Having narcolepsy as a human meant I might hurt myself. As a vampire, it meant I was always one step from my final death whether by someone hard-up for cash or the sun itself.

And I couldn't have that.

When he asked how I'd been coping, I met his wise, compassionate eyes and wished I could tell him the truth. His salt-n-pepper hair and deep wrinkles showed years of study and experience, which meant he'd probably be able to help me better if he knew the full story. But even as my therapist, I couldn't risk him upholding patient/client confidentiality when it came to me being a vampire.

So I smiled and lied. *Everything's great,* blah, blah, blah. We scheduled a time to meet later and I left, walking through the glass doors out into the light rain and darkness.

Preparing for my walk home, I pulled my hood over my head.

"Willow," a low yet startling voice spoke beside me.

I jumped.

Given my keen senses, I was rarely surprised—but in my

defense—Aaron had called to me as soon as I opened the door and stepped out.

"Thought you left," I said while zipping my jacket.

He ran a trembling hand over the top of his wet head. "No, I waited for you." Poor thing didn't have a hood or umbrella.

"What d'ya want?" I said coldly. He couldn't wait to get away from me while we were inside. Now he was waiting for me out in the rain?

"Can I drive you back to your motel?" he said in that low voice, eyes downward.

Motel, huh. This was too weird. It was Remi, but not.

"So how much do you know about me?" I said. *And hell no to the ride.*

"Not much. I don't think Remi knows much about you, but you're all he ever writes about."

"What did he write exactly?"

He tucked a stray lock of wet hair behind his ear. "That he sees you every Saturday night at some fetish club. He also mentioned you walk everywhere, and that he followed you to your motel. I imagine it's difficult to drive with narcolepsy." He glanced up to gauge my reaction. I shrugged. "Willow, let's get out of the rain. Let me give you a ride," he said.

I honestly didn't care about being wet, but I was curious about how much Aaron differed from Remi. I mean, how often did one find out the person they'd known had multiple personalities?

"Is that all he wrote about me?" I said.

He blushed. "No. He also writes about you and him…doing stuff."

I smiled. Remi would never have blushed about that.

This was becoming mildly entertaining. With all the supernaturals and their special gifts I'd met over the years, Aaron was quite possibly the most fascinating person yet. He was a gorgeous man with mesmerizing eyes and thoroughly whacked in the head…

"Sure, Aaron. I'd love a ride."

CHAPTER 14

"A Supreme Love" by John Coltrane was playing nice and mellow-like through the silver Jaguar XJL speakers. The smooth music and laid-back car were both evidence that Remi and Aaron were night and day.

Leaning my seat back, I found myself relaxing and enjoying the tune and the peaceful company. I glanced at Aaron. He was looking at the road…smiling. When he caught me looking, the smile disappeared.

"He never mentioned you liked Coltrane. Bet y'all don't play anything like that at the club," he said.

"Franco let's us use any music we like. There's just no easy way to slip in supreme love during our fetish performances."

"That's why I wouldn't go there. A fetish is something weird you gotta have to get off right?"

"More or less."

"Doesn't apply to me then. Only thing I need is love and that's not weird. Love is my fetish."

"So you're in love?" Fuck me—I was jealous.

"Not exactly. Dating doesn't work out well for me. I just wish I was in love."

Dating didn't work out well for Remi either. They had that in common. I'm sure it couldn't be easy to tell a girl *oh, by the way, I'm actually several people.* At least Aaron could leave off the part about liking death…or could he?

"You're not a necrophiliac?" I said.

He looked at me like I'd grown two more arms. "God, no. That's disgusting." Then he realized what he'd said. "No offense, Willow. It's just not me."

"None taken. I just perform for them."

"But how can you do that? Isn't that just as bad?"

Good point. "Yeah, I guess so." I turned away from him and looked out the window. Performing necrophilia shows was the least of my problems.

"I don't mean to sound judgmental. I'm just trying to understand you. I mean, I've been curious about who you are for the longest. Why do work there if you—"

"I'm good at it and I like pleasing people like Remi. That's why." That was a question I was used to answering. Even my patrons couldn't understand why I did it.

He popped a handful of tic-tacs in his mouth and offered me some, which I declined. It made me realize another difference between them.

"You don't smoke?" I said. He shook his head. "How can you stand for Remi to?"

"I have to make certain concessions to keep him happy. How can *you* stand Remi smoking?"

I smiled. "Guess we both want Remi happy. So what concessions does he make for you?"

"He only gets Saturday."

Huh. That had to be tough for Remi. He only got one day and night a week…and he chose to spend most of it with me.

We talked more about jazz and then more about Hades. It was definitely not the conversation-less ride I'd had with Remi.

I wondered how long before I stopped comparing the two.

When we got to my room, I didn't hesitate to invite him in.

Why? How the hell should I know? I was just going with the feeling, and it felt good talking to him, being around him.

When I turned on the bedside lamp, he looked around until his eyes landed on the heavily-padded window. "Can't take sunlight?" he said.

"I like it dark."

After tossing him a terrycloth robe and a towel, I went into the bathroom to change out of my own wet clothes.

"Remi asked me to move in with him, which is weird because technically I'd be moving in with you," I yelled from the bathroom.

"I know."

"How in the world was that going to work?"

"I don't know, but he threatened to go rogue if I didn't give in. He wants you badly."

It almost felt like Remi was speaking of himself in third person, but he wasn't. It was Aaron's softer, lower voice coming through the bathroom door.

"You've actually been good for him, kept him out of a lot of trouble. He's a bad boy, Willow."

"Don't I know it," I chuckled. "Was I just supposed to wake up next to him one morning and you'd be there? Was I not supposed to notice the difference?" I exited the bathroom in my satin blue pajamas, proud that I was well-covered.

He was sitting in the desk chair by the window with his wet clothes on hangers dangling from the heater. What I noticed most was his toned, hairy legs escaping under the bottom of the robe. I'd never seen his legs.

"The deal we made was that he'd explain everything about himself, about me, to you and if after full disclosure you agreed, then fine. I knew no girl in her right mind would go for that, but he seems to think you're different. That you care for him and accept him." He tugged on the hem of the robe self-consciously as if I was staring. I dropped my eyes so he'd be more comfortable. "Do you care for him?" he asked.

Guess Remi would have spilled the beans about Aaron if Max hadn't shown up while we were in the diner. "Yes. I do." I held up my index finger and thumb to indicate just how much and we laughed.

"He's right. You are different. Not many girls would invite a stranger to her bedroom after knowing he was clinically insane."

Naw, I wasn't worried. "You don't feel like a stranger to me. And I've always known Remi was off his damn rocker." *Plus, I'd drain you dry before you could say hubba-bubba if I had to.*

And suddenly I wanted to do just that. I turned away in a hurry and focused on the blank wall, willing myself to calm down. Since I'd already fed today, it wasn't an overwhelming urge so it didn't take me long to get it together.

"Please don't hurt him. I meant what I said about you keeping him out of trouble. I don't know what he'd do if he lost you," he said in his serious, soft tone.

Feeling better, I sat on the edge of the bed. I still didn't trust myself to be all up in his grill yet. "He mentioned he was kidnapped. I guess that means you were taken."

He leaned forward and put his elbows on both knees. "I was."

"When you were six."

"Yes. Remi saved me."

"How?"

"He killed my kidnapper."

CHAPTER 15

Whoa. Remi had killed someone? I was a vampire and I hadn't even done that.

"Don't be afraid of him, Willow. He'd never hurt you." He scratched his head. "He loves you."

"He's said that. He's also said he's fantasized about killing me."

"I said he wouldn't hurt you. I didn't say he wasn't sick."

True.

Silence.

It was awkward. This whole thing had me unhinged. I was trying to absorb it all, be cool with it…

"He never mentioned you were black," he said.

Here we go… "Is that a problem?"

"Not at all. Just funny he never described you physically. I wouldn't have been able to keep myself from doing so."

I smiled. "You're attracted to me?"

He blushed. *Adorable.* "I think you're beautiful. The color of your skin, the sound of your voice, the way you smile…it's all amazing."

Remi had described different features. "How can you tell?

You never look at me. Remi stares and you look at the floor," I mumbled.

He raised his eyes to mine. Ah. There. Simply divine. Still metallic blue, but less edgy, more guarded. From this angle, puppy-doggish—the kind you saw in the window and no matter where you were headed, you stopped and bought him.

"I'm just shy," he said.

Shy was okay. I could deal with shy.

"Which one of you added the permanent decoration to your wrists? Remi?" I said.

"No. He's not suicidal. That was Emmanuel. Twice. And once with a bottle of pills. Crazy bastard stays depressed. I hate when he shows up. Page after page of gloom and doom—"

"—Wait a friggin' minute. How many are there?"

"Ten. That I know of." I stared at him incredulously. He dropped his eyes, shutting himself down again. "I can leave if you want me to. I'm laying a lot on you…and I don't even know why. I've never shared this much with anyone other than my shrinks."

I continued staring. *Ten different personalities?*

He made a move to get up then settled down again. "I don't want to go, Willow."

"Now you sound like Remi."

"He says you're not judgmental. I could use a friend like that."

"Not my place to judge." I'd grown up with enough people who felt they had a direct link to God. Incidentally, that gave them the green light to judge and condemn everyone else. I'd pass on that. "Tell me about your personalities."

He did.

Turns out, Remi wasn't the homicidal one, Vlad was—a Russian assassin, to be exact. Remi was Aaron's protector, the one he couldn't live without. There was a girl, a homosexual, and a six-year-old Aaron in there somewhere. Of everyone, those were the ones who stood out to me most. His descriptions of them were light and humorous which made the whole discussion less creepy.

He truly was fascinating.

And that diary of theirs would be one hell of a read.

The real clincher was when he exhaled and thanked me for letting him get it all off his chest. It was the first time he'd been real. The first time, outside a clinical setting, he'd opened up about who he was. The first time he'd felt free to be himself without the threat of freaking someone out. He'd learnt the hard way that people didn't understand him and didn't want to. Aaron's own father had rewarded his uniqueness with a few years in a home for the mentally ill. Didn't visit him either. Helped Aaron realize he was a misfit, an outcast…insane.

Like he'd asked to be kidnapped when he was young.

I felt privileged he'd shared so much about himself. Considering how little he knew about me, it was a major milestone on his part. Made me an impostor since I was pretending to be a human whose only issue was narcolepsy. I'd even spun my job at Hades as something I did out of kindness for society's sexual deviants, like it was a community service project. I allowed him to believe I was the poster-girl for an after-school special when in reality, I was anything but.

I envied his willingness to be vulnerable.

Before I knew it, it was close to six in the morning. We'd spent all night talking. He had moved to the bed at some point and we lay side-by-side on our bellies, hoisted on our elbows. But as with all good things, our time had come to an end. The sun would be up soon.

"I should go," he said. "I've kept you up all ni—"

I leaned over and kissed him. Simple as that.

His lips were soft, nothing new there. But he didn't suction mine like they were something to rip off the way Remi had. In fact, he barely moved at all, like he was scared or inexperienced. When he did finally move, he was gentle and leisurely. His pace made me want more. Leaning closer to him, I ran my fingertips lightly across the hair on his thigh, prepared to hike up the robe and…

He jumped up suddenly, hitting the floor at a near run. "I have to go." He turned his back to me and started putting on his clothes like it must be done right now or he'd die. Like his car was about to turn into a pumpkin, his clothes to rags. "I'm sorry, Willow," he mumbled.

Remi would never have done that. He would have been all over me like mud on a pickup truck.

Oh, will you stop it! He's not Remi.

"It's okay, Aaron." From out of nowhere I asked, "Can I see you tomorrow?"

He paused halfway down buttoning his shirt and risked a glance in my direction. "Sure, I'd like that."

I smiled and got up from the bed. His eyes widened as I approached, but he continued dressing.

"It's late enough in the morning for the sun to rise so I'm going to have to hide in the bathroom until you close the door behind yourself." I helped him button his sleeves since his hands were trembling so badly.

"Why?"

"Because I'm a vampire."

CHAPTER 16

His eyes were so wide; I could have crawled inside them and took a nap. Heck yeah, he was scared. Heck yeah, he wanted to bolt. Anticipating he would try to run, I grabbed his arms before he did. Just in time. Staring in his eyes, I whispered soothing words until he relaxed and his pupils opened to the max.

"It's okay, Aaron. I won't hurt you. You're going to trust me like I trust you."

He nodded slowly, his subconscious making the agreement.

I explained how I had a great time with him, how I enjoyed talking to him and kissing him. Next, I gave instructions for our date tomorrow, erased any memories of my confession, and then disappeared into the bathroom. I stayed there until I heard the front door close. Then I got in bed to sleep the day away.

I slept like a baby.

Until there was a knock at the door, then suddenly, I was screaming and diving onto the floor and crawling under the bed for dear life. I'd taken the comforter with me, managing to protect myself from the incoming light.

"Close the fucking door, Bitch!" I yelled to the housekeeper who was trying to come in.

Good thing I had the chain on the door. Close call.

She shut it and begged my pardon over-and-over again.

This was precisely what I hated about moving to different motels. My old motel had gotten used to me and wouldn't dare pull this shit…but hell—it always happened at least once, no matter how many times I told the front desk to never come in my room. Paying extra a whole fucking week in advance usually did the trick. And they made out well considering I didn't ask for a refund when I changed motels mid-week.

Nothing like nearly bursting into flames to wake your ass right up. Since I couldn't go back to sleep, I did some online shopping, researched some narcolepsy treatment drugs, and checked my email.

When it was time to get ready for work, I was excited, though it had more to do with what would take place after work.

After I did my thing onstage, I mingled with patrons in the Graveyard room, took pictures with VIPs in the booth, and collected blood vials. By the time it was two a.m., I was giddy as a kid first going to Disneyworld. Looking at my watch for the eighteen-hundredth time, I smiled, knowing Aaron would be out back waiting for me.

I quickly changed into a black tank and low-rise jeans, throwing a fashionable scarf around my neck. Even though the cold didn't affect my body temperature, it was January which meant my leather jacket and boots were still acceptable. I put them on too. Then I said goodnight to my colleagues, ignoring their suspicious glares. They'd never seen me wear anything but a dull sweat suit once I got off work.

Not tonight. Tonight I had a date with Aaron.

As I headed down the hall towards the back door, it opened. Punch stepped inside and froze, nostrils flaring like he was sniffing the air. Then his head lifted slowly. I had a feeling

I knew what…er, *whose* scent he'd detected. Stopping in my tracks, I considered turning and running in the other direction, but couldn't move. The sound of his heart pumping blood into the arteries of his muscular body had my attention. My full attention. Every tall, chocolaty warm-blooded inch of him called to me even though he hadn't said a word.

I licked my lips thinking his blood was good…and I could use a dose of his power.

I'd never paid attention to Punch before because he was Fire's man. And I certainly hadn't been hot for him.

But things had changed.

I'd had his blood. And he'd made me come with barely a touch.

I'd made sure to stay away from him all night and sensed he was doing the same. Yet here we were face-to-face, neither of us able to run. When our eyes met, I couldn't tell which one I wanted more—the taste of his blood or its power. Either way, I was instantly starving for it. And sex was in there somewhere.

My mind was drawing a blank. Wasn't I headed somewhere?

His nostrils flared again, and I was betting he could smell my arousal. I was certainly getting a heavy dose of his.

"Do you need a ride?" he said in that baritone voice that made my cookie quiver.

The double entendre in his question was ringing in my ears. *Boy, do I ever.*

I shook my head, eyeing his jugular like it was the Last Supper. When my fangs elongated and pierced my lip, I knew I was in trouble. But I was lost in his glare, unable to tell who was doing the captivating. It was commonly known that were-animals had powers of their own except—other than becoming an animal—the details of those powers were a mystery. All I knew was at this moment I seemed to have been equally entranced.

Willing myself to regain control, I tore my eyes from his and focused on a spot on the floor. I prayed my eyes wouldn't turn. There'd be no holding back then.

"My truck's right outside," he said.

Startled, I looked up. When did he get so close?

He eyed the blood running down my bottom lip then rubbed his thumb across it. That's when I realized I had continued biting my lip, preventing it from healing. I stared at his full lips as he took the thumb to his mouth and sucked it.

His dark brown eyes immediately turned auburn and mine flashed red. I could feel it. I could see them reflected in his eyes. Tingling all over, I moved in even closer to his broad chest and palmed the pectoral over his heart. He dipped his head low enough for our lips to nearly touch. Oh, yes, his body was hot and strong and we were…

"You know, I used to like you, Willow."

Punch and I both jumped and turned in the direction of the voice that was harsh enough to break our trance.

Fire was standing a few feet away.

Although I couldn't see her eyes hidden behind red fringe bangs, I knew she was staring a hole in the middle of my forehead. But forget her damn eyes. Instinctively, I was more concerned about the smoke blowing from her boney nose. Her arms hung stiffly at her sides and her usually pasty white skin was beet red. Her stance reminded me of a fighting bull locked on its target. Only, I was no matador and I sure as hell wasn't holding a muleta.

I became conscious of my fangs, even thought about retracting them. Then figured they may be needed to fight.

Shit.

I really didn't want to go there with her especially since this drama was my fault. I'd been the one to cross the line in the sand, so to speak.

Punch walked towards her slowly, palms out. He was saying soothing things to her when I decided it was a good time to bust a move. Not only did I remember there was a hottie waiting for me out back, but I didn't need to press my luck with anyone who breathed out smoke. Where there was smoke, there was fire. Literally.

And me and fire didn't mix.

Nevertheless, with the way Punch and I had been carrying on, it was very likely I'd get another shot with Fire.

Undoubtedly.

And the next time I'd be armed with an extinguisher since I had a hunch there was more to Fire than I'd originally thought. When Franco had pulled his skin-burn thing on me, he hadn't been throwing off smoke. Which told me Fire was definitely one to watch out for.

All my anxiety went away when I saw Aaron's Jag waiting in the lot.

Curbing my appetite before I saw him seemed like a good idea since I was too high-strung at the moment. Couldn't risk being around him without wanting a bite. Knowing it was best for us both, I quickly downed half my blood vials then walked towards his car.

Later for Punch. My real interests were elsewhere. Remi was all about me. And if last night was any indication of how things were progressing with Aaron, it wouldn't be long before he would be all about me also.

"Hi. How was work?" he said as I got comfortable in the seat.

Double yum. He was looking too good for words...but I couldn't help trying to find the right one: beautiful, gorgeous, fine. They all came to mind, neither doing him justice.

It wasn't raining at all tonight, yet Aaron wore his hair slicked back again, this time parted on the side. He wore a cobalt blue long-sleeved dress shirt that made his eyes sparkle like diamonds beneath those thick dark brows and long lashes. The way his shirt tucked into black slacks was an exclamation point to all that was divine about him, from the chest hair peeking through the top of his shirt to the nicely-edged beard and mustache…

Remi was usually clean-shaven which made me wonder if they fought over facial hair. Did Remi win that battle every Saturday?

"What's wrong?" he said.

I shook my head. "Nothing at all. Just taking you in." I brazenly gave him the once over with appreciative eyes. "I think you may be the most beautiful man I've ever seen." That was saying something because he didn't have any supernatural enhancements.

And what do you know—he blushed the color of Heinz ketchup.

Looking away, he said, "So where are we headed? I can't remember what happened last night before I left your place. Don't even know how I knew to come here tonight."

"I'm glad you came. You agreed to help me with a situation." I gave him an address for his GPS and he started driving, didn't even ask what the situation was.

As he drove from the parking lot, Wham! played through the speakers and I was transported to the land of peace. Ah, yes. "Careless Whisper"…

A place where Aaron and I were the same species. A place where we were lovers and Max was dead. Really dead.

Oh, no. I was really digging Aaron.

"I didn't wanna be corny. I mean, I don't really know what's appropriate…but I brought you something. I hope you like it," he said. "It's in the backseat. I'm still not sure I should have gotten it. I'll understand if you don't—"

"They're beautiful." I picked up the bouquet of orange roses and sniffed. I'd thought the scent was car deodorizer. "Thank you."

I thought back to the last time someone had given me roses. My ex had been caught cheating and was trying to get out the doghouse. It had been too little too late.

But this gesture…this was special.

"You don't think it's too much?" he said.

Aaron was so thoughtful, so sweet, so romantic. I leaned over and kissed his cheek. "Not at all. They're perfect."

I felt warmness in my chest where my heart used to be. It slowly spread down my belly to my…

"Good. I was serious about needing a friend," he said. "I don't want to ruin what we have."

Scraaaaaaatch. What? *Friend?*

"No, *Friend*. They're perfect," I said.

He smiled, satisfied with himself.

Had completely missed my sarcasm.

I folded my arms and pouted the whole forty-five minute drive to Katy. He started several conversations and I let them fall away with one-liners and utter rudeness. My attitude made no sense. No sense at all, still I couldn't help feeling dejected.

Oh, this was bad. Real bad.

When we got out to the suburbs, it was dark and foggy and I contemplated bleeding him and leaving him in the ditch. No one would find his fine ass for days.

But I shook myself out of my stupor and explained to him what we were going to do here. At first, he refused. Then I explained *why* we were going to do it and he got onboard. Good thing, because I'd captivate him into compliance if I had to. I was trying to avoid that on account of how much I'd tampered with his mind already. Best to use that on him only when absolutely necessary from now on.

So once we went over the plan, we stopped at a gas station so I could get behind the wheel and he could crouch down in back. With no license and not much driving history, I was surprised he trusted me with his ride. He said that's what insurance was for. Okay then…

When we rode up to the iron gate, he kept quiet. I did the talking and smiling and hair flipping for the security camera until we were allowed in. It helped that the owner of the mansion had the hots for me and had told me so many times. Now I had the perfect excuse to show up at his house at three in the morning, looking good and sounding seductive.

The idiot actually thought I was coming to fuck him.

I walked up to the door as he swung it as wide as the shit-eating grin on his conniving face.

"Hey, Rafe," I said to Cindy's estranged husband. "You gonna let me in?"

CHAPTER 17

He licked his lips. "C'mon in, babe."

I wanted to gut-punch him right then.

I hated being called "babe" with a passion. It was just as bad as "gal", and both were almost as bad as the racial epithets Agent Monroe liked to throw around. "Baby" was okay, but only from a lover. "Babe" was totally unacceptable.

At least he'd given me the welcome I needed. Couldn't step in his house without an invite.

Showing both rows of my perfectly straight white teeth, I grinned big and fake. I'd need an Academy Award before the night was through.

"You mind if my friend joins us?" I said.

He threw his head back like the sex of his dreams was about to go down. "Oh, yes, babe. Where's your friend? Tell her to come on in."

If he kept calling me babe, plan A was out the window. I'd jump straight to plan Z, which included him in a body bag. That was the last resort—one that would end my friendship with Cin and probably secure my spot in hell—but still a viable option.

I grinned again and waved at the car for Aaron to come in. Then I stepped inside the grand foyer, closing the door behind myself, making sure it remained unlocked.

Rafe really gave me the heebie-jeebies, and I really didn't want to be around him at all. But with everyone Saybree confirmed was coming after me, I needed to tidy up the loose end with Cin. Didn't need her being desperate and ratting me out for money to fight this loser.

Looking around at the Roman sculptures, crystal chandeliers and marble fountain, I remembered the last time I was in the mansion awing over these expensive pieces. Cindy had plastered a smile to her face in honor of her daughter's birthday, but I could see right through it. Now Cin was living back with her mother, and Rafe was living really well. It wasn't fair what he was putting her through. She hadn't fought him for the house or one brown penny of her entitlement. She only wanted to keep their daughter and Rafe's spiteful ass was punishing her.

He handed me a glass of liquid poison and began sipping his own.

"I never thought you'd come around, Willow." He shook his head. "But I am sooo glad you did."

Sizing him up, I knew I may have to expose my nature to Aaron in order to get Rafe down. He was a huge dude, Punch huge. No problem. He was human. I'd skin his mohawked head in front of Aaron if it came to that.

Rafe came to me, leaning down to nibble my neck. I slipped from his reach and said through gritted teeth, "Let's go up to your bedroom."

"Shouldn't we wait for your friend?"

"We can go on up. Get things started."

He grinned. "Whatever you like." After hooking his arm so I could loop mine through it, he led me to the double staircase.

Felt like I was walking the plank.

"You're not going to ask how Cindy's doing?" I said.

"Nope. Why should I?"

"Maybe because you were married for eight years and have a daughter together? Or because you're suing for sole custody and you know how much that hurts her."

"Cindy's the one who filed for divorce. She brought this on herself."

"You cheated, Rafe. Several times," I scowled then quickly turned it to a smile. If I kept this up, I'd blow my cover. "'Course, I know it's because you're so passionate," I said. He grinned and moved his arm around my waist. *Gag.* "I just wish you and Cindy could be more amicable now that you're dissolving your marriage. Custody battles don't have to be so brutal."

When we entered the master suite, Rafe lifted his shirt over his head without preamble and threw it to the floor. "Are we gon' stand around talking 'bout Cindy all night or are we gon' get down to what you came over for?"

Well, at least I attempted to reason with him. "Oh, we're gon' get down to it."

He walked up close and slowly lifted my hand holding the full glass. "You haven't even sipped your drink."

"You look like you could use another one. Here." I held the drink to his lips as he drank. Once it was empty he let the glass of ice fall to the floor. Guess he didn't care about making a mess since the housekeeper he was last caught boning would clean it up in the morning.

In the next heartbeat, he leaned down to my neck and started nibbling again, like that was his go-to move. Backing up, I put distance between us and successfully kept myself from ripping out his spleen. "Why don't you show me what I'm getting?"

He looked suspicious, like maybe I kept dodging him for a reason. But all it took was a little wink from me for him to let his arrogance get the best of him. He dropped the caution and turned flirty, letting a devilish grin take over his face. Then he undid his belt buckle, stepped out of his pants and stood in his boxer briefs with his arms out like I should have been impressed. I twirled my finger around, indicating he should spin and show me the whole package. He did.

Not bad. Tanned muscles everywhere.

But he wouldn't have turned me on even on a famished day. His exterior was nice, but he was ugly on the inside.

Abruptly, he grabbed me and palmed my ass two-handedly. Pushing him away, I wondered what was taking Aaron so long. He was only supposed to wait five minutes then come on in and follow us upstairs. I certainly hoped he hadn't chickened out. He was critical to my plan.

"Lose the drawers," I said. "I wanna see *everything* I'm getting."

Rafe proudly hooked his thumbs in the waistband of his Calvin Klein's and pulled them down. They landed on the floor like a nail in a coffin, dick springing out like a jack-in-the-box.

I turned towards the door hoping Aaron would walk in.

No luck.

Rafe was hard…and he was aggressive…and I didn't want to hurt the dipshit before I had a chance to get what I'd come for.

"Well?" Rafe said impatiently.

How someone as sweet as Cinnabuns got wrapped up with Rafe I'd never know.

Fine. I'd do it the easy way.

I walked up to Rafe and locked his eyes on mine. "Go lie on the bed and wait for me."

He nodded and backed up slowly to the bed. Footsteps in the hall told me Aaron was finally on the way. About time.

"We're in here," I yelled.

Rafe was just getting comfortable on the bed when Aaron walked in.

"Whoa," Aaron said, covering his eyes from Rafe's nakedness.

"You still gonna be able to do this?" I said.

Aaron nodded, tossed me his digital camera, and started stripping. "Just so we're clear—I'm not touching his cock."

Guys fondling each other was not something I found disgusting. Not at all. But we were on the same page about Rafe. I didn't want to touch him either. "Fair enough."

I had every intention of turning around so Aaron could undress in peace, but couldn't take my eyes away from him. As sure as my name was Willow, I wanted a piece of that. Plain and simple.

Never a girl for body hair, I was surprised to find his so erotic. It decorated his skin like diamonds on an earlobe…elegant and subtle…on a body made to be idolized. Only, idolatry was a commandment violation so I'd settle with gawking shamelessly.

When he got down to his underwear he self-consciously cupped his groin like that was going to hide his package. Too late. I'd seen it all before anyway. Remi was not shy.

Feeling like a perv, I finally had the decency to turn away. "You ready?"

"Are you sure there's no other way?"

Rafe was a bully who only responded to bullying. "It's either this or I kill him and bury him in the backyard. Either way—I'm not letting him take Cindy through the ringer." I turned the camera on and waited for Aaron to join Rafe on the bed.

I'd promised Cin I wouldn't kill Rafe…and I was regretting that. He was rotten to the core and since I was already breaking a commandment by bearing false witness against him, I might as well just rid the world of his ass. Who would miss one pompous-ass athlete anyway? Oh, yeah—his daughter.

So this was the best I could come up with. I'd take

pictures of Rafe in a compromising position and dare him to continue waging war. If he didn't cease, these pics would be in every tabloid across the country by next nightfall. From what Cin had said about him, Rafe was such a homophobe, there was no way he'd let that shit ride. He'd rather be dead than considered a homo.

Good for him 'cause I'd rather him dead.

And since Rafe wasn't really gay, well…there went God's prohibition against a false statement that degraded a neighbor's reputation. Cin would have her daughter, but I'd no longer have a clean record in lying against my neighbor.

At least it was for a good cause…and technically, I wasn't lying. I was just the one taking the pics. Rafe was the one who decided whether they entered the media, and the general public would be the one interpreting them. I wouldn't be witnessing in court under oath so it wasn't so bad.

"Blackmail just seems wrong," said Aaron, inserting the obvious morality hitch.

"So is what he's doing to Cin."

He ran a hand over his head. "Why don't *you* lie down and I take the pictures?"

"Because he's a horndog. He'd post pictures of me and him on a billboard down 59 himself. No, it has to be a man." Enough with the questions. Time was a' wasting. Morn was fast approaching. I needed to hurry, get the ball rolling, and get back in my room before sunup.

Just stick to the plan.

"How do I know you won't use these photos to blackmail me too? My father's an important businessman. These pictures would be just as damaging to him."

"Thanks for the tip." He snapped his head up and I laughed. "I'm just kidding." After Remi's description of his father, I couldn't see why Aaron would care what happened to the old fart. Why not rebel, show dad he didn't give a shit about his reputation? Then again, I hadn't retaliated against my parents either. "You can keep the camera. Do what you will with the pictures."

He cocked his head to the side and considered that for a moment. "You'd do that for me? You'd lose your leverage if I deleted the pics."

"I know. Look, why are you asking all these questions now? Are you gonna help me or not?" *Or am I going to have to captivate you into submission?*

"Yes. I'll help. I trust you."

Was that because I planted *trust me* in his brain last night or because I sold the plan well?

Aaron walked toward the bed, eyeing Rafe. "Why is he just lying there like he can't move?"

I considered saying Rafe was drunk, mentally challenged, in a coma. But when it was all said and done, I spoke only the truth. "Because he can't."

Aaron looked at me then back at Rafe. "Why not? What did you do to him?"

"I sort of put him in a trance."

"You hypnotized him?"

I nodded.

Aaron sat on the edge of the bed and thought for a moment. "If you can do that, why don't you just *make* him drop the lawsuit?"

"Because I'm not certain the command would be sufficient or work permanently. If my hypnosis wore off, Cindy would be right back to Rafe ruining her life. And if he dropped the suit but decided to hurt her in another way…no, I need him to know he's gotta back off from her in all regards." Wow. How was that for candor? He was really good for my soul. All this purging, sincerity, honesty, openness…

Aaron leaned over Rafe, running his hand back-and-forth over Rafe's eyes like you would a blind man. "Have you hypnotized me? Is that how I knew to pick you up from work?"

Uh oh.

I just stared at him which was all the answer he needed.

"Jesus Christ," he said.

"You shouldn't use the savior's name in vain."

"He's not my savior, Willow. I'm Jewish."

Oh. Now there was wrinkle...one I should have seen coming. Guess that meant Aaron and I would be unequally yoked in faith as well as species. I could really pick 'em.

Holding the camera steady, I started snapping photos of the couple and explaining to Rafe what he needed to do in order to make sure the images never saw the light of day. The more I said the more flaccid his dick became. He clearly wasn't happy about the terms.

Aaron continued posing beautifully, but it wasn't enough. Rafe needed to appear aroused, to be enjoying Aaron's company. In order for him to back off Cin completely, the photos needed to be convincingly humiliating.

"Wait. He's soft." Grabbing Rafe's limp noodle, I squeezed and slid my hand up and down over and over. His head tossed from side-to-side as if he was trying to clear it and fight for control. It was purely a clinical action on my part until I realized how close nearly-naked Aaron was. He was watching me, and as sure as I wasn't a mule's ass, I was turned on by it. I started working Rafe faster and harder and the more he grew, the more I got into it.

Until I noticed there was nothing stirring in Aaron's boxers.

Surely, not everyone was a voyeur. In fact, some men would find a woman stroking another man in front of him downright offensive. But damn. Nothing?

When Rafe moaned, my attention turned back towards him. I dropped his dick like a hot frying pan. If I wasn't careful, this would be rape. And I wasn't into that.

I backed away and let my camera take over, sealing the deal. Aaron leaned in for poses without me asking. Modeling should have been his hobby, if not his bread-n-butter 'cause…

Rafe suddenly lunged upward with the force of two horses, head-butting Aaron in the nose. Blood gushed. Aaron yelled and grabbed his nose with both hands, falling back from the bed unto the floor. Blood ran down his fingers, arms, neck…

Oh shit.

My captivation power had worn off. I hadn't given Rafe another command after telling him to get on the bed and wait for me.

But forget what I did and didn't do. We had another problem…a bigger one.

My fangs were protruding, ready. My eyes were glowing red. My mouth was watering. The human I used to be was completely gone and my vampire instincts had taken over. I saw only one thing—blood. I didn't care about the Ten Commandments, Rafe staring at me in horror, or the fact that my plan had gone to shit. And though I felt bad Aaron was hurt, I didn't care enough to get him a wad of tissue.

His blood was calling me.

And I couldn't resist.

CHAPTER 18

Tossing Rafe out of the way like a sack of potatoes, I pounced on Aaron with the fierceness of a lioness attacking the last antelope in the wilderness. I sank my fangs into the bridge of his nose and latched onto his bleeding nostrils without regard for his pain or the damage I inflicted. He fought with everything he had but his strength was no match for mine. Pinning his body down, I had no thought for the feelings I had for him or Remi. No thought for the fear and panic he was in.

His blood was good and I was on a natural high.

At some point, I remembered two things: one, I needed to stop before I took too much, and two, things would get scary for me if I fell asleep while feeding. But ultimately, those thoughts faded with each gulp of his satisfying blood.

I'd had blood straight from the source not long ago. But this was my first Aaron feast. I was overcome with hunger, no, greed.

Did I mention how good it was?

I was vaguely aware of a tingling in my fingers and toes, of cool breeze on my neck, and the faint smell of sweet vanilla. I chalked it up to Aaron's energy seeping into my pores and sucked harder. He stopped struggling, probably passed out. I was too gone to care.

Hey, beauti—Ach Mein Gott! Willow?

Where was that voice coming from? And why was it speaking German? It was in my mind and I had the vague sense I should know, but the blood, the hunger—I couldn't think.

Tearing myself from Aaron's face, I looked around the room like a madwoman. Rafe's punk-ass was crouched in the corner with a phone to his ear. His hands were shaking and his eyes were wide like he'd seen a ghost.

Or a vampire.

"9-1-1? My address is—"

I lurched forward, backhanding him like the bitch he was. He slammed into the wall and plopped onto the floor. It had happened so fast he couldn't even think about blocking it. So much for being a super offensive lineman. He wasn't shit.

Willow, please tell me these are strangers you are planning to kill.

There was that voice again. It wasn't Rafe or Aaron. They were both out cold. Who the...?

Wiping blood from my mouth with the back of my hand, I looked around wildly. Aaron was on the floor on the far side of the bed, Rafe was on the floor by the door. No one else was in the room.

Willow, you have been a very bad—

"Not now, Max."

I slowly came to myself. To the realization of what I'd done. To the horror of my actions. Looking over at Aaron, I dropped to my knees in shame. He wasn't moving.

Wait—Max! I'd heard Max. He was here.

"Max, where are you?"

"Right here, darling." This time his voice came from right next to me, along with his unique vanilla scent. And it was no longer in my head, but audible. He was making himself visible to me even though he wasn't in the flesh.

This was one of those times I could have used his actual presence instead of his metaphysical manifestation. Nevertheless, I jumped in his arms and hugged him tightly. I had no experience with cleaning up the mess I'd just made because it had never happened to me before. Max would know what to do.

My bloodlust had scared the bejesus out of me. But worst of all, I'd hurt Aaron…sweet Aaron. He'd already suffered so much in life.

Oh, God. This was precisely why humans were killing us off.

Letting Max go, I rushed to Aaron's side. Having read my mind, Max beat me to him.

"He is alive. Barely," Max said.

The closer I got to Aaron, the worse I felt. His nose looked like it had been mauled by a savage animal. I burst into tears. I'd done that.

I rubbed Aaron's hair as my first tear fell on his forehead. "Oh, God. I did this to him."

Max looked at me with a weird expression. "You are a vampire, Willow. What do you expect? I told you to stay away from him."

Ignoring Max, I wiped my tears and leaned down to feel how strong Aaron's pulse was. Not very. I got a good look at him and winced. Such a beautiful face destroyed. I couldn't stand myself at the moment.

"He is not conscious so you cannot erase his memories. If he lives, he will identify you. You have to kill him, Willow. I will tell you how to dispose of the body so that—"

"No." I would not do that to him. Rafe on the other hand...

"It is doubtful your human will survive anyway." He went to check on Rafe. "Kill this one and make it look like a burglary. You must hurry before—"

"I won't leave Aaron here to die." I stood up. "I'm taking him to the hospital."

"You cannot risk it. It is nearly dawn."

Fuck.

There had to be something I could do for him.

Rafe started moving around and murmuring in the corner. Too bad for him.

Just as I was about to land a fatal blow to his head, I remembered all the reasons why I shouldn't kill him either.

"What are you waiting for, Willow? Finish him."

"I can't." When I explained why, Max especially thought killing him was best. Of course.

Instead, I tried several different commands. *Forget you saw me tonight* wasn't good enough. *Forget I'm a vampire* was just as inadequate. I finally went with: *You passed out drunk tonight and cannot remember anything at all.* Max suggested I email Rafe the photos tomorrow from an anonymous account and threaten him with exposure from afar. The affect should still be the same…maybe worse.

It was his best idea yet.

But Aaron was still out cold. "There has to be something I can do for him."

"I would forbid such bonding, but short of giving him vampire blood, there is no other way to end his suffering than death."

Ding ding ding. I didn't give a damn whether Max forbade it. My blood's rapid healing agent was what Aaron needed and so help me, I was going to give it to him.

Saybree had called it, hadn't she?

Kneeling next to Aaron, I cut my wrist open with my fangs and no second thought. I'd kill two birds with one stone: save Aaron and bind us forever.

Max grabbed my arm in a tight grip. "What the fuck are you doing, Willow? You would give this human your blood?"

"Yes." I jerked my arm away, lifted Aaron's head with the

other and fed him from my vein. I could feel my blood dripping in his mouth. It was giving him back some of what I'd taken, but more. Much more. He really should have consented to this but under the circumstances I hoped he would forgive me for forcing the decision on him.

Max fell back on his rear like he'd been clipped in the chin. I was fully aware that he could have used his metaphysical powers over me and prevented me from feeding Aaron, but he was too surprised. Surprised that I would blatantly disobey him and more importantly, that I cared enough for a human to risk angering my maistre. I was signing my own death warrant, motivated by something unexplainable. Something that felt close to love, and Max knew it. Oh yeah, he was surprised…and pissed…and insulted.

"You really care for this human," he whispered as if he couldn't believe it.

"I do." I couldn't either.

Max snarled like a vicious beast, "I have not given you permission to bond with this male. You are my bride!"

"Then I'll have to accept my punishment." I felt Aaron's mouth pull on my wrist wound. "Because it's done."

He grinded his teeth. "Yes. You will be punished."

And just like that, he was gone.

Whatever. I couldn't worry about Max and his threats right now. I'd worry about the consequences of pissing him off and bonding with a human with multiple personalities later. At least Aaron would be okay.

When he started coughing on my blood, I sat him up further. Oh, goody—his nose was healing.

Blood was everywhere, his and mine. And our skin was vibrant, humming with energy. I was curious about how deep the bond would go with a human, and we'd have plenty of time to explore and test its limits. Right now, I had to clean up any signs of us being in Rafe's house and get my ass to some shelter before it was too late.

Rafe was tucked in his bed, sleeping soundly when I carried Aaron out. By the time we reached the car, Aaron was completely healed.

And looking at me like I was the reincarnated Jack the Ripper.

"I'm sorry, Aaron. So sorry." I looked at the sky. Dawn was coming. Too bad it wasn't daylight savings time. I could really use an extra hour. "Are you able to drive?" It seemed terrible to have him chauffeur me back after all I'd done to him tonight, but I felt it was right to ask him since it was his car…and I didn't trust myself driving that far. Insurance wouldn't help if there was nothing left to insure.

He nodded and settled behind the wheel. "Guess I better speed so the sun doesn't get you."

"Please."

He did. Silently. We weren't short on tension.

As we pulled onto my motel's street, I was feeling the burn. Tucking my jacket over my head, I tried to shield myself from the light. I pulled my keycard out so it would be ready for quick entry once we arrived. By the time he pulled in the parking spot with a screech, my lips were tight, my skin was hot and sensitive to every stitch of fabric I wore, and my limbs were so stiff I could barely move.

I reached for the door handle and jacked my hand back with a scream. Light had only caressed it for a millisecond, but it had been horrific. I was in trouble. No way I'd make it inside in time.

There was rapid movement beside me, a door opening and closing. The whole car bounced with the impact of the trunk lifting and shutting. Then from out nowhere, my car door opened, Aaron grabbed the keycard and threw a blanket over me. He lifted me from the seat and carried me to my door. He opened the door one-handedly with the stealth of the hero he was, then closed us in from the sun.

I peeled the covering away as he laid me gently on the bed.

He cut on the lamp and stood still as a statue. I gazed at him.

After everything I'd done to him tonight, I couldn't believe he could be so sweet. From picking me up at work, to lying in his underwear next to a naked man and taking pictures, to getting me home safely—He was a saint.

Maybe bonding with him wasn't a bad idea after all. I felt love for him. I could be in a relationship with Aaron and to hell with the rest of the world, including Max. Maybe Aaron would spend the day with me. Just the two of us in my room…in my bed. I could be ready for something like that.

"Thank you for—"

"Will you please erase my memories too? Like you did for Rafe. I don't want to remember what you are…or any of this."

Gulp. So much for love and a relationship.

I took his camera out of my pocket and held it out to him. He shook his head, not even wanting it back. It contained memories too. Memories he didn't want.

I walked over to him and looked in his metallic blues thinking the last thing I wanted was to make him forget all we'd shared. No, I didn't want him seeing me as a monster. Didn't want him afraid of me. But I wanted to be real with him. I wanted him to know me like I knew him. That's what true intimacy was. Something I'd never had with anyone, I wanted at this moment with him. Maybe I could get him to see that.

When I extended my hand to smooth the black curls from his face, he flinched.

Damn. I'd blown it.

Trust was a vital part of a relationship too and we no longer had that. We'd have to start over.

Willing his brain to obey my command I spoke softly into his soul, "Aaron, forget everything you saw tonight. Forget what I did to you. Forget what I looked like. Forget I'm a vampire. Remember you picked me up from work and we went for a walk. We talked about our hopes and dreams and passions and desires. I opened up to you and showed you my true self. I was beautiful, loving, kind. And I thanked you for a lovely evening." Then I planted a seed for tomorrow's date.

As long as his memories remained hidden we could have a do-over.

I blinked away a tear and kissed his cheek before he backed away like a zombie and I retreated to the bathroom. I slid down the bathroom wall until I landed on my bottom. I stayed there sad, lonely, and ashamed for hours after he was long gone. I'd known desolation as a human, not as a vampire. Thought that part of my brain had been shut down...until I met Aaron. Now, I'd severed a connection with him I hadn't known I was desperate to have.

And it sucked.

Priority #1 was getting it back.

CHAPTER 19

At some point I fell asleep on the bathroom floor. When I finally got up, first thing I did was setup a fake Facebook profile and sent Rafe a message. I sent him copies of the pictures and dared him to pursue his vendetta against Cindy. And for her trouble he had to throw in a large sum of money so she could buy another place. He could afford it if he laid off a maid or two.

Then I deleted the account. No response necessary. Not to me anyway.

Even though I'd been the one to attack Aaron, I blamed Rafe for making things get out of control. If he hadn't used Aaron's head as a piñata none of this would have happened. Sure, if I hadn't been a vampire it wouldn't have happened either, but Rafe's insolence was the catalyst for my drive-by to begin with. I would have been perfectly content having another all night talkfest with Aaron.

Now, I risked Aaron remembering what happened and hating my guts.

Yes. It was all Rafe's fault.

Almost wished he'd fuck up so I could use the images to

destroy him. Only thing was Aaron's face was in the pics too. And he had no memory of taking them.

I put the camera away before I was tempted to out Rafe on general principle.

Next, I emailed a response to Dr. Floyd confirming we'd meet at his office tomorrow.

Also had to login to my bank account. Yep, like clockwork, my payroll check had been deposited. I remembered when Cindy had set it up for me so that I could bank online. She hadn't even asked why I couldn't do it during bank hours. I hoped we could get back to the way things used to be.

I scheduled a contribution to American Red Cross as I'd done with every check. Since I'd stolen blood from their bank a few times when in a pinch, I felt it was only right to support their cause.

My parents would say it was sacrilege not to give my tithes to church, but I read the bible to say "storehouse" not church. I'd seen enough mismanagement of church funds to know they weren't all functioning as storehouses. Although I gave occasionally to churches I'd watched on Sunday morning television, I had more faith in non-religious affiliated 501c3s. At least I didn't have to worry about them using my tithe towards a building fund or an outlandish pastoral lifestyle then claiming God said to do it. No, the Red Cross used it where needed, where it saved lives. And they made financial statements available. This humanitarian organization had more accountability and integrity than most churches I knew. And I knew A LOT of churches. Besides, the bible spelled out "church" so many times that it could have been specific about tithing to *church* if God wanted to say church.

So fuck 'em. I didn't let anyone tell me who to give my money to. Religious whackos had run my life long enough.

Just as I was about to shut down my laptop, an instant message chimed:

Hey, Willow. It's Mom.

Ha! The irony. *Hey.*
How've you been?
Fine. You?
Good. [pause] *Miss you.*
Me too.
Pause.
Long Pause.
Well, now that we got the niceties out of the way, clearly she had something on her mind. Let's just get down to it, shall we:
What?
Your dad's birthday is coming up and the church is having a dinner for him.
Tell him I said Happy Birthday.
Willow, I want you to come. It's been years since I've seen you.
I don't think so.
Your brothers will be there. They miss you too.

Good try, but I knew better. They missed me about as much as a wart. My older and younger brother were both threads from the old cloth, both preachers like dad. Only thing they hated more than me was sin. I'd always been the black sheep of the family and not just because of my narcolepsy. No, I was the one who snuck away to listen to secular music and watch "Dungeons and Dragons". The one who refused to take the purity vow but read erotic magazines instead. And uttered curse words to emphasize points or because it felt good rolling off my wicked tongue.

But I'd never seen in the bible thou shalt not say "shit" or "fuck".

Honor thy father and mother was in there though. Which was the only reason I still corresponded with her via the internet to begin with. Even though they didn't know I had no intention of seeing them again, I'd honorably said goodbye to my family before going to stay with Max and giving up my human life. No intention of building a relationship with them now.

129

Please, Willow. I love you. Please come.

I considered disconnecting her then decided against being rude. I loved and missed her too, imperfections and all. But I was not going to be guilt-tripped with *I Love You's*. There was no way in hell I was going to my dad's church dinner. Still didn't hurt to be nice about it.

I'll think about it.

* smile *

Yeah, I'd given her false hope, but at least she was smiling.

We chatted awhile and then it was over. Done. Until another few years from now.

It was for the best.

As soon as I got to work, Cin rushed up to me, grabbed my arm, and dragged me to the nearest room. Her sweet cinnamon scent was overtaken by the smell of budussy that hit my nose and nearly knocked me down the second we entered. She hadn't even noticed she'd closed us in the AsSmother/Toe-rrific room with the face-sitting/foot fetish crowd. I came here once every blue moon to collect blood, but Valentina frequented this room and boasted of the subs' expertise. She'd trained a few herself.

If Cin was looking for privacy, we wouldn't get it here. Then again, no one paid us any mind. They were too busy sucking and fingering so we were invisible.

Trey Songz's "Love Faces" was playing all erotic through the speakers. And how appropriate was that.

"I take it Rafe has talked to you," I said, yanking my arm back.

"What the hell did you do to him? He called me crying, begging me to call the mafia off him. The mafia!"

I laughed. He was really melodramatic, wasn't he? "Is that all he said?"

Someone was coming in the far corner and apparently it was intense. Made me want some of that. The effect of my session with Max was wearing off. Focusing on Cin was getting harder.

"He also said I could have whatever I wanted: Lucia, money, the house. I know you must have gotten to him, but how?"

"I can't tell you without incriminating myself and a friend." I glanced in the corner as a thick blonde with ripped pantyhose got up from a bench where she'd been sitting on a man's latex face. Only his glistening mouth was visible. She looked completely satisfied and a little wobbly on her feet but was nice enough to unzip his mask so he could breathe through his nose. I tore my eyes away to concentrate on our conversation.

Cin crossed her arms. "The friend you got all dolled-up for last night?"

Too close to home. I'd said too much. "Just be glad he's off your back. Name your price. I'm sure he'll pay it." My eyes wandered again.

"I suppose I should thank you."

Well, duh.

The man who'd worked the blonde over thoroughly got up zipping his pants. He'd been manually working himself out too.

I was over Cin's drama. I'd done my part. There were other things on my mind now. Looking at her meaningfully, I had to ask, "So we good? You and me?"

She smiled. "Oh, yeah. You're a dangerous enemy."

I nodded. "Don't you forget it."

We shared a stare then she gulped, blinked and walked out.

I didn't move because I had half a mind to get friendly with Mr. Tongue who was spraying down the bench with sanitizer, wiping it clean. I didn't have to wait until after my set to collect blood and I could use a good workout with a submissive. It may even keep another catastrophe like what happened last night with Aaron from happening tonight. And wouldn't it be grand if Aaron could end the night with his memories and nose intact.

After the job I'd just seen Mr. Tongue pull, he'd be good for blood and orgasm.

Looking around, I noticed two other couples enjoying themselves and a set of five who looked like they were playing naked *Twister*. I'd have to get him further in the corner or take him to the restroom to go unnoticed.

By the time my eyes made it back to Mr. Tongue, I nearly swallowed mine. He was looking straight at me and I could see his features clearly enough to recognize him. The room was sparsely lit with yellow neon light, but it didn't matter. I'd recognize those sapphire blue eyes, pale skin with pink undertones and choppy dark brown hair anywhere because it belonged to Ivan, my first love…the one who'd cheated and broken my heart.

There were no hard feelings, but I'd better get the hell away before I broke that dick…or tongue of his.

CHAPTER 20

He was walking towards me. Fast.

I was so out of here.

"Willow! Wait!" I heard him jogging to reach me.

Okay, I could do this. "What?"

His smile was breathtaking. "Is that anyway to greet someone you once loved?"

"Keyword: *once.*"

He went on to explain how he was happy to see me, how he missed me, how sorry he was for how things ended yada yada. I was over it. Really. But that didn't stop me from being immature. So just for the hell of it, I slowly raised my hands to the sides of his face and brought him forward like I was going to put a wet one on him. I captivated his brain instead, planting a seed about him loving me forever but never having me again. How he'd yearn and ache and remember the one good thing he had and lost. When I let his unconscious go, I told him to go fuck himself and walked off, swinging my hips as I went. I could feel his eyes on me. Good. *Get a gander at what you'll never touch again.*

It was petty, I know. But what good are supernatural

powers if you can't use them for self-gain every now and again?

As I hurriedly left the room to disappear before he tried to talk again, I ran smack dab into Queen Ming. This was partly her crowd, after all.

"Wow. You're in a hurry. Seen a ghost?" she said.

I shrugged but didn't slow down. She kept up with me. "You're in a hurry too it would seem."

"Headed back to the dressing room. I can't take another minute watching that girl—what's her name? Fiery Red Beast? She's playing Fucky Ducky tonight and it's creeping me out."

I laughed. Hysterically.

It was always funny when people saw our shows for the first time. Apparently, even other performers could be amazed…and sickened.

Fire, AKA Fiery Red Beast specialized in bestiality and on the real—that shit was nasty weird. I didn't blame Ming for being squeamish. Fire did it as tastefully as possible, but like necrophilia, there was no soft and easy way to make it appear normal. I always thought anything between consenting adults was okay—and that was the problem with mine and Fire's specialties. The dead couldn't consent and animals shouldn't.

I'd seen Fire perform Fucky Ducky before with feathers everywhere, but it was nothing compared to some of her other costumes: Smoking Tigress, Titty Kitty, Moo Moo Baby, Bitch in Heat, and Nasty Piggy. It especially crept me out when she dressed as Medusa with her red hair swarming around her face like snakes and scales painted all over her naked body. She called herself Horny Serpent then. Patrons loved it, especially when she stuffed herself with a rubber snake. Freaks. As long as she didn't bring in a real snake, we were cool. It was all fucked up, but I preferred her shows when she brought stuffed animals and simulated sex with them rather than dressing up as the actual animals.

She was smart too, had a masters in anthrozoology, which made her somewhat of an expert in animal/human interactions…and a formidable foe. She also had intimate experience with an animal considering Punch was a beast of sorts. Hell, sex with were-animals probably redefined bestiality in the same way sex with vampires did necrophilia. But never mind her sexual experience with the fetish. Recent developments indicated she may have even more intimate knowledge of beasts, like firsthand look-in-the-mirror-at-yourself type knowledge.

Anytime I thought of Fire now, I thought of possible beasts who breathed fire just to prepare myself for a showdown. Whatever I came up with made me want to shit my pants.

She was nothing good.

Shuddering at the thought, I switched my brain to what was to come after work. And there it was again: a smile, warmth in my chest, and overall sucker-like giddiness. There was undeniable anticipation circulating throughout my body anytime I thought about seeing Aaron later. I liked Remi, but I was hot for Aaron. I wanted him as my friend, my lover, my companion.

Aaron was my muse.

And as soon as my spirits uplifted they were stomped down again. Severely.

Truth was, I was bringing nothing but heaps of shit to Aaron's life. In addition to harming him physically, all my mental manipulation was harming his brain. Unfortunately, that was just the beginning. Max was pissed at me, which meant Aaron was in danger of further collateral damage. As a matter of principle, jealousy, and ego-bruising, Max would make Aaron pay for my rebellion. Me wanting Aaron was nothing but trouble for both of us.

Rubbing the hollow part of my chest where my heart used to be, I thought of how many ways Max could punish me. He had all the tools he needed. Maistre vampires were powerful by anyone's definition but particularly to their clan of vamps.

As sire, they held all power over us. He could have exercised his power and summoned me already if he really wanted to be petty and I would have been compelled by supernatural forces to do his bidding. No doubt, he was just trying to make me come around so that I would go back compliantly on my own. He'd always admired my strong-will. Plus, rogue vamps were controllable but irritating.

Then again, with the current war against us, he didn't need my shit. It would be better for him to make an example of me. He certainly didn't want other vamps getting ideas, requesting to leave the clan house. He would either have to let them go or risk looking like he was playing favorites with me. No, they wouldn't win a mutiny against him, but he wouldn't want to be surrounded by a bunch of angry brides and clan brothers.

Funny—none of that bothered me as much as knowing the harm he would inflict on Aaron.

Maybe it was time to come up with a plan to protect him. Running wasn't an option. Max could and would find me anywhere. I was a fighter, and though no match for Max, I had to put up a fight. But I couldn't kill him. His death meant mine and hundreds of others. And if he didn't die, he'd be back with a vengeance nightmares were made of. I just couldn't win which meant I couldn't protect Aaron.

By the time I was done performing, collecting blood from Mr. Cash, and dressing, I felt depressed. There was no way I could fight and win against Max. I was as good as meeting my final death really soon. The best I could do was save Aaron by staying away from him.

But that wasn't all.

Mr. Cash had returned from his trip to D.C. where he'd attended the Humans Against Supernatural Beings Summit. Turns out, he'd been working hard to help pass legislation that would make sex with vampires punishable by imprisonment. It wasn't enough that vampires and humans couldn't marry, but once these laws were passed, they couldn't get caught having sexual contact either. The government was working hard to crack down on humans who harbored and aided vampires in any way and they considered sex fraternizing that would lead to us evading extermination.

It was all bull.

Mr. Cash had told me and anyone who would listen to him about his political endeavors. He never had a problem tooting his own horn. It was the same way every time he came to Hades and sat at the bar and had a few drinks. He'd do all that talking then start propositioning the employees for sex. Guess we were supposed to be turned on by his political power.

Not.

Just meant I needed to have sex with Aaron soon while there were no legal consequences for him. So staying away from him would have to come after that.

When I got in the car next to Aaron, I kissed his cheek and buckled up for appearance-sake then waited. But he didn't start the car and drive off.

He spoke instead. "We need to talk. Strange things have been happening to me and I think you know why."

Okay. This talk was inevitable. "Like what?"

"When I woke up this morning, I couldn't remember details about last night. I remembered hanging out with you but only that we did. I can't visualize anything. Not where we went or what you wore…and…"

"And?"

"I had blood on my clothes. Lots of it."

"Oh." I rubbed my temples. Big booboo. I'd been so distracted by Max and struggling with my emotions regarding Aaron, I'd forgotten to cover my tracks. Hadn't even changed motel rooms as I normally would have.

"And I had energy today like you wouldn't believe. Ran ten miles, ate about five thousand calories. I could hear, see, smell, feel things from distances that just aren't humanly possible." *You don't say.* "What's happening to me, Willow?"

He looked at me with those gorgeous puppy eyes and I melted. "And I've missed blocks of time. Taylor and Reese had new journal entries." He smoothed hair down over his head. "I haven't heard from them in years."

Alternate personalities? I'd caused him to shift?

I owed him an explanation. What could I say that would be adequate and evasive?

I needed guidance. Max had said stay away from the human. Saybree had said to bond with the human. I was confused as hell.

At least he hadn't regained his memories. That would buy me a little time to figure things out. I'd half expected that would have happened by now and fully expected his senses would be enhanced after having my blood. For how long was the real question.

"Would you believe me if I said I didn't know what was happening to you?" I said.

"No. You know something. I can almost hear you thinking."

Uh oh. "What do you mean?"

"I can't make everything out. It's like I need to tune in to the frequency or something. But I know you know something."

I sighed. "You're right, Aaron. I do. But I need you to trust me. I can't tell you everything I know."

"I thought we were friends."

There was that word again. Ouch. "We are...and that's why I have to keep some things from you."

"To protect you or me?"

"Both."

"Fine. Don't tell me...but Willow, if you know how to stop what's happening to me you gotta do it. If this continues, I'll have to get back on medication. I *hate* medicine. Such terrible side effects."

"I'm sorry. I don't know how to stop it."

He sat for a minute. Then another and another. Finally, I gathered my duffel bag to go. I could see he didn't want to let it go and he certainly didn't want to have a romantic evening with me.

"Wait," he said as I opened the car door. "Am I still human?"

"Yes."

"Are you?"

I closed the door and sank back in the seat. How to answer this…

He surprised me by answering first. "Okay. I get it. You can't tell me that." I remained silent. "Well, tell me this—did we kill anyone last night?"

I shook my head.

He relaxed. "Good. 'Cause I can't go through that again."

Any other time I would have opened dialogue with him about that, but I was thankful he was accepting my half-ass answers. I didn't want more questions. "We didn't. I promise."

Without another word, he started the car and drove so we could hang out and have a real date.

At least it was a date to me.

CHAPTER 21

I'd fallen asleep twice while we were at the SkyBar lounge. Once at the table, once on the dance floor. Aaron was there to catch me each time. Other than that, it had been a wonderful night. Most importantly, nothing bad happened that needed erasing from his mind. We'd officially shared pleasant times that could evolve into pleasant memories.

Rolling over, I snuggled closer to him and buried my head in the crook of his arm. Ah…nice. He smelled good, felt warm, didn't snore. Too bad he'd fallen asleep before I had the chance to seduce him. I didn't want to wake him since, due to his insomnia, he said he'd been up for days.

We were both fully clothed, resting atop the covers. I sooo wanted to be naked with him, bumping and grinding, but this was what humans did—they took it slow. I could do that, right?

No way.

Running my hand lightly along his arm, I kept going until I got to the top button of his shirt and began undoing them. Enough with the waiting. Soon sex between us would be illegal. Soon Max would be on my ass. Aaron was already in bed with me. No time like the present.

Suddenly, he grabbed my wrist and stared in my face. "W-W-W-Willow?"

I jerked upright. The voice was all wrong, his eyes too fearful, too crazed.

"W-w-w-where am I?" he said.

"Shhh. It's okay. You're here with me. No one's going to hurt you." I leaned over and slowly began to button his shirt. His eyes were wide, but they weren't on me. They were on the ceiling, the door, the walls, everywhere at once like someone scared to death. "Shhh. It's okay. I rubbed his head urging him to calm down. "You've read about me right?"

He finally focused on me and sat up. "Yes. I kn-kn-kn-know who you are." He rested his head on my shoulder. "Why am I awake?"

"Aaron's been under a lot of stress lately. I think his brain is scrambled." I hugged him tightly. "I'll help you."

I was so glad our clothes were still on. It would have been all kinds of wrong for lil' Aaron to wake up to me fondling the body in his six-year-old mind.

"I'm M-M-Mason, by the way."

What? "Mason? I thought you were lil' Aaron."

"No. I'm the only one who st-stutters." *Well, I'll be damned.* "I woke up yesterday out-of-the-blue. First time in months, jjjjudging by the dates in the journal. Your name was everywhere. Aaaaaron wrote that we should introduce ourselves iiiif we shifted. He said you'd know what to do."

Aaron had more faith in me than I did. I was no psychologist.

I got up from the bed and paced. This was my fault so it was my responsibility. But if memory served correctly, Mason was the one with the eating disorder, as in gluttony. Which meant I couldn't just cut the TV on and have him entertain himself. Aaron had said Mason ate waaay too much so he only got one day every six months. I had a feeling this wasn't supposed to be the day.

I looked at my watch. Fuck. I didn't have any food for him to eat and since it was broad daylight I wasn't going anywhere for a while.

"I'm ssso hungry. Got anything tttto eat?"

"No. I'm sorry."

We sat leering at each other for a long while. I suspected he thought I should be a good host and fetch him something, but I was more concerned about getting him back in Never-Never Land. Fast.

"I know y-you don't w-w-want to be stuck here with me. Go. I'll try to g-go back to sssleep. Maybe Aaron will c-come back."

I wondered if he could hear my thoughts. My blood was probably still running strong through Aaron's body.

"No. I won't leave you." Resolved, I climbed back on the bed and urged him down next to me so I could rub his head. "I'll hold you 'til you get to sleep."

We stayed that way at least an hour but sleep eluded him. Made me wonder if he had insomnia like Aaron.

Bet he'd fall asleep if I fed him a cheeseburger. And if I stayed in a hotel with room service that wouldn't be an issue. Hadn't thought of it until now since I hadn't made a habit of receiving guests. Maybe I should look in to that.

Finally, I decided to try something risky since the damage had already been done. I captivated Mason's eyes and forced Aaron out by calling his name. Just like that. Took all of ten seconds. Funny, he had no clue as to what I'd done. Acted like he had just woken up. I thought it better to leave things that way. What he didn't know wouldn't hurt him…no more than it already had.

He showered and put his clothes back on in a hurry saying something about being late for a meeting. Without any prompting from me, he said he'd pick me up from work tonight and we'd hang out again. I was all smiles.

Perfect.

When nightfall came I was whistling a tune. Maybe it was because in spite of everything, Aaron and I were getting closer than ever. And I was planning to get a piece of that. Tonight.

I refused to think of the ramifications.

Just in case, I tried reaching Max metaphysically to mend things. I needed to reason with him, remind him that even though I had feelings for someone else, he would always be my maistre. Besides, he had many brides. He could grant me one extra-relational affair.

He refused to answer. Just turned his back to me and shut down his brain wave. I couldn't see where he was or what he was doing. Which was scarier than his anger.

It sealed the deal on my plans for the night, however. I was going to fuck Aaron good. No sense in holding out considering Max was already pissed. I'd pray to God for forgiveness afterward and hope he'd make an allowance this once since he knew how much it meant to me.

After donning a sweat suit and changing motel rooms, I skipped on over to Dr. Floyd's lab. He had to run some new tests on my blood for compatibility with the new drug. It was a requirement for each new clinical trials group.

Seemed like I had to go through this once a week. Hoped that meant new developments and advancements were being made.

Though nothing had worked for me yet.

He usually had to send the samples to another lab for testing, but now that his new lab was up and running, everything could be completed there. And I didn't have to wait forever for results.

When Dr. Floyd pricked my arm and took ten vials of blood I burst with laughter at the irony. Then I read through a stack of literature detailing new narcolepsy research studies while he put my blood through various lab procedures.

Sometime later he told me he was calling in several colleagues who were expert hematologists and that he'd have to run the tests again. Time was getting by so I used a courtesy phone and called Franco to let him know I'd be about an hour late.

Their expert analyses did not take long. Each left the lab shaking his head.

When Dr. Floyd asked me into the private confines of his office, I knew things were about to get interesting.

He explained a bunch of medical mumbo jumbo like how the whole composition of my blood had changed. And something about it being predatory. It couldn't metabolize the drug because it attacked and destroyed the properties intended to help me. It wouldn't work on my blood and therefore, its healing agent wouldn't work on my body. Bottom line: I wasn't eligible for the study.

Leaning back on his desk, he folded his arms over his white lab coat and looked over the brim of his glasses. In his smart British accent he said, "I had to have a fresh sample of your blood for this new drug, but I wasn't expecting the make-up of it to be completely different." He took off the glasses. "And you don't look surprised at my findings." I sat in the chair and rested my face in my hands. My existence was getting out of fucking control. "Sooo. Is there anything I need to know about your blood, Willow? Anything at all?"

There was that patient/physician confidentiality, right? Since he wasn't supposed to tell anyone, not even VET whatever I told him, I may as well give him full disclosure. "Yes. There is something *confidential* you need to know." When I opened my mouth again to confide in him he waved his hand, cutting me off.

"Willow, you have been my patient and friend for years. In fact, you are like the daughter I never had. I want to help you. You know that."

"But?"

"But if you tell me something that violates the law, I am required to give that information to the authorities. That is an

exception to the confidentiality rule."
    Oh. Well, damn.

CHAPTER 22

"Maybe you can keep looking. There's bound to be another drug that will work for me. I'm willing to pay for the research. Say...ten thousand dollars?"

I had nothing but motel rooms and clothes to spend on which meant I had accumulated quite the savings. Giving towards his silence—I meant, *research* on narcolepsy—was just as good a cause as any.

He put his glasses back on, moving to sit behind his desk and cross his legs. "Don't say another word. I told you you're like a daughter, Willow. I don't need to be bribed. I'll search for a cure for you no matter how long or what it takes."

When I had first read Dr. Floyd's email about him opening a sleep disorder treatment facility in the Medical Center, I had been hesitant about leaving Max and coming back to Houston. I had not wanted to get my hopes up because after years of human treatments and medicines and therapy, nothing had cured me. So why would I believe his studies and clinical trials would cure me as a vampire? At least I had special gifts that could make my existence more bearable. And if I stayed with my clan, I stood a good chance of surviving as a narcoleptic vamp.

Yet Dr. Floyd had been so positive, so persuasive. Had even promised free services in exchange for my participation due to a federal grant he had received. I had felt it was worth a shot. Now, I could fully appreciate that decision. Fully appreciate him. I still had narcolepsy, but if anyone could find a cure, it would be him. And if anyone would help me without reporting questionable findings, it would be him as well.

He went a step further and said he'd explain my blood sample was contaminated if any of his colleagues inquired about what they had seen. I nodded and left his office with a smile. I'd still give him the money. It would be the best tithe I'd ever spent.

Going through the motions at work was nothing new. That's how it was whenever I was bored. And I was bored tonight. Would be until Aaron picked me up.

My countenance lifted as soon as I saw him. He smiled nice and big too. Oh, yeah. Tonight was the fucking night…pun intended.

I didn't want to seem too easy or overly zealous about it though. He needed to work a little for it. So I let him drive us to a restaurant while he had dessert and I watched his lips wrap around the spoon over and over. Slowly and deliberately…and sexy as hell.

I wanted to mount him while we were at the table.

But I kept my cool.

When we got back to my new room, Aaron asked why I'd moved. I told him I liked change. Then I changed in to something more comfortable: my bra and panties.

Subtlety was not my strong suit.

Walking up to him, I nudged him back on the bed until he sat awkwardly, hesitantly. That was okay. I could handle things. No problem being the aggressor. So I straddled him, planted my hands in his dark curls, and stuck my tongue in his mouth. Probing, sucking, moaning, grinding…I did it all while he held on and let me have my way. I had enough passion for both of us.

When he finally palmed the part of me that wanted him desperately, I nearly slipped my skin. If I didn't have him within the next minute I was going to scream.

Thumbing the side of my panties, I ripped them off. Didn't need that barrier.

Boy was I ready, beyond ready.

"I want you so bad," I said. And it surprisingly had nothing to do with blood.

Reaching down between us to let him know exactly what I expected next, I palmed his genitalia through his slacks and found him thick, long and…soft like Charmin. He, most disappointingly, was *not* ready.

I froze, probing his eyes for answers. He immediately looked away.

What the fuck? He didn't want me. This was so embarrassing.

Dismounting, I smoothed my hair back from my face. I was flustered. I was humiliated. I was confused.

I turned my back to him. Couldn't look at his lusciousness knowing how bad I wanted him and how much it was unreciprocated.

"I should have told you. I'm sorry, Willow."

"Should have told me what?"

"I'm impotent. Always have been," he said.

Swinging around on him like the desperate woman I was, I said, "No, you are not. I have seen you aroused. I've seen your erection…and it is spectacular." I laughed at the absurdity of this conversation. "If you don't want me, that's okay. No need to make up shit."

"I'm not making it up. I really am impotent." I looked at him like the freak he was. He stood and walked towards me. "I'm not Remi. When are you going to get that?" I looked hard at that gorgeous face with the mesmerizing eyes and beautiful hair. I couldn't believe this mess. "No, there's nothing physiologically wrong with me, but me—Aaron—I can't get hard. I'm still a virgin no matter how many times my body has physically done the act."

I gritted my teeth and stalked to the bathroom mumbling, "This is just too damn bizarre."

I was sexually frustrated, but I didn't have to be. I knew how to get myself off. Fuck Remi…or Aaron, or whoever the hell was in my room.

"Don't shut me out," he said. "I thought you enjoyed hanging out with me. Nothing has to change. You can hang out with me and have sex with Remi. Isn't that the best of both worlds?"

"No. It's creepy as hell." I slammed the bathroom door shut but not before I saw his eyes watering.

Ah, hell. I'd hurt his feelings. Hadn't meant to do that. Plopping down on the toilet lid, I covered my face with my hands. I hated being cruel to him. He had been nothing but sweet to me. But I was a vampire and cruelness was in my nature. Just because he didn't know it, didn't make me any less a bloodsucker. I slowly rubbed my temples and wished taking several deep breaths would help but knew it wouldn't.

"I've never done oral sex before, but I wouldn't mind doing that to you if it'll help," he said in a soft voice through the door.

Ha! Tempting, but not good enough. I wanted a big hard dick like the one Remi had.

I slowly opened the door. "You should go, Aaron."

"That's not fair, Willow. Please don't do this."

"It's not safe for you here anyway."

"What do you mean?"

"There are some dangerous people after me and I don't want you to get caught in the crossfire. It's not your battle."

His eyes met mine. "Why didn't you tell me this sooner?"

Because I wasn't thinking clearly. Because I was letting my

fucking emotions get the best of me. Because you look and taste so damn good. "I don't know. Just...I guess I just wanted to hang out with you anyway. But it's not right."

"You're saying I'm no longer worth the effort because I can't have sex with you." He looked hurt.

"No. I'm saying it's not worth it for *you*."

He walked to me and wrapped his arms around me. "You're worth it to me."

He just wasn't getting it. "And what about Mason? Is it right for him to get caught up in my mess?" He stepped back abruptly, making me lose my balance. I bumped in to the wall, but I didn't care. It was best we got all this out. "That's right, I saw Mason today. This morning. He woke up before you did. That's what hanging out with me is doing to you."

He palmed his head in his hands, backed up to the bed, and slid down to the floor. I sat next to him.

Long moments passed before he spoke. "I can't make love to you, Willow. God, I'm sorry about that, but you are the best friend I've got. I'm not willing to let that go. I don't care what the consequences are."

I laughed. "You don't know all the consequences."

"And I don't care."

Grabbing his camera from a dresser drawer, I flipped to a picture of him lying next to a very excited Rafe.

He hissed. "What in the world—"

"That's what else hanging out with me is doing to you. I can manipulate your brain, make you forget you did stuff like this."

He covered his mouth like he was horrified and choking back vomit. Then he took a deep breath, closed his eyes and said, "I still don't care." He opened his eyes, looking straight ahead. "I trusted you enough to take the pictures in the first place didn't I?"

Well.

I hadn't told him everything, but I'd told him enough. And

he still wanted to hang out, still wanted to be friends. It was a bummer about the sex, but not a deal breaker. Saturday night, I'd see Remi again. I knew his mind would be in the game. Blood would fill his lower region faster than I could say *fuck me*. Just had to wait until then.

Aaron and I got on the bed for the second night in a row and talked until I fell asleep. I wasn't sure when he did, but I knew he would. He'd said being around me was causing his insomnia to take a break. He was sleeping better than he ever had…since he'd been abducted. Of course the downside was that his alternates were waking from dormancy. But hey, you win some, you lose some.

When I woke up, his breathing was deep and slow. He was still sleeping. I lay staring at him awhile until I had to touch him. Started by rubbing his bottom lip slowly with my index finger. Man, I wanted to seal the deal with him. But that wasn't going to happen. Hmm. Not unless…

I felt his eyes on me. He was staring blankly and then he was staring with purpose. His pulse and breathing had quickened like he was aroused.

Aroused? That couldn't be…

He licked his bottom lip from one corner to the other like he was tasting remnants of my finger. Yes, definitely aroused. Then as quickly as his blood boiled with testosterone and high-octane lust, it dulled then simmered with anger. I could feel all this from his aura. His mind. His body. His energy was radiating with it. My blood was still running within his veins and it was his normal personality…on steroids. But it wasn't Aaron.

"Remi?" He wasn't supposed to be around until Saturday.

"Yeah." He sat up, hair naturally falling over his eyes. "That's fucked up, Willow. You tried to fuck him last night, didn't you?"

CHAPTER 23

Busted.

What could I say? Not a damn thing. Except: *Yeah, you're right. It was a disaster.* Judging by the way he had said "tried to fuck", he already knew Aaron was impotent.

No use arguing over something that didn't happen.

I grabbed a handful of his hair and pulled him down on me, locking our lips the way he liked it. Locking my legs around the backs of his knees. Pushing my hips upward so his groin had a nice, soft landing.

It was full-on surrender. Hot as hell. Wet. Delicious.

Remi was here with heaps of lust spewing from every molecule of his hot body. Gave me an idea.

Sure, he was pissed, but this would help him get over it. He was as necessary as darkness for me at the moment.

Our clothes started ripping away. His, mine. This would be brutal. It would be fast. And it would be right on time.

He locked an arm around my waist and held me tight. Though sinful, it felt heavenly when he breached my threshold by ramming himself into me with one deep, smooth stroke. Raising my hips to meet him, I gave him all the access he could possibly want. Access we both wanted. I grabbed his butt and squeezed hard, throwing my head back to yell in pleasure and completion.

Good thing I was a girl who could take it rough though because Remi was coming hard and he was coming strong and he was taking no fucking prisoners. He was above me, resting on his hands, letting the bottom half of his body swing freely, powerfully. As my bonded human, his strokes rivaled Max's—which made me lose my head and get completely out of the moment. Bad time to think about my maistre.

Remi was staring down at me and must have sensed when things had changed. "What's wrong?"

I shook my head and that was all the answer he cared about. He resumed his thrusts, slamming me into the headboard repeatedly.

"Oh, fuck. Oh, shit. Oh, fucking shit," he said.

He must have been close. And as wonderful as it all was, I couldn't let him finish. Not yet.

His eyes were already zoomed on mine so it was easy to lock him in and call Aaron. When I first whispered Aaron's name, Remi frowned like I'd call him the wrong guy. Then he twitched, groaned and dropped his head. Energy swirled around his body, humming, vibrating. When he lifted his head, he looked confused, disoriented…scared. He looked down at me, at himself.

"Oh, God." He looked at my lips, my breasts, my stomach like a man who was starving then he hissed, "Am I in you?"

I smiled. "Yes, Aaron." Then swiveled my hips to let him know just how deep he was.

"Ohhhh. My. God," he said, positioning his hands on the bed beside both sides of my face and dropping his head to my neck.

I was hoping to continue the eye contact, but knew that sort of intimacy would be asking too much from him right now.

"Can you do that again?" he said.

I did.

We both moaned. I swiveled again for good measure and to let him get used to the sensations. Didn't take him long. Virgin or not, just as his body instinctively knew to blink, it knew how to give him the most pleasure. He started moving in that age-old primal motion until he found a rhythm that was good for both of us. Slow, deep, passionate.

It was so good. I told him so.

Pushing Max and Remi as far from my mind as possible, I gave myself over to enjoying Aaron's first time. I grabbed his butt and squeezed as he retreated and buried himself in me again…and again.

"That's it," I encouraged. His breathing became ragged. It was the most erotic thing I'd ever heard and it tickled my ear, provided an added stimulus to my already overcharged body. I was so close I dug in his back begging him to keep it right there.

"Oh, God, Willow. Oh, God that feels good."

The vibrations of his voice rattled me to the core, heightened my pleasure to near agony.

He kept his strokes slow and deep, just like I knew he would. The only thing that became urgent was his moans and "oh God's". His heavy breathing and erotic whispers told me just how much he enjoyed my slippery walls. Turned me on just as much as what he was doing down below. I was so caught in the moment I missed the change in him. We were both right at the edge, straining for release…and then something changed. He jerked up, looming over me with his thick eyebrows dipped low and angry. He pulled out like he'd seen a herpes breakout and sat back on his knees.

Uh oh.

"What the fuck is going on, Willow!" Remi was pissed. How had he switched so suddenly? "I was there with you one minute and the next I wasn't. What the fuck did you do?"

I rolled away from him. He'd just screwed with my orgasm, one Aaron and I desperately needed. I wasn't pleased. "I don't know what you're talking about."

"Like hell you don't." He grabbed my arm to swing me back around to face him, but I didn't budge. "Willow, you switched us didn't you? You…"

He removed his hand like he couldn't bear touching me. I turned to him expecting to still find anger but saw disappointment and hurt instead.

"Aw, Remi. Don't look like that. I just wanted Aaron to have the experience."

"No. You just wanted Aaron." He got up and jammed his legs into his underwear. "You found out he was a pussy and you used me." I watched as he put on the rest of his clothes. "I thought we had something. I thought you finally wanted me inside you because you liked me." He laughed sharply. "I can't believe it was a ruse just to lay with Aaron. That's fucked up."

Anticipating his next move was opening the door, I grabbed the comforter to cover myself from the sunlight and sunk on the floor next to the bed. Right in the nick of time. He slammed the door on his way out.

I threw the cover off and stared at the ceiling. I'd really fucked up.

Too much fucking up, not enough fucking.

CHAPTER 24

I had half a brain to call Franco and tell him I wasn't coming in tonight. I felt like stinking poop and my attitude wasn't likely to change anytime soon. After pacing my room with the tiny four walls, I decided to go in anyway. Didn't want to be stuck in my room all night with my thoughts…and I needed to collect more blood. My refrigerator stash was dwindling.

Should have stayed in my room.

First thing I encountered at work was Ivan. And right after I grimaced at Ivan's smirk, Franco introduced him as the newest employee. But no, he wouldn't be a cocktail waitress. Due to overwhelming demands from Hades's rising female customers, Ivan was our first male performer. He'd be putting his magic tongue to good use. And Franco was giving me the pleasure of showing Ivan around. I had the wonderful task of helping him acclimate to the workplace.

Great.

Ivan walked behind me the whole time. I could feel his eyes on my ass, the heat radiating from his body. Yep. He wanted to fuck. I knew the minute he was about to open his mouth and ask about hooking up later. Turning toward him just before he did, I inhaled his familiar scent, thinking about how I owed him a beat down for hurting me.

"And that completes your tour," I rushed to say before I thought too hard about revenge.

"Go out with me."

"Fuck off." We had to work together but we'd never be best buds. I turned to storm off, but before I took a step, I fell asleep.

What a whack exit.

When I was able to open my eyes again, I recommitted myself to finding a cure for narcolepsy. I was going to die if something was not done soon. This was a vulnerability I didn't need, dammit.

I didn't care that Ivan had caught me and kept me from hitting the floor. First thing I saw when I opened my eyes were his thick dark eyebrows and intense sapphires. I thought about how they'd looked from this angle the first time I'd opened my legs for him. How painful it had been, how gentle he'd tried to be. Then I thought of the other women who'd had close-ups just like this when Ivan was supposed to be my man. Scoundrel.

At least Max was open and honest about his many brides.

I pushed away from Ivan. Even though I couldn't...or *wouldn't* kill him, I was glad to have at least used my power of captivation. There was some closure, some revenge in that. When he let me go, I stormed off. Finally.

And wha'd'ya'know—I ran right into Ming. Again. We had to stop making a habit of this. Was she following me or something?

"Are you following me?" she laughed.

"I was just about to ask you the same thing."

"Of course not. But hey—you wanna get a drink at the bar? We can get to know each other a little better."

Drinks were free for employees, but I obviously never

made good on that fringe benefit. "No, thanks."

Her lips thinned to a disappointed line. "Okay. I get it. I'm the new girl. No one wants to give me the time of day. If I was hot like the new guy...well, then that would be different. You were just falling all over him." Then she turned to walk away.

"Ming, I *fell* on him. As in, I fell asleep."

"Oh." She turned back towards me and stuck her chin out proudly. "Sorry." She licked her lips and threw her head back, succeeding at moving the hair from her neck, exposing a beautiful neckline. I gritted my teeth. "So it's this place? Yeah. You probably would rather go somewhere else to have a drink. How 'bout after work? Say—Belvedere?" She batted her thick lashes. "My treat."

Was she coming on to me? "Uh...I have plans. Maybe another time." I walked away as fast as I could then yelled over my shoulder. "By the way, you *are* hot like the new guy."

Work was cool. Nothing to scream about. I was busy trying to figure out how to make amends with Remi. I'd have to explain myself...but what exactly could I explain that would make this situation better?

Maybe I'd have better luck figuring out what was going on with Aaron's mind and fixing that. I'd been captivating Remi for a while with no major side effects. What had changed? The frequency? It had gone from once a week to every night. Had that made a significant difference? Was it the stress of having his nose bitten off? Or having my blood heal him?

When I exited Hades's back door, I had a brief moment of anxiety...no, excitement. For the past few nights Aaron had been waiting there for me so my mind told me he'd be there tonight as well.

No such luck.

Focusing on him all week had robbed me of any time I normally spent enjoying the darkness and fresh night air. It was perfect for clearing my head. Yeah...a nice leisurely stroll was just what I needed to iron out conflicting thoughts and pesky feelings. I found myself casually walking through an overgrown cemetery and realized that was where I needed to be. Plopping down on an unmarked plot, I closed my eyes to appreciate the peace and stillness.

Not sure whether God still listened to me, I prayed anyway. But not for myself. Didn't waste time on that. I prayed for Aaron. His body, his soul, his spirit.

By the time I got to my room I felt better, more settled, calmer. I had come to grips with a truth I hadn't wanted to accept. I was an evil being. I'd died and instead of letting nature take its course and allowing my soul to journey toward my destined eternity, I'd made a deal with an evil being. I was no better than the man who'd made a deal with Franco or whatever the hell his name was. I'd willingly traded my human life for "immortality" in an animated shell of my former self. The real kicker was the magic that animated my body was probably satanic since it also came with the need to survive off others to exist. What kind of being could have done what I'd done to Aaron? Certainly not a Godly one.

I had to accept that I was soulless. No salvation for me. No heaven in my future. I could only hope there were different levels of hell. Maybe a purgatory 'cause no paradise was waiting for me. Ninety degrees had to be better than one thousand degrees of fire, right? If it was possible to be punished for my transgressions with some leniency, I'd aim for that. No way of knowing if that option was available, but one thing I was finally certain of—I was headed to hell or some other place where the soulless went once I met my final death. My reasons for becoming a vampire didn't matter.

Another realization: I was responsible for watching over Aaron as long as he lived since I was the cause of his current degenerative state. As a vampire, I was unredeemable, but dammit there was still hope for him. I'd do whatever needed to be done to protect him. At least one of us had a stab at a heavenly hereafter.

I stopped abruptly once I got to my door. It was ajar and I never made the mistake of leaving it open even when I was most distracted.

Someone had been here, had been *in* here.

Looking around to see if anyone was waiting to ambush me, or if there were witnesses, or if there was anything unusual, I saw no one. Whoever had been here was either long gone or still inside.

I stepped in cautiously then shut the door behind me.

My room had been turned upside down as if someone had been searching for something. My bedside lamp was on, clothes were strewn about, each drawer was pulled out and left in various parts of the room. Even the beautiful bouquet Aaron had given me was in ruins. Surprisingly, my laptop was still on the desk which meant it had not been a random burglary. Aaron's camera was still in one of the dislodged drawers which meant Rafe hadn't found me and tried to steal evidence against him. In fact, nothing seemed to be missing.

I inhaled, hoping to pick up a scent and did. Oh, no…

Listening for sounds, I detected a subtle drip in the bathroom. No…

Hair on my arms and back of my neck stood. What eyes couldn't see through the closed bathroom door, my other senses picked up and were already on red alert. Smelling blood in my bathtub where water had been running recently was not a good sign.

I slowly opened the door half-expecting the Boogie Man to jump out, but he didn't. The strong aroma of death greeted me instead. I didn't have to cut the light on to see the body lying in the tub of overflowing water. I cut it on anyway to verify the identity of what my senses were already processing.

Ivan was lying naked in a pool of his own blood waiting for me to find him.

And wasn't that a perfect ending to a fucking fantastic day.

CHAPTER 25

Don't know how long I stood leaning against the doorjamb reflecting back on good times with Ivan. He was my first love after all. Funny how we can only remember things we liked about people after they're gone. The fact that he was a cheater meant nothing now. He didn't deserve this.

He'd been so sweet to me when we first met. And yes, he loved for me to sit on his face back then too. Now that I think back, that must have been his thing. He probably didn't have the courage to tell me as I didn't have the self-confidence to do it often. He didn't have the extra tongue speed or the bonus of tuning into my head so that he knew exactly what worked and when like Max did. But he was great at it, nonetheless, especially for a human.

Water under a bridge.

He was dead now and I hadn't even given him the courtesy of a stranger when I'd last seen him.

Looking his body over, I finally shook the cobwebs from my head and considered my predicament: there was a dead body in my motel tub. What if the person or supernatural who'd done this had also called the cops? Who could already be on the way. I'd be fucked. Blood was everywhere, all over the floor, ceiling, mirror, commode. He'd actually been killed here.

Ordinarily, seeing this much blood would have thrown me into a blood thirsty tailspin. But no. I wanted to throw up instead, especially with his beautiful sapphire blues frozen straight ahead.

I sure hoped he hadn't suffered.

Who could have done this to him? Couldn't have been Max. First off, there would have been no blood left. Secondly, Max would be here to take me out too.

Then it dawned on me: whoever killed him and left him here had intended to set me up. Boy, that really lit a match under my ass. I had to clean this mess up ASAP, get rid of his body...wait—what would I do with it? Dump him in the dumpster?

I went to sit on the edge of my bed. Before I knew it, I was calling Franco and explaining it all to him. He was completely calm and after I told him where to find me, said he was on the way stat.

Somehow, instinct told me he'd know how to handle this. And Saybree had said I could trust him.

I could tell the moment he and Punch arrived because I started twitching all over, my body responding to Punch's energy. Finding a spot on the floor to focus my eyes on, I meditated on darkness and void until the twitching was gone. I simply felt relieved they were both here to help. Franco made sure I was okay then they put on gloves and got busy. They wrapped the body in Aaron's old blanket and loaded him on the back of Punch's truck. Then they cleaned up the mess while I sat on the bed hugging my knees, wandering how much trouble I was in and what to do about it now.

"Get your things. Best for you to come with us," Franco said.

I didn't question it. Didn't argue. Didn't stall. I'd asked for his help and I was taking it.

Once at Hades, I numbly followed them through a secret passageway and down to the basement, which had another secret passageway. It was like this place had been built for secrecy. I wondered only for a moment why we were taking Ivan's body to Hades but then I saw why. Behind a large stone door was an incinerator. With no hesitation, they lifted the body-filled rug and hefted it inside.

"Wait!" I'd become sentimental, realizing I should say parting words or pray before Ivan was nothing but remains. But it was too late. Fire had spread all around the rug, eating it, devouring it whole.

"It's best this way," Franco said.

"How are you so certain what's best?" I said. I appreciated his help but I was still peeved, maybe even grieving. Who would tell Ivan's mother? His dad had been a racist piece of shit, but his darling mother had always been kind to me. "Come to think of it, you didn't seem too surprised when I told you he was swimming in my bathtub."

Franco motioned for Punch to leave us. When we were alone, Franco said, "I've been around a long time, Willow. I know what's best here and you know I do. That's why you called." I nodded slowly. "I'm sorry for your loss," he said. I searched his eyes. "Yes, I know of your history with him. And no, you cannot contact his mother. It would only bring heat your way."

The frustration I felt must have shown on my face because he led me to the stonewall and told me to sit. There were no chairs in the small room so he squatted next to me.

"You weren't surprised were you? Franco, what is it you're not telling me?"

"I was surprised that his body was in your bathtub not that he was dead. I knew the moment he died. His soul came back to me."

My eyes narrowed. "What the fuck are you talking about?"

163

"Ivan and I had a deal."

Oh, no. This was bad. My skin started crawling. "What kind of deal? He was a Christian. He wouldn't have made a deal with a demon."

"I wish he could be here to explain himself to you. The deal was I would help him get what he wanted most and he would give me his soul."

I gasped and clutched my throat, feeling like he'd just slapped me because somehow I knew I was to blame for this. "Please tell me I have nothing to do with this."

He cleared his throat. "I collect souls. It's not just what I do, Willow, it's who I am. It's the reason I exist…and I've existed as long as dirt. I bargain for souls and I keep them for eternity when the time comes."

"You mean when they die."

"Yes." He jacked his thumb back towards the incinerator. "I wasn't expecting to collect on him so soon since I'd only recently made good on my end of the bargain, but shit happens and I'm not the Grim Reaper. I have no say on when they go."

I thought about asking him if he knew G.R. personally and decided to stick to the subject at hand. What the hell did Ivan bargain with Franco for and what did I have to do with it? "You're going to torture Ivan for eternity?"

"No. He just won't be able to enter the pearly gates. No streets of gold. No mansion or crown of jewels. No respite. Just an eternity of mental unrest. Because he met his demise before getting what he wanted most out of life, he'll torture himself for eternity. I won't have to. He'll spend eternity pining for it. For you."

Oh God. "For *me*?" Terrible. Terrible. Terrible.

"Yes. You're what he wanted most in life. I saw him here the other night and his desire for you was strong. He said he'd done everything he could humanly do to get you back."

Oh hell. This was worse than I thought. Not only was I

the reason he'd forfeited his soul to Franco to begin with, but I'd planted the seed in his mind to want me so badly. Before that mental plant, he'd just wanted to hang out. Five minutes before that he'd been busy enjoying Sushi in the fetish room with the hot blonde. If I'd just said hello and left him alone, none of this would have happened.

I'd bet my left titty Franco knew I'd planted the desire in Ivan. He had capitalized on it as soon as he'd gotten the chance. Was probably what he did at Hades every night on unsuspecting folks. Was probably the reason he even opened the club. "You knew I planted that desire in him, didn't you?" He nodded. "So you're like a genie who grants wishes, only you take the most important thing from people when they die and make them suffer. You are pure evil, Franco."

He laughed, which shocked me. Then I thought about it. Yes, I was being all high and mighty like I wasn't an evil predator. Like I didn't use Hades for my personal gain. Like I didn't prey on unsuspecting folks for sustenance too, draining their life force because I could, because I had to. Bloodsucking was not just something I did, it was who I was. At Hades, I had home-court advantage and Franco knew it.

"Yes. I know what you do here night after night. You and me aren't so different. Look, I know you feel guilty. And I know it's easy to blame me, but Willow, he understood the details and consequences of our arrangement. He knew the sacrifice. He *knew*. Trust me. It's what he wanted."

"He didn't know what he wanted. No one wants to spend an eternity like that. It's cruel. That's why when people die humans say 'rest in peace'. Peace is what they want after death."

"Is that what you wanted? When you allowed your maistre to cut your heart out and bind you to him in exchange for your supernatural existence as an almighty fucking vampire? Is that what you wanted? Peace? No way. You wanted to be a *vampire* and you were willing to suffer the consequences. No more sunlight. No more church. No more garlic or silver or food. But who cares. Look what you got in return." His voice had continued to rise until it was loud by the time he was done.

He had a point, but it didn't matter. I was already responsible for Aaron. I couldn't be responsible for Ivan too. "What if I bargain to get his soul back?"

"Sorry. Doesn't work that way. The minute I started making good on my end was the moment he became mine. It was a tragedy he was murdered before making good on his."

My mouth felt dry. "What effort did you make?" I had a feeling I already knew.

"I gave him a job. Made sure he was going to be working closely with you. First guy I ever hired to perform here."

"Fuuuuck!" I screamed and slammed my fist into the wall. Damn it hurt, but I didn't give a shit. All Ivan's efforts at getting me back had occurred years ago. Why had he gone straight to supernatural involvement this go 'round? Why didn't he just pursue me like a sane person?

"Love makes you insane," Franco whispered. "And because you used your supernatural influence on him first."

I was tired of him reading my mind and tired of discovering how bad I screwed up. Franco, on the other hand, looked pleased with himself. "I bet you just love your job," I said hoarsely.

"I love my power. Don't you? Don't you love being more powerful than humans? Don't you love being higher on the food chain? Don't you relish in the power you receive from their blood? Each soul I take elevates me, and yes. I *love* that." He reached for my wounded hand and rubbed my fingers and palm. "There, there. It's okay. Don't worry. You'll see him again."

He was dropping all kinds of bombs tonight. "What do you mean?"

"As a supernatural, you'll see his spirit soon enough. He'll wander the earth, still trying to gain his heart's desire even as a ghost."

I swallowed the lump in my throat and jerked my hand back. That was worse than him just being dead and Franco having possession of his soul. "When? When will I see him?"

"When he's ready."

"That's great. That's just great."

"You'll learn how to tune him out." He walked to the wall opposite me and propped his foot against it. "We have bigger fish to fry, Willow. Ivan was murdered. Any idea who would do that and leave him in your place?"

Ahhh. Yes. That was definitely a bigger fish. "Not a clue."

I told him all the lengths I went through in order to stay hidden. Apparently, frequently changing motel rooms wasn't enough. Someone had been watching me, but for how long? Scary thought.

The last thing I wanted was for my story to turn in to a murder mystery. I was freaked enough with the idea it was about to fit in to romance, but that was better, and more exciting than trying to figure out who killed my ex. Besides, discovering his killer wouldn't bring Ivan back. But romance could fill some lonely nights and satisfy my carnal desires.

"You need to stay here until we figure it out," Franco said as a command not a request.

He held his hand out for me to grab it. I stared at it a moment then took it, stood, and followed him to an empty bedroom where he gave me the combination to the door and said I had everything I needed here, including a bathroom. He reminded me he was preparing a sanctuary for supernaturals and was ready to accommodate me. His only rule was no humans. Fine. I could do that. Tomorrow night I'd see Remi upstairs anyway.

I had to admit my room was secure, soundproof, completely dark, cozy. Not much furniture or decorations, but I didn't mind minimalism. It wouldn't be permanent. Couldn't really stay here long-term. Franco collected souls and probably hid them somewhere underneath Hades in one or more of these locked rooms. And one of those newly soulless ghosts was my ex-boyfriend, Ivan.

Just seemed all wrong.

CHAPTER 26

No use trying to sleep after you've found your ex's body and then watched it burn.

Saying I tossed and turned all night was an understatement. When I did finally get sleep, my parents were there. Brothers too. And this time we were at a family reunion when I was sixteen and forced to wear a helmet in case I fell asleep…and fell. It was an absolutely ridiculous get-up, but not as bad as when I wanted to listen to Johnny Gill sing "My, My, My" in my cousin's headset. I'd taken my helmet off long enough to listen, sing along, and get caught. My oldest brother went squealing to my parents…who came squealing to me. I had to spend the rest of the day standing in a corner, holding one foot up…with my helmet on. All because I enjoyed "Satan's music".

Completely humiliating.

Not as humiliating this time around, more maddening. Couldn't have a restful sleep that way. Was setting myself up for some nasty narcoleptic episodes later tonight.

I also spent time pondering who could have murdered Ivan and tried to frame me for it. Remi and Aaron knew where

I was staying. I just couldn't see how either of them could have done something like that. But what about another personality? I hadn't met them all. That Vlad guy seemed like a murdering douche. Maybe he'd done it. But with what motive?

It just didn't add up. None of my scenarios did.

Just meant that it was someone I was totally oblivious about. Someone I didn't know was watching me, stalking me, planning my demise just like they'd planned Ivan's.

I dressed in a hurry so I could get upstairs. Couldn't wait to see Remi. Last time we were together, he'd been pissed with me. But after the night I'd just had, I needed his friendly, loyal face. And he needed to know he was important to me. Conditions were perfect for hot make-up sex.

Fate would think differently.

Because for the first time in a year of seeing his sexy ass with the I-dare-you-to-fuck-me-hard eyes, he was a no-show.

Unbelievable.

I looked, sniffed and listened for him everywhere. Then I panicked like a mother-fucker. I'd seen close-up what Ivan looked like as a corpse. Had the same thing happened to Remi? Oh, God, no!

Bursting into Franco's office like a madwoman, I demanded he look up Aaron's membership info and give me his address. Stat. No time for playing around. Hopefully, I wasn't too late.

As usual, Franco didn't look surprised to see me. After mumbling something about violating club policy, he unlocked a cabinet near his desk and retrieved a file folder. He knew better than to argue with me on this. I stood directly in front of him with my hand out, waiting as he wrote everything down.

Just as I was about to walk out the door in a blur, I stopped and eyeballed him. "Please tell me you haven't made a deal with Remi."

"Who's Remi?"

"I mean Aaron." His name was on the driver's license to

apply for membership, after all.

"I've made no deal with him." He leaned back in his chair, smirking. "Given the way you're running out of here like a bat outta hell, I'm preeeetty sure he's closer to his heart's desire than I could ever get him."

Wincing, I looked down at the folded paper in my hand. I knew the location. It would take me two minutes to get there if I ran. "You think I'm foolish to go after him, don't you?"

"Heck naw. He spends a shitload of money here. Go get him." He crossed his ankles over the desk casually. "But Willow? Take one of the bouncers with you. Not Punch. I need him tonight, but somebody else."

"No can do. Gotta do this alone."

His eyes penetrated mine, letting me know he knew what I was up to. Tonight's plans for Remi did not include a third-party tagalong and Franco knew it. "Isn't your maistre going to have your head on a stick for fucking that human?"

"Yep."

He shook his head like I was up the creek without a paddle and swiveled his chair around so that I faced his back. "Well, be careful."

I didn't respond. Just ran across town with the strength of ten horses, the speed of hurricane winds. I had to get to him in a hurry. Just in case.

Wow. My eyes popped when I saw his high-rise building. Very ritzy. Made me look at the address again to make sure I had the right place. Yep. This was his residence all right.

I surveyed the place to see what I was up against. Cameras everywhere. A concierge. Valet. Two maintenance workers and three guests…

Good thing I was good and fast at climbing because I certainly wasn't going through lobby security. Didn't have time to sign-in, get frisked, get approved, and get escorted to the key-activated elevator before going to his door. So after one last cursory look around to make sure no one was watching, I ran around back and scaled the wall like a four-legged spider. Since I could enter a building without personal invitation, just not individual apartments, I broke a hall window on his floor and climbed in. Smart enough to know the break would set off a silent alarm, I scaled the hall ceilings until I got to Aaron's door to avoid security cameras.

Dropping to the floor like a thief in the night, I banged on the door like Remi's life depended on it. If he didn't answer, I was fresh out of ideas. I couldn't get inside without his invite and I wouldn't know the first place to go look for him. Didn't even know if there was still a him to look for.

No one answered and there was no sound from inside.

I banged again, risking waking his neighbors and getting caught because sometimes you gotta do what ya gotta do.

Then it dawned on me—maybe this was a good time to see how strong our bond was. Since he was the first human I'd fed my blood, I wasn't quite sure what we were capable of metaphysically. What were our limitations? How strong would our blood connection be now considering he had used most of its power to heal?

No more wasting time. I owed it to him to at least try to find him psychically, use my blood in his body like a tracking device.

But I could only track him if he was still alive. His energy could only be picked up if blood was flowing through his veins, if there was brain activity.

Closing my eyes to concentrate, to alleviate tension from my body, I shut down my physical senses and opened up the psychic ones.

Opening my mind, I threw out a short psychic net to test the waters. Not like ringing a telephone. More like my energy traveling through the walls, through space, searching for his energy. It wasn't the same connection Max and I shared, but I reached Remi's energy source quickly because of his close proximity.

The link to his aura was stronger than I expected given how much time had passed since he'd had my blood. Alarmingly so.

My energy tickled him lightly like a feather, awaiting access to his mind, seeking an opening as though he were in a deep sleep and needed gentle prodding to wake. His subconscious responded with despair and sadness and self-pity.

I pulled back sharply before I got images to go with the emotions. Didn't need his turmoil floating in my head too. At least I knew he was alive.

Just as I heard footsteps marching down the hall toward the window I had broken, he began stirring inside. Stumbling to the door. Cracking it open. Standing there in black boxer briefs with thick, dark bed hair.

Given the way his hand gripped a liquor bottle, I figured he'd been passed out drunk instead of sleeping. Had I mentally awakened him or had he finally responded to my knocks?

And the bigger question: Was this Remi or Aaron…or neither?

"Willow? What the fuck are you doing here?"

Hmmm. His slurred words took away from his vocal register so I still didn't know who he was. He recognized me at least…but didn't they all? Bet that diary included a description of me to go along with my name ever since they'd started switching randomly. "Uh, can I come in?"

"You can't be here. Security has to call me when someone's here." He shook his head like he was trying to shake off his buzz. Stepping into the hall, he looked both ways through squinty eyes and said, "I must be dreaming." He tried to put the bottle to his lips a couple of times, missed, then used both hands to help steady the bottle.

More footsteps and mumbles were coming. Staff had cleaned up the glass and were now looking for what broke it. I'd bet an ass cheek they didn't think a vampire had climbed the high-rise and done it so they were probably baffled, looking for an eagle or…miniature airplane.

But I needed to get out of the hallway. I'd be a suspect for sure.

I snatched the bottle from his grip before he could take another swig and caught him from stumbling backwards with my other hand. Gripping his chin, I pulled him close to my face. "This is not a dream. Aren't you gonna invite me in?"

He blinked slowly a few times and slurred his words, "Youwannacomein?"

"Yes."

"Well, comeonin."

I still didn't know who he was. Didn't matter. I had plenty of time to figure it out now that I knew he [they] were safe.

Letting go of his face, I hooked my arms around his waist and carried him inside, kicking the door shut. The feel of him in my arms and the grandness of his place immediately caught my attention. In lieu of appreciating either, I found a comfortable-looking oversized couch and plopped him on it. He looked over at me through heavy lids when I sat next to him.

Dammit. He was still gorgeous. Still insane. And I still had no clue which personality was sitting next to me. Setting the bottle on the coffee table, I offered to make him coffee. Hopefully, I still remembered how.

"You have no idea who I am do you?" he said. I shook my head. He barked out a laugh. "Tonight's Saturday night, isn't it? Remi's night. His night for the past few years…and now…"

I waited for him to finish. When I realized he wasn't going to, I spoke up. "And now what?"

"Now, we're totally fucked up." He threw his head back on a pillow.

I stared at him and started going through my checklist: he had nearly a full blown beard, was making eye contact but not staring, wasn't smoking and was making no moves to jump my bones. Not Remi. Plus, Remi wouldn't have spoken of himself in third person. On the other hand, he was drinking and cursing and his hair wasn't slicked back. Not Aaron either.

"I knew being without medication would totally tank us. I told Aaron not to stop the goddamn drugs. Now look at us. All mixed up." He looked down at his wrist and rubbed the scar with his thumb.

Bingo! Only one suffered from that level of depression.

"I spent all evening going through the journals catching up. Funny both Remi and Aaron are in love with you. Aaron just doesn't know it yet. Not too bright. Hell, neither are too bright if you ask me. Didn't take me long to figure out what you are. Remi says you're always cold...he never feels a heartbeat. Hell, just lookatya'! Idiots can't tell you're not human." He half laughed, half cried. "Reese is the fucking braniac, but even I can figure that shit out."

Okay. He had to go, but I had to handle him delicately. "Emmanuel, it's okay. Aaron's going to get back on his meds. I'll make sure he does."

"I sure hope so, 'cause I can't take this. I don'twannabehere."

Oh, hell yeah. Aaron was getting back on his meds. Taking care of Aaron was my responsibility and obviously it was time I stepped up to help. And the first way I needed to help was making sure Emmanuel didn't attempt suicide while he was occupying Aaron's body.

Tears ran down his face as he repeated how he didn't want to be here over and over again.

Had to put this poor bastard out of his misery.

Leaning towards him, I placed my hands on both sides of his face, commanded his pupils to open to me and whispered, "Emmanuel, I need to talk to Aaron, okay?"

He nodded. "You gon' do that hypnosis thing?"

"Yes."

"Well, can you make it where I don't ever have to come back?" He looked hopeful like a child telling Santa what he

DICEY GRENOR

wanted for Christmas.

Baffled me what was so darn depressing about his existence that he couldn't stand it for a few hours. But hey—I was no therapist. Had no interest in counseling him. "I'll see what I can do." After rubbing away his tears, I said, "Aaron? We need to talk."

He blinked rapidly then smiled. "Willow, what are you doing here?" Well, that didn't take long. Emmanuel had been eager to let the body go.

I smiled back then told him what had happened since we'd last spoken. Even told him about finding Ivan's body, left out Franco and Punch's involvement. Told him about my conversation with Emmanuel and encouraged him to seek medical treatment so his personalities could be managed again.

He swooned as he tried to rise from the couch which reminded me Emmanuel had been drinking all evening. I told him to sit tight as I got up to fumble around in his decadent kitchen to make coffee. The stainless steel appliances, granite countertops, and brown-stained custom-built cabinets almost made me wish I ate food. Almost.

He followed me to the kitchen anyway, leaning against the island as I looked around for everything I needed. I could tell he wanted to talk and judging by the sheepish look on his face, he wanted to talk about sex.

"Sorry about what happened last time we were together." He started smoothing his hair down across the top of his head. "It was so amazing. I couldn't believe I shifted in the middle of you and Remi making love. I've never done that before. He wrote that he felt betrayed. I can't have him upset with me," he said as I dumped coffee grounds into the filter.

"I'll make it up to him. He blames me not you." He looked puzzled like why would it be my fault. Ha! *Because he knows I forced the shift.* "Um…because I didn't tell you to stop. Because I enjoyed being with you."

He blushed. "So I wasn't disappointing? I didn't know

what I was doing."

I smiled and turned the coffeemaker on.

Men and their delicate egos. Aaron and his innocence. "Being with you was absolutely heavenly. I think you knew exactly what you were doing."

He leaned down towards his elbows on the island to hide his smile. "Too bad the only way I can do it again is to shift when Remi's in you. Interrupt your lovemaking again. Betray him all over again." He shook his head and blew out a deep breath. After several quiet minutes, he said, "This is a mess. I have to control my personalities. I can't let them control me. I'll make an appointment first thing later this morning."

I nodded.

The sooner, the better. Things were definitely better when they shifted upon my command. This random shifting was too much, too unpredictable. Maybe once Aaron got on his meds, I could go back to shifting him in while Remi and I fucked, without worrying about Remi shifting back like he did last time or any other personality showing up when least expected like Mason and Emmanuel already had.

After handing him a warm mug, I looked around to appreciate the glory of his penthouse, which Remi had severely understated as a condo when he had asked me to move in.

Aaron sipped his coffee as he showed me around. I awed over its grandeur. My motels had nothing on this.

With all the sculptures and paintings lying about haphazardly, there was no need for him to tell me he was an artist, but he did anyway. And he definitely was not starving. Between Daddy's trust fund and Aaron's talent, he was living well. No studio apartment or bartending on the side for him.

His specialty was landscaping: beaches, deserts, mountains, canyons…

Lost my train of thought when I came across his collection of willow trees sketched in charcoal, painted colorfully in abstract and realism, molded to different sizes, in moonlight and sunshine, snow and rain. He said they were in homage to me.

Well, duh.

He'd gotten a contract with a nationwide hotel chain to buy exclusive rights to his "Sleepy Willow" collection. Ah, the irony.

As I was about to congratulate him and say how I was impressed, flattered, and profoundly touched, we walked in his bedroom and I was distracted in to silence. It wasn't the big 'ol white contemporary bed with black linen and pillows or the matching zebra print rug on the floor. It wasn't the magnanimous view of Houston from the twenty-seventh floor windows extending from high-ceiling to polished hardwood floor or the red lighting that gave the room a romantic glow. No, it was the oversized white desk against the east wall where stacks of leather-bound books lay.

Could it be?

One look at his embarrassed face told me they were indeed volumes of his infamous diary, the most current one opened midway with a pen stuck in the center. Finally, laying bare before me were recounts of his life, experiences of his personalities, written renditions of his soul…or souls, plural.

How did that work exactly? Would he be judged based on actions of each personality?

"I don't mind if you read it," he said, sitting on the edge of his bed, sipping coffee, waiting for me to invade his privacy.

It was my chance to learn everything there was to know about each of them. Had one of them killed Ivan? What had happened to Aaron to birth all the other personalities in the first place? Were Aaron and Remi truly in love with me?

He'd never shared his diary with anyone. This was a rare gift. A privilege. Reading it would be putting together a puzzle, a riddle.

Or I could just ask everything I wanted to know. Call up each personality, stare in his gorgeous eyes while watching his lips move. Ease my curiosities the fun way. Or…

I could just accept every part of him, secrets and all. Keep things mysterious, exciting.

Instead of walking over to the desk, I made a detour, ending my tour of his home with his bathroom. Surprised us both.

He moved in behind me. "I thought you'd want to read it. To know everything about me. About us."

Maybe Emmanuel was right. For Aaron to share something so private, he must really be in love with me.

"We'll have more to talk about if I don't read it," I said without looking at him. He was standing so close, my body had started responding to him. I was afraid my teeth and eyes would start changing.

Picking up each bottle lined neatly on the counter, I sniffed each scent, read each label, and discovered Remi was a Perry Ellis Night man and Aaron wore Acqua Di Gio by Giorgio Armani. I figured LA Looks gel was for Aaron's slick look and Remi just shampooed with L'Oreal and went. The counter was full of grooming cosmetics mind you, but I didn't care who the other scents and products belonged to, although the eyelash curler and mascara did give me cause to pause.

These details were just as intimate as any verbiage his diary could have held.

Though tempted to use the opportunity to seduce him, I left the bathroom when he mentioned wanting to take a shower. His walk-in closet kept me plenty busy with separate sections of an array of clothing styles. Apparently, one of his personalities was Goth. Made me laugh out loud. Someone was actually creepier than Remi.

Didn't even want to know who the blowup doll on the closet floor belonged to.

When Aaron emerged from the shower, I was mindful of his shyness and dared not turn to face him until he was dry and clothed. When he asked if I would lie next to him since he couldn't sleep unless I was there, I agreed to stay until he got to sleep. He'd drank three cups of coffee so it was probably going to be awhile. Either way, I had to leave before sunrise and time was a' ticking.

I sat on the edge of the bed until he cut off the light and got settled. Then I pulled the sheet back to climb in bed with him. Lo' and behold, he was stark naked. Thanking God for small blessings, that was all the invitation I needed to take it from here.

His eyes tracked each of my movements as I stripped slowly. He had missed the foreplay before and seemed intent on missing nothing this go round. Maybe he thought his body would respond differently since he'd already done the deed. There was just one problem—this time wouldn't be for him. Well, two problems 'cause his body still wasn't cooperating.

Cupping his flaccid dick, I climbed on top of him, kissed his forehead, his cheeks, his lips. Then I said, "This is for Remi."

Locking into his eyes, I palmed the sides of his face and kissed him gently again. Nothing was happening down below on his part but I was consumed by heat. I stared into his eyes and commanded him to open to me. I felt his resistance. Maybe subconsciously he knew what was happening. "Remi, please come out. I want to be with you."

Aaron didn't move for a while, not even his eyelids. His hands rested next to him on the bed. His chest rose slowly, evenly, as he breathed.

Suddenly, he jerked, his whole body jerked, his spirit and aura changed…and his dick twitched.

"Remi?"

He looked around then focused on me. "How'd the fuck did you get in here? What the—"

I kissed him hard, sticking my tongue so far in his throat, he'd gag if he didn't push back with his own. He groaned and grabbed my hips like I was a lifejacket. I felt him swell to full, painful hardness and I couldn't wait to have him inside me, easing his ache. He rolled me over his erection, which caused us both to gasp. I was already slick, covering him with glossiness.

It was time to get down to business.

I grabbed him and lifted myself to sink down on him when he did something surprising. He stopped me. "No! You don't want me. You want Aaron." He tried to throw me off, but I held my ground, locking my knees against his hips, my heels against his legs.

Okay. I was horny as fuck but that didn't give me the right to come in and take some dingaling without talking to him first. He'd been pissed when were last together. I had to keep the peace if I wanted a piece. "I'm sorry. Okay?"

"No. Not okay. You're just saying that because Aaron's cock doesn't work. If you could fuck him, I'd never see you anymore. You two would find a way to switch him in permanently. That's what you're planning to do now. Isn't it?"

"No. That's not true. It's you I want right now. I like you a lot."

"But you love him."

Silence. I didn't know how to answer that really. Wasn't sure I possessed the capacity to love anymore. "I don't know, Remi. I enjoy hanging out with both of you and it's confusing as hell when you look like the same person to me."

"But you know we're different. We've shown ourselves to you completely."

"And I think I love you both a little for that." There. That was the truth. It didn't have to be all or nothing did it? "What about that? Would you have me if I wanted to be with both of you?"

He looked pensive.

At this rate, I'd lose them both. Attempting to sweeten the deal, I bared my fangs. "You know I could kill you with these."

He hissed in shock and horror. "Sweet Jesus!" he cried.

CHAPTER 27

I let his blasphemy slide so my revelation could sink in…and I could absorb the feeling of his dick twitching beneath me, titillating my most sensitive spot. "What about now? Will you have me now?"

I already knew the answer.

Like taking candy from a baby.

His eyes narrowed with desire. He smiled. Big. "Fuck yeah." He turned his head to the side, exposing his neck and pulsing vein. "Fuck me, bite me, do whatever you wanna do to me. Right now."

I did. I rode him like a stallion, fed from him like a fountain.

We came hard, him filling me up as I contracted around his erection until it softened. He rested for about three minutes then asked me to fuck him again and bleed him dry.

I did him one better. After ripping my wrist open with my fangs, I held it to his mouth as he nursed, filling himself with my power. Bonding us even more, even tighter. I had to do something or risk killing him.

Man, I did love Remi. I loved them both. And wasn't love

antithesis of soullessness?

Never mind the implications of being soulless and in love. Time to revel in my victory. He was mine. Aaron I still had to work on. But Remi was mine.

With my blood flowing strongly through his veins, I could barely tell he was human. Didn't know how long the effects of my blood would last, but for the moment, his prowess was outstanding. Unnervingly so. Remi wasn't lasting as long as Max, but his lower region was filling with blood again fast after each orgasm. Refractory period, my ass. I knew that wasn't normal. He hit hard and deep, rocking my whole world, making me see stars. Then he paused long enough to stiffen and shudder before he was back at it again.

Given how much blood I'd taken from both sides of his neck and groin, his skin should have felt cold by now. Yet it felt feverish. At each crescendo, he stuck his wrist in my mouth so I could take more of his nourishment as he pumped my body full of his.

Sometimes, when it started off leisurely, we dialoged like old lovers. But by the end, we were so overcome with passion we could only writhe and make unintelligible sounds.

"I've never fucked like this before. Goddamn. I feel so strong, so sensitive," he said as his hips moved in long, slow strides.

"My blood will enhance your senses. You'll experience some of my strengths with none of my weaknesses."

His face tensed up like he was about to explode again.

"Just breathe through it, Remi." I smoothed his hair back from his face so I could watch his pleasure. Sweat beaded on his forehead, his skin was red, his muscles were tight. I could watch him all day if it weren't for having to leave before sunup.

"Your eyes are weird…glowing…and red," he said.

He lifted his torso from me, raising my legs outward so he could stare down at where we were joined. When I put my heels on his shoulders, he ran his tongue over the tips of my toes then sucked my big toe in his mouth and slurped gently. It heightened the already intense sensations of his thumb gently rubbing my clit. I could barely speak, but I tried. "My eyes change when I'm aroused, angry, sad, any strong emotion."

"Can you control it?"

"Sometimes no, but meditation and deep concentration help a little."

His strokes quickened, his breathing changed. He was close again. "That's it, Remi. Fuck my pussy."

"Ahhhh," he said from low in his throat and gradually rose in pitch. "Ahhh. Ahhhhh," he continued moaning as his hips pumped too fast to keep his hand in place. His mouth tightened around my toe, his tongue swirled around it. As I watched his abs move sensually, I wanted to tell him I was coming, but all I could do was hiss. I knew the moment he realized it and that was almost better than talking filthy. Just as I contracted around him, squeezing, stroking, his eyes flew open and his hips punched fiercely, faster and harder than a human, until he buried himself deep within me and shook so hard the whole bed moved. He didn't shout. He moooooaned his pleasure as I moaned mine. It was harmonic music.

Then he made a funny, exhausted face. I laughed while raking my nails lightly down his chest to his abs, to curly black groin hair. He shook some more. I laughed some more.

He finally pulled out and collapsed next to me, chest heaving while he struggled to breathe. Once his breathing returned to normal, we pillow-talked about how I'd been able to go undetected as a vampire by using my phlebotomy kit and blending in at Hades and that I'd trained myself to survive off feeding once a day. When I confessed to taking blood without his permission in the past, he said he had never noticed puncture wounds. True to Remi form, he said he had enjoyed the razor cuts and wished I would have used my fangs on him long ago.

Gotta love that.

"Do you miss the sun?" he asked, laying his head on my chest where it held no heartbeat, no breath…only vibrations from my voice. He oddly found the stillness comforting. And I knew this from his thoughts, his energy.

"Nope. I'm more concerned about the fate of my soul."

"But not enough to remain human."

Touché. "No. I guess not. I thought being a vampire would cure my narcolepsy."

"You don't need a cure for narcolepsy. That's what makes you unique. You're perfect the way you are."

I swallowed the lump in my throat. No one had ever said anything like that to me before. Even my aunt, who had been the only one to understand what I was going through, had tried desperately to be cured herself. Her hope had been a small comfort, but the other part of her time was spent in denial about her condition altogether. And that was just plain sad.

Where had Remi been when I was human, struggling with the disorder? Alone. Scared. Unlovable. Willing to do *anything* to get rid of what made me different.

Yeah, well, he was just saying all this because he was captivated by my vampireness, high on my blood. He hadn't known the human me, the weak Willow. The one who cried when she was picked on and was too ostracized to have childhood friends or…

I fell asleep at some point and that suited him just fine. He climbed on top of me and pumped his way to another orgasm. When I woke up, he was just finishing, sweat beaded on his forehead, heavy-breathing and all. Kinda made me wish I hadn't missed the whole encounter.

Remaining inside me, he rested his head on my shoulder and breathed, "Sorry."

"No, you're not."

His chin hair moved indicating he was smiling. "You're right." He sighed. "I've been wanting to do that since I first saw you at Hades."

Good time to ask what I'd been wanting to know. "How do you get turned on by death anyway? Why do you like sex like that? Most men want a responsive partner."

Flashes of his brain waves told me he was remembering something…a pretty girl, black hair, blue eyes. After moments of silence he finally said, "My first sexual experience was with a dead girl…and I liked it."

Holy shit on a stick. I didn't know how his kidnapping fit in to that, but I knew it did somehow. He must have been forced. "I'm so sorry."

"Don't be. Not for me anyway. Aaron didn't like it. I did. Be sorry for him."

I held him close, resisting the urge to ask if that was when he first shifted. Didn't know if remembering and talking about it would traumatize him or help. There had to be more to the story than a six-year-old boy kidnapped and forced to have sex with a dead girl. Did "first sexual experience" mean actual intercourse? Had he been capable of that at six? Maybe he had been captive for years. Maybe he'd been kidnapped at six and hadn't had the experience with the corpse until he was eight or ten.

It was all too inconceivable.

Could he handle opening up about it? Could I?

He raised his head and looked down at me. "By the way, how old are you? Couple hundred years?"

"Nope. I'm a newbie, turned when I was twenty-one and I'm only twenty-four."

"So your body's always gonna look like this?"

I nodded. "And since I knew I'd be frozen in time, I got a Brazilian wax, relaxed the hair on my head so it would always be straight and long, got a mani-pedi…" I laughed. "Turns out, none of that mattered. My hair and nails grow as they did when I was human."

"Really? How is that? Aren't you dead?"

"As a doorknob. I guess the same magic that animates my body makes my hair and nails grow too."

"So everything functions normally?"

"Not exactly. My tear ducts work, I make saliva, but I don't pee or poop. Don't sweat either." I had never shared this much about myself with anyone. We were both treading on uncharted territory tonight.

"Can you fly?"

"Hell no. But I can move really fast and jump really high. Human eyes wouldn't know the difference."

"Damn, that's hot." He kissed my cheek. "Hey—I'm not going to turn in to a vampire now am I?"

"No. The effects of my blood will wear off."

He exhaled. "Good 'cause I'd never want to be a vampire. I love dead things, but I don't want to be dead. There'd be no thrill of nearly-dying again and there's no greater rush than coming close."

I wondered if he'd change his mind if he truly was on his deathbed. "I can't turn you anyway. I'm not strong enough. It takes a maistress vamp and powerful witch to do it."

"Who's your maistress?"

"I have a maistre. Only men can sire female vamps, only women can sire male vamps." I wrapped one of his long curls around my finger. "It's kind of like a marriage."

He stiffened…and not in a good way. "You're married to a maistre vampire?"

I caressed his shoulders to ease the blow. "Yes, but it's not like you think. He has hundreds of brides. He can have as many as he wants. We're not exclusive."

"So he's okay with me laying up in you like this?" He rocked his hips for illustration, making me lose myself momentarily.

"Uh…not exactly. But don't you worry. I've got it all under control."

"I know y'all burn in the sun, but how do I kill him at

night? Just in case he comes after me."

I laughed. The likelihood he'd survive a one-on-one fight with Max was nil, but that wasn't the point. "I can't tell you that. If he dies, so do I and his whole lineage."

"Really? Shit in a creek."

"That's why maistres and maistresses have to be so strong. Their power provides our life force. Their blood mixes in with our blood and sustains us. Kill them and it's lights out for the rest of us."

"Damn. I hope he's somewhere safe then. I heard VET has just about wiped out the entire vampire species in the U.S. Every country has passed anti-vamp laws, but none of the others seem to enforce it as well. I wouldn't want to lose you." He smiled and kissed my cheek tenderly, belying the sadness in his eyes. "Where is he anyway?"

"Can't tell you that either. Nowhere in this country though."

He relaxed.

We lay in peaceful silence until he yawned and I knew it was getting close to time for me to leave.

"I came in you a lot. You can't get pregnant, right?" he said sleepily.

"No sexually transmitted diseases either."

"Cool." He searched my eyes. "Most women want kids. You're okay with not having any?"

"God, yes. I never wanted any. Can you imagine me falling asleep while feeding a baby? Or passing this gene along?"

"Know what you mean. With my mental state, I would never want to be responsible for a child and I sure as hell wouldn't want to bring one up in a world where things like what happened to me happens."

"Will you ever tell me what happened?" I asked.

Suddenly, flashes of his past coursed through my mind like a whirlwind. I saw a man, a dark cellar, a cot, a machete slicing through his hairy back as blood splashed about...

Remi threw the memories from his mind like vomit. Few more minutes and I would have known the whole story without him telling me.

Maybe if I told him the effects of our bonding he'd stop broadcasting his feelings and memories so strongly.

"It's probably best that Aaron fills you in." He put his head back down. "I'm so tired right now."

I caressed his back. "I've taken a lot of your blood."

"You gave me so much of yours too. My body still feels like it's on fire. Like if I dipped in the pool it would boil instead of cooling me off."

"I'll take less next time."

His dick jerked violently within me. "I like that there will be a next time. I want to come in you over and over again. But you don't have to hold back. Ever. Take whatever you want. Whenever."

I enjoyed him coming in me too. Ivan and I had always used condoms and Max had always withdrawn at his critical moment, so this was the first time I had experienced it. But there was another person to consider when it came to sharing blood and bonding.

"I'm so glad you feel that way but I don't think Aaron would like that," I blurted before thinking of Remi's reaction to my comment. I was cheapening our moment by making him feel like he played second fiddle to Aaron. Not to mention it was a terrible time to bring up Aaron's feelings in all this after I'd spent the past few hours feeding Remi and feeding from him.

He tensed. "Aaron doesn't have to know. He doesn't have to know we fucked or what you are or that you were even here. You are *mine*. I'll rip that damn diary to shreds before I write a lick about it."

This was the jealous streak I'd glimpsed when I mentioned my relationship with Dr. Floyd to him. And that relationship was innocent. I sure hoped jealousy between two men in the same body wasn't going to be a problem. Remi's possessiveness mirrored my sentiment for him, but he'd forgotten I wanted both of them. I had been forthright about my feelings for Aaron. Maybe not the next time we had sex or the next, but one day soon I would switch Aaron in and fuck the shit out of him too.

"That's sweet of you, but he already knows I was here," I said. "I saw Emmanuel then Aaron."

He slowly raised his head like it weighed a ton and stared down at me. "Emmanuel?" I nodded. "Holy shit, we're fucked. If he's shifting again, we're all in trouble. He gets NO shifting privileges anymore."

"He doesn't want it either. Don't worry. I can help with him like I did tonight. And Aaron's gonna get back on his meds."

He just stared at me, his jaw ticcing, then he withdrew from me and got up from the bed. "You realize that may be the end of me? Or is that what you and Aaron are planning. You want me out of the picture."

I blinked. "No, I didn't know that. He said there would be side effects. I didn't know…"

"Aaron's the host, Willow. If he gets on meds to control shifting to alternates, what the hell do you think will happen to me?"

I hadn't thought it through. I thought the meds would just help him *manage* the alternates. But what the hell did that mean exactly?

Oh, no, Remi was right.

He grabbed a pack of cigarettes from the dresser, went to the bathroom and closed the door.

What in the world were we going to do? I didn't want to inhibit Remi and I had a good feeling Aaron felt the same. He needed Remi, relied on him, in fact. They were a package deal. Couldn't see a use for Mason or Emmanuel or Vlad, but we needed Remi. They were co-dependent, two peas of the same pod. We'd all be screwed if Aaron got back on meds.

Couldn't let that happen. Had to think of something.

But time was suddenly of the essence.

I went to the bathroom where Remi sat on the floor smoking near the shower. I told him I had to go and kissed his cheek. He just stared. I told him not to worry I'd think of something but I definitely wanted him. His face softened and he asked me to stay. He reminded me of his offer to move in with him. He would close the blinds and curtains to keep the sun out for me. Would even get a coffin or clear a spot in his closet.

While spending the day shut inside with him appealed to me more than I was willing to admit, I thought of the secure room I had waiting for me at Hades so I declined.

"Besides, I like watching Christian TV on Sunday mornings and I know you're Jewish."

"Actually, I'm atheist," he smirked.

CHAPTER 28

Atheist? Oh, boy. I should have known.

I'd thought Aaron's soul stood a chance as a Jew since he was one of God's chosen people. But Remi, an atheist? If his beliefs affected Aaron's soul, they didn't stand a chance. At least I was a believer. They needed my help in more ways than one. He needed to be converted fo' sho'.

He laughed. "This is wild. I can almost hear your thoughts. A minute ago, I swear you were worried about me being jealous of your feelings for Aaron and now you want to convert me, don't you?"

Guess he was discovering the benefits of our blood connection on his own. Although I preferred the upper hand, him reading me was only fair. And seriously intimate. If he fine-tuned his psychic connection to me, he would hear my thoughts even clearer. I'd keep that part to myself for now. "Yep. That's what I was thinking."

He shook his head. "A Christian vampire. Isn't that an oxymoron?"

"Maybe. But who can be sure?"

I mean, the bible said to confess with your mouth and

believe in your heart that Jesus was the Son of God and you'd be saved. I didn't see any stipulations like if thou art a vampire all bets are off. On the other hand, as conceded earlier, I'd given my soul away in exchange for being undead. Realistically, I watched church on TV out of habit from my upbringing not for any real effect on my spirit, soul, or body.

Not wanting to get too deep in that just now, I kissed him long and thoroughly to distract him from my thoughts. Then after verifying his multiple bite wounds had healed, I got my patootie out of there in an instant. Had to run like hell to beat the sun, but I made it.

No, I didn't captivate him into forgetting the sex or my confession. Couldn't risk messing with his brain any more than I had already. Not until I talked it over with Saybree. She had known there was something different about him yet she still said he'd be a great day companion for me. Surely, she would have some guidance as to how to keep him safe.

And truthfully, I wanted him to remember.

When I got back to Hades, I snuck back in the basement through the private corridor and shut myself in my room. Still felt strange calling it mine, but I was definitely glad to have it.

I didn't waste any time running my bathwater then plopping down. Soaking in the tub was therapeutic, relaxing. Gave me time to think.

Things were looking up. I had a safe place to stay, a companion—or two companions, depending on how you counted Remi and Aaron—on top of an interesting place to work, with a resourceful boss and loyal colleagues. Maybe I'd bested Saybree's warning. Maybe no one was coming for me after all. Or if they were, they wouldn't be able to get me. Not in Franco's sanctuary.

Then again, Max was still an issue. Maybe that was the evil coming for me she'd been referring to. And he could get me anywhere.

Laying my head back and closing my eyes, I focused, tried

calling him again. We really needed to work this out. There had to be a way we could both be happy.

Darkness. Silence.

More darkness. More silence.

Then the darkness slowly lifted. Vanilla assaulted my nostrils.

There he was lying on his bed, uh…relaxing. He was stretched out, eyes closed, skin starkly contrasting the black silk sheets and mop of kinky black hair covering his groin. Judging by the fact Max's name was tattooed on her forearm, it was Mercedez, one of the clan's human vamp whores—I meant, willing blood donors.

The fro was moving up and down, obviously the source of his relaxed state. His mouth was slightly ajar revealing long, bloody fangs, indicating she'd pleasured him in more ways than one. No blood was spilt, indicating he had been characteristically neat and greedy.

He wanted me to see this. Wanted to rub in what I could have if I went back to him. Or wanted me to be jealous about him being with her. Or wanted me to see he wasn't pining for me.

Didn't bother me a bit considering the time I'd had with Remi.

I was just glad Max was in a good enough mood to open his brainwaves to me. And since he was having his moment with a human woman in lieu of a vamp bride, I hoped this was a good time to make up with him. Appeal to his mercy…oh hell…just try to reason with him.

And beg for forgiveness.

Digging one hand in her hair, he yanked her head back and grabbed the base of his dick for a strong tug. Ah, yes. He had to see his money shot, had to see evidence of marking his territory.

Except, this human was having none of that. She caught him off guard, clamping down on his head to drink all he had to offer. Tenacious little thing.

Since Max never shared his blood with humans, those addicted to sex with vamps, particularly sex with him, would ingest anything they could to have a piece of him inside. He hated sharing his power with them as they were only meant to serve our superior species so she'd been slick. And it would pay off with inhuman strength.

He jerked, cursed, but didn't use his strength to remove her. I waited patiently as he unloaded himself in her mouth. The better mood he was in, the better for me.

Once his spasms ceased, he pulled her face back, kissed her lips then slapped her hard enough to land her into the wall across the room. She'd known it was coming, that he would inflict punishment. She got up smiling, totally unfazed. For what she'd gotten from him, it had been worth it all.

I got out of the tub and wrapped myself in a towel.

She turned as if she'd finally sensed I was there and grinned nice and big for me. I waved. She'd been a favorite donor of mine. The perfect playmate. Absolutely loved pleasing us.

There were humans out there who wanted the benefits of vamp blood (and other fluids) without the hassle of dying and becoming a vampire. Some just wanted sex, others just friendship. Just to say they knew a vampire. Of course, things were changing. That kind of interaction with us could get everyone involved killed nowadays.

Mercedez knew the consequences, but she stuck around anyway. She and a handful of others who were addicted. It was worth the risk to them.

What I liked most about her was her convictions. She and I philosophized about human nature, love, life's purpose, religion, you name it. She didn't want to be a vampire because she didn't want to relinquish her soul. I agreed with many of her points, but in the end decided I'd take my chances.

So here I was.

Dead. Animated by magic. Soulless or at best, with a darkened soul, a heartless one. Bonded to Max and now Aaron, Remi, and whoever else was in that body.

Oh, yeah…I was also an illegal villain with enemies on every corner.

Reminded me why I was desperate to get on Max's good side again.

"You come pretending to make amends after you've given the human your blood, MY blood," he looked at me venomously, "and after you have fucked him." I stood still. Best to let him speak his mind. Get it all out. "Whatever happened to all your moral shenanigans or were they pretend as well? Need I remind you, you are my bride? That means you committed adultery."

"C'mon, Max. That doesn't really apply to us, does it? We're vampires." What I'd done probably constituted adultery and definitely was fornication, but I wouldn't take it back. It had been too good. "You were just with Mercedez. She's human, not one of your brides. Would you really hold a double standard against me? We're not monogamously wedded. The rules are different for our kind and you did the same thing I—"

He waved his hand, cutting me off. "I forbade you and you did it anyway. You must be punished." He snapped his fingers and we were instantly transported to a place of darkness that gradually became brighter. There was no evident source of light so I figured Max's sudden glow was illuminating the area.

I nodded. "I understand. I will take whatever you feel is—" I said as I looked around. A sick feeling started in the pit of my stomach. We were in a circular room that looked like a huge pantry, infinitely high. There were shelves of jars surrounding Max and they were all full. Full of human hearts. Still beating.

"Shut the fuck up, Willow. Are you trying to be stoic or

humble? Rational or brave? You confuse me to no end."

"I am truly sorry to be such a thorn in your side."

"Pain in my white arse, you mean."

"That too."

The glow intensified. "Do you know where I am right now?"

"Not the exact location, but I know you're surrounded by our hearts. The hearts of your vampires." No one knew where he kept them and reasonably so. Anyone with possession of them controlled us.

He grinned wickedly. "That's right, love." He began levitating and rising, then slowly twirled around midair until he grabbed a jar from a high shelf. "Do you know whose this is?"

My throat was dry as I watched the heart pound, but I managed to whisper, "Mine."

"Right again, Willow. And do you know what I could do with it right now?"

"Yes." I was truly scared, my legs shaking.

He continued floating in the air, glaring at my heart-filled jar, his eyes glowing neon green. Making me tense. Worried I'd just spent my last night on earth. When I was certain he was going to drop it to the ground and stomp on it, he returned it to the shelf.

His short blond hair and strong jaw decorated his face so perfectly, it was a shame to ruin it with the menacing look he gave me. "There is only one way you can make amends and you already know what that is."

I gulped, taking a moment to think. I shook my head. "I'm not rea—"

"Then get out of my face, Willow! If you are not ready to come back to me, I am not ready to be kind to you. Come back on your own and all mine is yours again. Make me drag you back and I will not kill you until after I have let you marinate in a coffin for one hundred years first." He was about to disconnect our brainwaves.

"Wait!" I needed answers. "My ex's body was found in my tub. Do you know anything about it? Did you send someone?"

"How dare you question me," he snarled. "If I had put a body there, yours would have been in pieces next to it."

That's what I thought. I rushed my next line before he cut the connection. I wanted him to know why I was not ready to go back. "Max, I love my job. It gives me purpose, keeps me busy. Please understand that. And Dr. Floyd is helping to cure my narcolepsy. I'd finally have a shot at being more normal."

"*Normal?*" He laughed. "You will never be normal. You were not meant for such mediocrity. And what of your human fraternizing? How do you explain that?"

My voice came out small, "He has multiple personalities and needs my help. He's getting worse because of me. I can't abandon him now."

That got a deep, rumbling laughter from him. "Multiple personalities? You're in love with a lunatic? That is about the funniest thing I have ever heard. Call him. Ask if he put the body in your tub." Then he shut our link down. His evil laughter still echoed in my head four minutes later.

CHAPTER 29

I'd said to myself a million and one times that Aaron and Remi were insane. But criminally insane? No way. Remi had killed whoever abducted him and had done God-knows what to him. Justifiable, not criminal. And that made all the difference in the world, didn't it.

Despite my current predicament, I watched hallelujah TV then slept well. No dreams, no unsavory memories, just rest. And when I awoke, I called Saybree from the phone on the nightstand. She answered before it even rang.

After explaining as briefly but thoroughly as possible what had happened to Ivan and what had been going on with Aaron and Remi, Saybree expressed sorrow over Ivan's death and mentioned she would prepare an amulet for my boyfriend(s). Ideally, a crucifix would work best to ward off human and supernatural evil, a silver Star of David protection necklace, second best. But they weren't exactly vampire-friendly so she would make a gold and brass medallion to protect my boys from Ivan's fate. Of course, it wouldn't prevent them from shifting, but one issue at a time.

Planning to visit her at nightfall, I sat on the bed with my laptop to place an order on Amazon and check my email. Since I didn't have to work tonight, I had no need to go upstairs...except then I discovered the WiFi reception was not strong enough to maintain an internet signal.

Bummer. I'd gotten good reception at the motels.

First strike.

Not that I was looking for reasons to leave Franco's sanctuary and move in with Remi and Aaron or anything.

When I got to Franco's office, I was surprised to find his door shut. First there was mumbling from inside. Then there was louder, more distinct arguing about club policy and...me. When I recognized the other voice, I turned on my heels to flee.

But not fast enough.

The door swung open. "That's her! That's the girl from the pictures," said a raspy male tattletale.

I turned to face the music so to speak even though the only music I wanted to face was away from Franco's office and towards Hades main room where Pitbull and T-Pain were jamming "Hey Baby" while two nude girls mud-wrestled onstage.

"Ms. Willow! I'm so glad you're here. Your boss said you didn't have to work tonight, but I urged him to ask you to come in for questioning. You must be a mind-reader because we were just about to leave," Agent Monroe sneered.

Blind bastard.

He was nice enough to move out the way so I could step in the office then he closed the door.

Weren't we being nice.

Unsurprisingly, he had not come alone this time. There were two musclemen standing with their arms folded, eyeing me like I was week-old trash that needed to go out immediately. Without being asked, they confirmed they were co-exterminators by flashing badges that held their credentials.

Okay, so they'd come for me. Fine. But I wasn't going

down without a fight. Monroe would need more than Tweedle-dumb One and Two to take me out. They'd better be packing silver bullets, crosses, holy water…

I glanced at Franco, who was sitting behind his desk. I wasn't sure he'd help me once things got cranking, but it didn't matter. I didn't want him caught in the crossfire. He'd already done enough for me. Probably the main reason I'd survived as a narcoleptic vampire so long without the protection of my clan. Wish I could have thanked him for…

He gestured for me to keep quiet by putting his finger to his lips.

"Ms. Willow, we are here because Ivan Somerset has been reported missing. We've learned that he was recently employed here and he is your ex-lover."

Franco was right that I should keep quiet. They had shit. Still fishing for evidence. "Do you have a question?" I said.

His cheek started twitching. Boy. I really got under his skin. "When was the last time you saw him?" he said through tight lips.

"Uh, I believe it was Friday night." *Answer only what's asked*, I told myself.

He asked a series of questions like when was the last time we were intimate, how did I feel about Franco hiring Ivan, why had we broken up and if I held a grudge.

My patience had finally waned.

"Is there a fucking point to this? He likes to sleep nude and watch me pee, but none of this has anything to do with his current whereabouts. You three jackoffs should turn this over to the real police and let them get out there and look for him instead of being here harassing me again."

That made him snap. "You smartass! I know you had something to do with his disappearance. Your colleague even said you had words Friday night. See, I think you finally saw an opportunity to get back at him for cheating on you. Now that you're the big badass vampire you had motive, opportunity, *and* means to kill him. So where the fuck is he?"

Ming should have kept her fish lips shut. If I managed to keep myself from jail this time, I'd have a long talk with her about over-sharing about me.

Definitely not the way to fit in around here.

Franco was standing behind his desk. "That's enough, Agent. Either you have something to arrest Willow for or you get out of my club."

"Forget arresting her," Monroe said calmly. *Uh oh.* When he grabbed a Subway sandwich bag from a chair and shoved it at me, I had a pretty good idea what he had in mind. "Eat," he said.

I opened the bag and saw a meatball sub. My stomach lurched.

"That's your favorite sandwich isn't it? That's what your mother told us. So EAT!" he yelled.

When the hell had he spoken to my mother? He'd been a busy ass bee. Never mind. I had a bigger problem.

He got out a gun from inside his jacket and pointed it at my forehead.

"I do not have to have proof that you killed Mr. Somerset. If you don't take a bite of this fucking sandwich right now, I'm going to put a silver bullet through your skull because I'll have enough evidence to prove you're a heartless blood-sucker." He cocked the hammer back. "You got five seconds."

"Wait—you can't expect her to eat something *you* brought." Franco said. "I'm sorry, Agent, but I don't trust you. You've been too overly-zealous to hurt Willow. How do we know that sandwich isn't poisoned?"

Monroe snarled. "Then have something brought from your bar. Anything. And she better eat it or I'm shooting her and arresting you."

Silence.

One way or another, I was dying today. At the hand of a blind man.

So much for being at the top of the fucking food chain.

Franco picked up his walkie-talkie and called Punch, telling him to bring a fruit cup from the bar for me to eat. I would have loved to have seen Punch's face when he heard that.

Already feeling like throwing up, I wondered how I was going to pull this off. "Can you lower your gun, Monroe? Vampire or not, no one likes a gun pointed at them. Accidents do happen," I said unsteadily, knowing full well if he lowered the gun even a half inch, I'd break a commandment and kill him. One of his Tweedle boys would probably take me out before I could get at them both, but at least I wouldn't be alone in hell today.

"If I pull this trigger, Ms. Willow, it will not be by accident. It will be because you thought it was best to try and kill me rather than eat food." He raised his other hand to support the one holding the gun.

Couldn't get anything past him, could I.

Punch came in ten minutes later, not even blinking at the scene before him. I was glad someone could be calm about all this. Then again, he wasn't the one about to experience instantaneous sickness from food in order to avoid getting a bullet between the eyes. The food would be poisonous and debilitating to my body until it was out. I knew this because Max had punished another bride in the same manner. It had not been pretty. I wouldn't die the final death from excruciating pain, but I'd wish for death.

Come to think of it—I may as well take the bullet 'cause sure as my name was Willow, Monroe was going to shoot me once he saw my reaction to the fruit.

I went back to gauging whether I could kill Monroe before he had a chance to get a fatal shot off. Then I noticed there were only red cherries and red strawberries and red watermelon in the cup. I mean, *really* red.

And I caught an unmistakable delicious copper scent.

Thank you, God!

I didn't know whose it belonged to, but I was certain there was blood in the fruit.

CHAPTER 30

Having Punch and Franco on my side was the best thing that could have happened. I trusted them to take care of me, to make sure things turned out well. So far, that trust had not been misplaced. Internet in the basement was cow's manure compared to that.

Without another thought, I tossed back my head and emptied the cup into my mouth.

Good thing the pieces were cut small. They slid down my throat smoothly without me having to do much chewing. But not so fast that I couldn't recognize the yummy taste of Punch's blood.

He'd done all he could for me. His efforts just couldn't hold off the inevitable.

My whole mouth—lips, cheeks, tongue, gums, and throat burned the moment fruit touched it. Then my chest and stomach. Felt like my guts were on fire…and the flames were spreading. Rapidly.

I managed a smile, holding my arms out like *violá, I'm still standing*.

But it wasn't going to last. I really needed Monroe and his

goons to leave ASAP.

"Agent, I think it's time for you and your boys to leave. Willow did everything you asked of her," Franco said as he stood by the door and motioned for Monroe to exit.

Monroe stood still and I stood tense. Heat had spread up to my head and down to my toes. I was so glad to be caramel brown at the moment. Hopefully, my complexion hid my internal burn, my rising sickness, my bubbling poison.

Ugh…didn't know how much longer I'd last though.

Monroe continued standing starkly, staring blankly with pupil-free eyes. He surprisingly had excellent aim as the gun remained between my eyes with only the slightest tremble.

I felt like a hot teapot about to blow its top off and whistle in agony. And this was only the beginning. My body would begin to protest, to expel the bits it wasn't meant to ingest. Any second now…

After what seemed an eternity, Monroe snorted and put his gun away. Then he unfolded his walking stick, straightened his tie and left with his buddies.

Sinking to the floor, I held it together until I could hear Monroe down the hall. Didn't want him to hear me…

Heave.

There was no holding back.

Involuntarily squeezing my eyes shut, I heaved again.

Who knew fruit soaked in blood would have bought me a little time. It had. But only a little. I was out of time now. Sick to my damn stomach. Heaving up red fruit.

There was frantic movement all around me. Franco was barking orders, scrambling to contain the mess while I was lost in pain racking my entire body.

Not sure how long I stayed there. Purging myself of poison. Ruining Franco's carpet.

When I was sure the heaving had stopped, trembling began. And then more heaving. Seemed like there was no end to it.

I wanted to yell, to die. Again. For good.

Then I was lifted and carried, the motion causing more nausea. Made me remember what it was like to be seasick. Made me lose count of how many times I puked. When I finally felt the cushion underneath me, I guessed I was back in my room on my bed. The steadiness was welcomed and not a minute too soon.

An overwhelming sense of gratitude engulfed me when my puke-soaked clothes were peeled from me. Even more so when I was cleaned with a wet cloth and wrapped in a sheet. But nothing compared to the taste of fresh, uncontaminated blood as it hit my dry mouth. The wrist smelled wild and beastly…

If I had not already figured it was Punch saving me again, his deep growl and big, heavy body on top of mine through the sheet would have been a giveaway. His weight was just right in making me feel grounded and his blood was so good. Too good. Soothing. Refreshing. Felt like it was sealing up holes the poison had created.

Then his teeth sunk into my wrist. I felt each pull all the way to the tips of my toes and finger. He was sucking my blood, removing the poison. Saving my animated life.

Bonding me to Fire's man.

Ahhhh. Relief for me. Pleasure for him.

I could tell he was fighting hard to refrain himself, but it was no use. He couldn't prevent the hard-on or his increased pulse or breathing. Alas he gave himself over to the pleasure, rocked against my thigh and released his tension. Remaining still, I let him use me in gratitude for the gift he'd given me. I was too weak to move an eyelid anyway.

But I was gaining strength slowly. The blood transfusion was working.

He slowly disengaged his canines from my wrist then carefully removed his wrist from my mouth. Positioning himself next to me on the bed, he rolled me until my head rested on his massive chest. Then he hummed—would you believe—"Twinkle Twinkle Little Star". I listened as his breathing and heart rate gradually slowed and then the hand he used to stroke my hair grew still. The lullaby tapered off and he was asleep. Snoring.

I knew I needed to get up. Needed to finish my internet mission. Needed to get him off my bed and out of my room. But I just didn't have the physical strength or mental willpower.

Finally giving up the fight against joining him in sleep, I relaxed my mind and let it go. Napping safely in his arms after a meal was tantamount to heaven at the moment. Especially since I wasn't used to anyone caring so tenderly for me. I had done nothing to deserve this. Nothing to deserve his loyalty, his compassion. Yet, I craved it.

Another tender moment I could remember was Aaron keeping me safe from the sun even after I had hurt him. Aaron dropping his head to my shoulder and stroking slowly when he realized he was inside a woman for the first time. Aaron giving me a bouquet of roses, painting willow trees, offering his diary for me to read…

My sweet Aaron.

Thinking of him was a great distraction while I healed. Now that I had Punch's blood, my body would heal itself. Thoughts of Aaron would heal my mind.

It had been an exhaustive experience. One I would not soon forget and never ever wanted to repeat. And as loving as my thoughts for Aaron were, I had nothing but contempt for one determined VET agent.

Maybe it was time to be proactive. Time to find out where that fucker lived. Find out who his family was. Do damage control like I did with Rafe and Cin.

Or maybe next time I saw him, I should just kill Agent Fucking Monroe's ass on the spot.

CHAPTER 31

I was awakened by a disturbingly sharp object dragging down the side of my face yet instinct told me to lie still, make no sudden moves. Throwing my senses out, I assessed the situation, discovered I was in a heap of shit. The sharp object was a claw. The claw belonged to a wild animal. The wild animal was not Punch because I still lay on top of his slow-rising chest. And the wild animal was not in a friendly mood.

Awww fuck! It had to be Fire. Punch hadn't locked the door.

I panicked.

But before I could leap up, the hand attached to the claw grabbed a handful of my hair. One strong tug and I went flying through the air, crunching into the concrete wall so hard I saw stars.

Then I heard the ugliest, loudest animal war cry I'd ever heard come out of the ugliest fucking animal I'd ever seen. The room was dark, but there was no mistaking the humongous eyes, pointy horns, red scales on a long, thick torso…and oh, shit—wings that were not fully extended! If I survived, I'd spend time pondering how the fuck her big ass fit through the door of my room. Quick guess—she transitioned to a red fire-breathing dragon *after* she caught me laying up with her boyfriend.

Speaking of fire-breathing—

"Punch! Puuunch!" I screamed as I dodged the first blast aimed at me by moving in a blur towards the door.

I had to get the hell outta here. I hadn't escaped Monroe's bullet and food poisoning to become a crispy critter so soon.

But as I reached the door, I caught a backhand from her huge, clawed hand that sent me back in the direction I'd just left.

Shaking my head of the daze, I screamed again, "PUUUNCH! Get your bitch!"

He appeared in front of me, his back to me, hands out at his side in that familiar non-threatening approach. He was trying to calm her down. Help her see reason.

Fuck that. Kill the bitch.

He wasn't going to do that, but thankfully, he wouldn't let her kill me either.

Once he saw logic wasn't working, and she was rearing her head back to send another burst my way, he quickly grabbed me from the floor and leaped across the room out of the fiery path. Then he dropped to all fours, jerking, popping, expanding…and expanding some more until his clothes ripped and his long, black locks turned in to fur and spread over his whole gigantic body. His face elongated. His ears, hands, and feet too until a huge charcoal black wolf occupied the space where Punch used to be.

Just in time to pounce on Fire before she had a chance to light her torch again.

The large black werewolf was magnificent as it sprang up and forward, landing in such a way that sent them both rolling along the floor, slamming into the dresser.

Good thing the room was larger than my average motel

room—another point for staying at Franco's sanctuary. With only a bed, a nightstand, and one large dresser with a mirror, they had room to fight, though not much.

And good thing Punch was huge. He just may have a shot at handling her.

Except they ended with him on his back and Fire foaming at the mouth so bad, it ran from her fierce, snarling mouth to his face. He screamed with each drop, and each drop dissolved his skin. Apparently, her dragon saliva boiled like water and burned like acid.

His claws were wrapped around her neck, hers around his and neither looked like they were going to budge. If either used their teeth, the other would be fatally wounded. So that wasn't the plan. The beasts were just making a show for dominance. They'd be dead-locked indefinitely if it wasn't for her acid drips.

Maybe I should have ran when I had the chance instead of inciting her, but I couldn't let Punch go out like that. Especially since he was defending me against the woman he loved after saving me several times already. "Get off him you red bitch!" I screamed as I jumped on her back and started pounding my fists into her skull.

She let out another horrible war cry but I didn't let go. I'd pound a hole in her ugly head before I let her up and give her a chance to blow fire towards me again.

Pound, pound, pound…

Suddenly, I was air-born again. Only this time I didn't smash into anything. I remained mid-air, levitating the way Max had done earlier. But I didn't have that power. What the…

Then Fire was air-born. Next, Punch.

All the snarling and howling and screaming stopped. Time stood still.

A shirtless Franco, covered in tattoos, emerged from the doorway looking pissed. So pissed that he cursed in Spanish for a while before reprimanding us in English. "You goddamn, children! How dare you fight in *my* house. You are all guests here." There was more Spanish cursing accompanied with hand gestures then more calmly he said, "Do NOT do that again. Ever. How many times must I say 'we are all supernaturals and must stick together'. Huh? Whoever cannot live—or in your case, Willow, un-live—by that motto can get the fuck out of Hades right now. There's the door." He pointed to it for effect.

We all looked like unhappily scolded children, none making a move to leave.

Tension began to ease from the room and I began floating back down to the floor. How the hell did he do that?

"Fire, I told Punch to care for her. Blame me." She looked down at the floor, though I couldn't tell if it was in shame or out of respect for Franco. He walked to her and patted her head. "Do not be jealous, my child. Her heart belongs to her maistre and whatever affections she's capable of is bestowed on a human. And Punch only loves you, though his body responds as a man's."

Not sure I would have been able to calm down by now if I had seen Remi or Aaron laid up with another woman, but hey—whatever worked. Blood transfusions were intimate, but at least Punch and I had not had sex. And we were definitely not in love.

As Franco comforted her, smoke blew from Fire's tennis ball-sized nostrils. Not able to stand the sight of her any longer, I looked closer at Franco's tattoos instead. I'd never seen him without clothes, never knew how plentiful they were. They extended from his lower neck to all the way down to the base of his wrist where a shirt would cover him. My guess was they went even lower in to his slacks covering the lower half of his body.

The patterns were intricately designed with angles and colors and shapes, so much detail they looked like everything and nothing simultaneously. The more I looked, the more the patterns seemed to re-shape, re-form. Spelling out words, drawing pictures, showing faces. Oozing energy. How odd...

I leaned closer as a familiar set of eyes began forming. Sapphires so intense, so disarming, I reached out and ran my thumb across Franco's skin where they appeared to beckon to me.

He jerked, dropped Fire and stood. "Never touch my tattoos," he said icily.

But I'd already gotten a jolt of energy along with an image from his skin where it whispered to me. I'd already read the drawings, felt their essences...discovered his source of power.

Franco was not covered in merely ink. Each pattern told a story, held a history...a life. The sapphire eyes had belonged to Ivan as the rest of Franco's tattoos belonged to other claimed souls.

My mouth gaped. "So that's where..."

"Yes. That's where I keep my souls," he said.

CHAPTER 32

It had been one hell of an evening. Extraordinary events had transpired while just getting on the internet seemed like mission impossible. Would have to do that later since I had already spent waaaay too much time in the middle of Punch and Fire's drama.

Or causing them drama, depending on how you looked at it.

But never mind them. According to the clock, too much time had already passed.

Leaving Franco to mediate insecurities and relational issues between Fire and Punch, I showered and dressed in a hurry. Other matters needed tending now that it was dark.

And I was feeling great! Punch's energy soared through me like electricity. Whistling and humming were uncharacteristic of me, but here I was doing both along to the thumping beat as I walked through Hades to the back exit, out into the night air.

Ah, yes. It was good to be undead.

Once I picked up the medallion from Saybree, I'd mosey myself back over to Aaron's, maybe make a deal with Remi so

Aaron and I could pick up where we had left off. Yeah. Give him a shot at an orgasm of a lifetime. And since his place didn't have fire-breathing jealous girlfriends on the loose, maybe I could give Remi's proposal some consideration. We could at least talk about...

WHACK!

Never even saw it coming. All I knew was a huge, heavy object had slammed into the back of my head and I now had a mouthful of dirt and was hovering close to unconsciousness.

Had Monroe and his Get Fresh crew come back for me?

Was it the same person or persons who had killed Ivan?

I hadn't seen or smelled anyone. And since Punch and Franco were down in the basement, I was on my own.

I tried to get up. *Somebody's gonna pay for th...*

WHACK! WHACK!

Okay. Nothing I could do about that. I saw a two-by-four drop to the ground next to my head, then it was lights out.

When I first awakened, I realized I was hanging upside down by chains binding my legs. My arms were bound too, behind my back and judging by how bad my skin was burning, the chains were silver.

Next, I realized I had the migraine from hell and someone was standing close by. And oh, yeah—I was naked.

Well, that made sense. As twisted as it was, I understood how obsessed some patrons could be. Evidently, this one wanted a little hanky-panky on the side. My performances weren't gratifying enough. Fine. Hopefully, if I did everything asked, I would be set free soon.

"You know, I don't have to be upside down to fuck you," I said, my head throbbing with each word.

No answer.

"I know you're there," I said, opening my eyes to look around. Bright light made my migraine worse so I squeezed them shut again, but not before I saw the black boots and denim legs.

Still no answer.

"Please let me down. The fuck will be better if I'm comfortable. I'll lie real still until you're done."

No movement. No sound. Just the steady beat of his heart—at least I thought it was a "he". Boots were too big for a woman.

"You've got a nice rack, Sleepy Willow," he drawled.

Definitely a "he". And I thought I knew that voice. "So are you gonna let me down so you can suck on them?"

"I don't think so."

Yep. I'd heard the voice before. "Look, Mister. I don't know what you're in to but I specialize in necrophilia. If you want some dom/sub stuff, you should have taken Bloody Valentina."

"You always call me Mister," he chuckled. "My name's Dario."

Dario? Dario. I didn't know a Dario. I called *him* Mister?

"Well, Dario, if you want some pussy, can we go ahead and get it over with? I have some errands to run before morning."

He laughed heartily like I was Jerry Seinfeld doing standup. "Willow, I'm not interested in your pussy. Sorry to disappoint you."

Wait a minute—that voice belonged to someone I'd called Mister. Someone who wasn't interested in fucking and had hit me over the head and dragged me back to this…

"You attacked me in the club, didn't you!" I said, angry as hell.

And frightened.

"Bingo. I knew you'd figure it out. Being a bloodsucker must make you smarter too."

I blinked rapidly. So the silver chains weren't by accident.

How did I keep finding myself in deep shit?

"You're an agent?" I asked, surprised VET would have sent another agent after Monroe had been working so steadfastly.

"Nope. Try again."

Left only one other type of person dumb enough to chase vampires. "Bounty hunter." Which meant he could be bought. "Let me down and I'll pay you whatever VET is offering."

"I'm not interested in money either." He had walked closer to me, his heart beating louder, but not faster. He was cool as a cucumber.

Meticulous. Deadly.

"What do you want from me, Dario?" The sinking feeling in my stomach told me Saybree had been right about this guy. *You will see your attacker again. He will not stop until he captures you because his motivation goes beyond the bounty on your head,* she'd said.

"Revenge," he said quietly. "I want you to suffer the way you made my wife and child suffer and then I'm going to drain you and kill you just like you did them."

What???

At least now I knew why I was upside down. Easier to drain my body from the heaviest end first. Easier to clean up too.

So far he had been calm, but I needed to see his face to gauge his emotions, to see whether he was rational enough to comprehend what I was about to say. "Listen to me, Dario. I have *never* killed anyone."

"LIAR!" he yelled, slicing a blade across my body.

I yelled too. He was definitely NOT rational.

"You bloodsuckers are all the same. That's what you do—kill, destroy lives. Never thinking of consequences because you're soulless animals," he said.

My thigh, groin, stomach, and underneath my breast all stung from the invasion and my blood ran down to the floor. He had cut deep, but I was full of Punch's blood, his power. I could already feel the wounds healing twice as fast as they normally did. At this rate, I'd be completely healed in less than a minute.

Hope he didn't notice since he was bent on making me suffer.

He sighed. "You're healing much faster than I expected. You must have just fed from someone. I'll have to go slower to make it last longer."

He'd done his homework and was astute on vampire biology. Not good.

He put a picture on the floor underneath my head of a smiling blonde woman holding a child look-alike. "This is the family you took from me," he sobbed.

Though familiar with Stockholm Syndrome, I felt no empathy. Nevertheless, I realized he was probably too overcome with pain, anguish, and loss to listen to me. I still had to try sounding genuine. "I'm sorry they're dead, but I have never seen them before." The last part was true.

"Denial is not going to make this any easier on you."

He stepped away and I felt relieved.

Until I heard a drill. Sounded like a power saw.

Uh oh. Nothing good would come of having missing parts. Sure, they'd grow back, provided I wasn't burned in the meantime, but it was still a bitch getting by without a finger or spleen…or vaginal lips.

I'd seen Max inflict that punishment before too. And that was only because one of his brides had said she was going to find a maistress to help her turn her brother into a vampire. At the time Max had not wanted any men in his clan. Once vampirism became illegal, he changed his mind and combined forces with a maistress vamp as old and as powerful as himself. When our clan doubled in size and strength, Max was pleased.

But that had not changed the months his bride managed without her missing lady parts.

"I'm going to start with your fingers since you removed April's," he said, revving the motor of the saw.

"Wait!" He sure was prepared to make some heinous moves based on some big assumptions here. "Of all the vampires in the world, what makes you think I'm the one who did this?"

He walked closer to me and I tensed, certain he was going to strike at any moment. He'd given no warning last time. "I worked in a blood lab back when you bloodsuckers were legal. Back when my family was taken from me," he said through gritted teeth.

Not making the connection, I asked, "What does that have to do—"

"I kept the blood samples taken from the crime scene at my house. I took them everywhere with me as I hunted down and killed every soulless one of you I could get my hands on."

Was I missing something? What in the hallway of hell did any of that have to do with *me*?

"I hunted vamps by night, continued working in the lab by day until I had almost given up finding you. Then one day I got lucky. Your paperwork came through needing to be tested…for a new narcolepsy drug therapy treatment, I think."

Ohhh. I was starting to see where this was going. "And let me guess—my blood matched a sample taken from the scene."

His answer was to grab my tightly bound arms from behind my back and slice right through my middle, ring, and pinky fingers. I screamed as they fell to the floor and more of Punch's blood spilt with them.

Dario screamed too. Though he wasn't hurt physically, he was forcing himself to relive the horror that had befallen his beloved. I also got the feeling he wasn't used to torturing women.

But I hurt too badly to pity him at the moment.

Struggling to get a handle on the pain, I choked, "It wasn't me. When were they killed?"

"Ten years ago," he whispered then fell to his knees in sobs. "Your blood matched just a few weeks ago."

When my blood had been drawn from Dr. Floyd's lab and

sent off for testing in order to participate in one of his new clinical trial studies. I hadn't even gotten the results back from that analysis yet and I was already being punished for it.

"Dario, you listen to me and you listen good: It. Was. Not. Me. I could not have done it. I've only been turned three years."

"I may not have your superior intelligence, Willow, but I'm no fool. How could you only be a vampire three years but your blood match a vampire murder scene from ten years ago."

I thought back to the transition ritual. To the part where Max had cut out my heart while it was still beating, while I was still alive. To the part where he drained me of blood and filled me with his own. To the chant Saybree made while my body convulsed and died and reanimated.

Thinking back on a few days ago when Dr. Floyd had analyzed my blood in his own lab and had said the composition of my blood had changed, I realized I had been wrong about Max's blood *mixing* with the composition of mine. His blood had completely taken over. Though I still didn't know who had killed Dario's family, I knew whose bloodline it had come from. We all shared Max's blood. And his alone. It took over the body of every vampire he sired, meaning someone in Max's bloodline had done the deed.

"Tell me how it's possible!" he said, waving the saw in front of my face.

"Because your blood samples belong to my maistre vampire. Anyone of us in his bloodline who has been a vampire for ten years or more could have done it."

Silence. Pacing.

Maybe he will let me go.

More silence. More pacing.

"Then I must kill this maistre vampire of yours. You will tell me where he is," he huffed finally.

CHAPTER 33

Fat chance in hell of that happening. "Fuck you."

His hand came down across my back with that saw three times, making me scream and spin around like a Tasmanian devil. He didn't even care that blood was landing all over his picture.

Grabbing a handful of my hair, he pulled my head up and forward long enough to spit in my face then dropped me to swing around again.

"I don't want to do this to you. Really. I don't. Torturing a woman, alive or undead, is not in my nature. But revenge is." He walked away to put the saw down. "I want the bastard who killed my family. I kill your maistre, I kill all o' ya, right?"

Struggling to talk, I mumbled, "No incentive to tell you anything then, is it? Go ahead and kill me now."

I heard him pick up something from the table and walk over to me a second before I felt agonizing burns across my back as he spritzed my wounds with liquid. It was the equivalent of a human having salt poured in a gaping sore. It hurt like hell.

Just my luck to have a creatively sadistic fuck on my hands.

"Know what this is?" He'd waited until I was done screaming to taunt me. "Holy water. Yep. All kinds of new ways to hurt you with it." He laughed. "Bet you were wondering why you didn't pick up my scent outside the club. 'Cause I washed myself in holy water. Guess you can say it gives me a protective coating."

Interesting. Humans took the business of exterminating vampires seriously. Apparently, torture methods had been perfected as well.

And *we* were the bad guys?

"You say you didn't kill them. Fine. Help me get the one who did. I wouldn't be killing any innocents. You vamps have mercilessly killed and lived off humans. It's only fair that y'all die in exchange for the lives y'all've taken. Allow me my justice."

"I already told you I've killed no one. I don't believe in murder. Goes against my religion."

He laughed. "Religion?! You're kidding, right?"

It was no use. He wouldn't get it. "And don't give me that 'no killing innocents' bull. You killed Ivan. Other than using his dick too freely, he had hurt no one."

"What? I don't know an Ivan."

And he called me a liar. "Riiiight. Regardless, I ain't telling you shit."

He paced a minute then stopped. "Tell you what, Willow. I don't have the stomach or patience for this. I'm going to get a few reinforcements and I'll see how you feel after that."

Lovely. Couldn't wait.

He cut off the light and exited quietly.

Since I hadn't yet felt burning rays from the sun that I was sure was in the sky by now, either I was underground or he had the windows covered and the door led to a hallway instead of directly outside. Listening carefully, I heard nothing. No dripping faucet, no chirping bird, no crawling rats...I smelled nothing either. Nothing but the iron in my own spilt blood. He must have washed the place down with holy water, making it difficult to figure out how to escape.

I was glad he was gone but it was disconcerting.

Sort of felt like the calm before the storm. And the reinforcements would be coming in on a cloud of barbarianism with lightning from Lucifer. I was sure of it.

So where the hell was I and how the hell did I get out of here?

My last thought before I fell asleep.

When I awakened, I had a feeling I had only been out a short while, which was a bummer. The pain from my lacerations and amputations hit hard. Since I'd lost so much blood, I was healing slower and wished I could have stayed asleep while my body repaired itself. Could have really used a longer break from the pain.

No such luck.

See, when you're a vampire, you feel things more intensely. Pleasure is soooo good. Pain is…well, it's something awful.

And I was feeling awful. The power boost Punch had given me was running dry because of all the stress my body had been under since.

Thinking of Punch made me remember how much of my blood he'd taken. It acted as a drug for him, an aphrodisiac, something that made him euphoric for a while, then the high was gone. The bond was not.

Vampire blood in another supernatural established an indefinite magical bond that grew less intense over time if the supernatural did not continue drinking vamp blood. But the bond would not go away completely without supernatural intervention like a spell or ritual. A human would have to re-charge his vampire blood intake more frequently since the magic was one-sided, but not a were-animal. Punch, the werewolf, was mine.

I'd taken a lot of his blood too. Maybe he could find me,

rescue me.

My mind called to him on its own before I had a chance to think through the ramifications.

Punch...

It was like a whisper on the wind that floated through the air, through the molecules of the wall, out into streets and into his home, until it found him and landed on his skin, his essence. He sucked in air as if to keep from drowning and looked at me. I looked at him. Fire looked at me. Then I threw myself from their bedroom where Fire was no longer the red fire-breathing dragon, but a pasty white woman with freckles, riding her chocolate stud as they were close to simultaneous orgasms.

Didn't want to watch. Didn't want to interfere. Didn't want to call him to help me when he and his woman were making love. Making up.

Then I heard footsteps. Heavy boots. Several sets in no hurry, but coming steady and they were going to be here any second.

The door opened and I opened my eyes to one, two, three, four sets of boots entering the dark room. Someone cut the light on so they could all see me better because it certainly wasn't for me to see them. I could see just fine in the dark and I was sure they knew that.

Someone said something in a language I didn't recognize and the salacious *mmmm* at the end was not the giveaway for what he had in mind. His hand sliding up from my bare breast to my crotch was.

It was going to be a long day.

Unfortunately, there was no Calgon to take me away.

"Told you she was hot. But don't let her fool you. She's no Mary Poppins. I'd stay away from her fangs and keep her chained up with the silver or you'll be sorry," Dario said. "And she has narcolepsy. So don't think she's dead just 'cause she passes out."

"A narcoleptic vampire? Ain't she special," said one of the thugs.

"So you want us to beat her without killing her?" a different guy asked.

"I don't care what you do to her as long as she coughs up the location of her maistre vampire," Dario said then stepped towards the door. "I would do it myself, but I lost lunch and dinner after what I did to her earlier. Let me know when she talks."

Things didn't get better. In fact, once Dario left, I was closed in with three of the horniest, most disgusting "reinforcements" to ever walk the planet. Made Dario's torture seem pansy-ass. Also made me feel sorry for Houston single women.

But I'd never give up Max's location.

Because truthfully, I had no idea where it was.

CHAPTER 34

"I don't know," I said hoarsely.

I had screamed so much I was barely audible. Yet, they continued.

And *we* were supposed to be the soulless, heartless, merciless creatures.

They had taken me down some hours ago, wisely leaving my hands chained behind my back and my feet chained together. I thought that, along with my physical strength, would keep them from wedging themselves between my legs. But never underestimate the determination of a horny man with access to a naked woman. They managed to enter. Several times.

Better than having them use the saw though.

After coming once they'd grown more creative in ways to inflict pain on me. Guess they had less pressure on their balls and more blood flowing to their itty-bitty brains. Valentina could use them in her shows provided they learned the concept of "safe word". One had even cut off my nipple when I mentioned he had a baby dick and fucked like a turtle.

My bad. Note to self: never insult a man's manhood while

you're chained up even if he really is under-endowed.

So in order to keep their minds off the saw, I had resorted to titillating them, pretending my vampire libido wanted them. Encouraging them to insert dicks in my orifices rather than sharp metal objects. I was not having a good time, mind you, but Dario would be pissed to learn I was not suffering. That they were no closer to extracting Max's whereabouts. That I'd survive awhile longer with more time to plot their demise.

And sure as shit stinks, their demise was coming since I'd discovered a few clues about my prison. One, while lying on the floor, I had detected faint scents of bleach and Lysol which told me this was already a sterile environment before Dario had doused it with holy water. And two, now that I was no longer hanging upside down, I got a good look around at all the white cabinets and white tables covered by clear plastic to catch my splattered blood. There was not much else to go on since my abduction had been premeditated, but these clues were more than I had before.

Unfortunately, no one had been stupid enough to get a blowjob. My fangs were itching to bite a dick off.

"Where is he?" Little Dick asked for the fifteen-millionth time.

Lying on the cool concrete floor, I just shook my head back and forth. How many ways could I say I didn't know?

Max had sired hundreds of female vampires (though I wasn't sure how many still existed), joined forces with another vampire clan, and accumulated more power, more possessions, more wisdom than anyone I'd ever known. He had been around for over two thousand years and he'd done that by shrewdness and careful planning. We all came to him blindfolded. We left only after he scrubbed our brains of his location. It was a safety precaution for all of us. No one feared the other would turn on him and thereby kill us all. It had been smart. It had been effective.

And it would be the reason I met my final death alone

today if I did not figure out how to escape.

Little Dick looked at his watch then straddled my chest. He'd obviously decided he had wasted enough time. "Where is he?" he asked.

"I don't kn—"

I never finished the sentence because he had punched my jaw so hard it cracked. And he was wearing metal mesh gloves so I couldn't bite through his skin.

He punched again.

I could take it. Been taking beatings since I was a child. This was nothing. Only thing missing was the prayers to God for my salvation. Which would have been nice.

Unless God wasn't going to answer.

"Where. Is. He?" he asked, accentuating each word with a kick to my side.

Yeah, that's really going to make me talk, you overcompensating motherfucker.

Pulling my knees to chest, I tucked my chin to shield myself from the beatings as much as possible since his fists and steel-toed boots were packing more power than my parents' belts.

I was happy to feel my consciousness slipping from me again…

"Hang in there, Willow. I'm right here," came the sweetest sound I'd ever heard. The voice of love and concern. "You're not alone this time," he said.

Squinting through swollen lids and bright lighting, I saw him crouching in front of me, smiling warmly, rubbing my shoulder.

Comforting me like he'd done years ago when I had confided in him about my childhood.

I forced a smile. Because either I was delirious with pain and imagining things or Ivan's ghost had picked the perfect time to show up.

CHAPTER 35

When I reached my hand out to touch Ivan, Little Dick ceased his ministrations and stepped back. "Man, this bitch is crazy," he said to no one in particular.

Tuning them out, I stared into Ivan's sapphires and thought of how beautiful they were, though not as mesmerizing as Aaron and Remi's. Not as creepy as when Remi peeped through them, not as innocent as when Aaron did.

Just realized I had a thing for eyes and not just because they were the windows to the soul I used for captivating brains. In fact, an argument could be made that my men's eyes were so beautiful, they captivated *me*.

And it wasn't just about eye color. Sapphire or metallic blue, emerald or neon green, smoky black, it didn't matter. It was also the thickness of the brows and where the bridge of the nose fit between…

The non-English-speaking guy had come over and started smacking my face around, so I mentally withdrew unto myself. Focusing on my men and their eyes…and their captivated brains.

My mind wandered all over the place. Anywhere was better than here.

Speaking of captivated brains…

Emmanuel had asked me to make it where he never had to come back. What if I could use my power of captivation over each of Aaron's personalities and command them to appear only at pre-approved times? Maybe I could repair some of the damage I'd done to their brain that caused them to shift randomly by forcing them to shift according to a calendar schedule. Mason could go back to shifting only once every six months, Remi every Saturday, and Emmanuel not at all. It wouldn't be permanent, of course, but it may buy us a little time. Time without Aaron's medication.

If I survived today, I'd have to try it.

Provided Aaron was still alive since I hadn't gotten the protection amulet from Saybree yet.

Hopefully, Dario was nearby, focusing his efforts on breaking me instead of going after Aaron in the meantime. While I was preoccupied with reinforcements.

Who were breaking me down bit-by-bit.

Going in and out of consciousness was no longer helping my mental state. Meditating on everything other than pain no longer kept me grounded. I was a ball of nerves, a cesspool of desperation. Wondering if this was the beginning of insanity.

My mind had begun reaching out to Max for help, knowing that was a bad idea in all regards. One, although I didn't know exactly where he was, I could still sense he was miles away. Still well-hidden in another country. Two, even if he was close, it was daylight. And three, if by some swing of the devil's dick Max would come rescue me, he'd be putting himself and the clan in danger. If he was unsuccessful in saving me, I was truly dead anyway.

I crashed the brain signals as quickly as possible to keep from alerting him to my situation.

Had Aaron gone through similar torture? Guess I should have read his diary after all. Would I have split personalities after this?

Remi had killed his abductor. And for some reason that made me laugh.

Here I was stronger than any human and I couldn't get out of my mess. Yet, he had escaped when he was a whippersnapper. Looks like he had the balls I needed right now.

Yeah…I needed Remi.

In my delirium or desperation…or weakness, I stretched my mind out to him.

I should have been ashamed. What if he wasn't the one inhabiting the body right now? What if it was lil' Aaron?

Enough with the what ifs. I had to try.

So I did, stretching my energy as far and as wide as possible. It traveled down the highway, through the walls, calling him. *Remiiiiii.* And regardless of whose mind was in the body at my moment of contact, Remi eagerly answered the call.

Willow, he whispered, grabbing his chest and swerving into incoming traffic. He was behind the wheel of his roadster, looking confused, wary. *Where are you?*

"I've been taken. I'm in danger and need your help, but…" Hell. First off, I didn't know where I was. Secondly, if I did, I couldn't risk him getting hurt. There were three men here, maybe four if Dario was waiting nearby. What could Remi do against them? I couldn't lure him here for the slaughter just to save myself.

I'm coming to get you, he said, pulling over on the side of the road. *Tell me where you are.*

"No! Don't. I'm sorry. I shouldn't have reached out to you. You'll get hurt." I pulled away from him quickly, shut down the link, and squinted at the fools in the room with me. The view with my physical eyes was much worse than the one with my mind's eye.

Willow! Tell me where you are.

Remi's voice had startled me. He had pushed back and opened our connection again. His emotions were strong enough to choke me. Wary anxiousness. Profound protectiveness.

Little Dick and his friends backed away from me to survey the damage. One whistled because he was so impressed, which told me just how bad I was. "Go get Dario so he can pay us. This bitch ain't talking and I'm tired. I need a cig and some sleep," he said.

Who the fuck is that?! Remi asked hysterically. *Is that the guy who took you?*

"Can you see through my eyes?" I asked in total shock, unaware of all our blood bond capabilities. But I was a fast learner. Logic told me if he could see what I saw, he may be able to figure out my location. Maybe he could get word to Franco that I needed help.

Yes! Remi said. *I've never seen him before. Where are you?*

"I'm not sure. That's what I need you to figure out."

He paused. *Looks like a medical facility.*

"Who the fuck is she talking to now?" Little Dick said.

One of the guys left, presumably to get Dario. I stared in the hallway past him when he opened the door hoping Remi could collect clues from whatever was outside the room. Then I started looking around so he could see as much of my surroundings as possible. I also wanted him to get a good look at the pervs just in case they got away. They'd be at the top of my hit list once I got out of here.

Slow down. You're moving too fast. There's a trillion hospitals here. I need to figure out which one you're at.

I slowed down my view. Although I still felt nervous about involving Remi, this was the best shot I had at getting out.

"Remi, get Franco and Punch to help. Puh-lease do not come here alone. It's not safe."

The door opened and in walked Dario and his gofer.

Since I'd been chained up when he was here before, I didn't get a chance to see him. Now, from the floor, I had a front row seat to a whole lotta man. If I wasn't in such bad shape because of Dario's directions, I would have thought he was a hunk: tall, well-built, tanned, dark spiky hair, dark eyes. He looked just as good as when he'd first tried to abduct me from Hades a week ago.

Never mind that. I just wanted to bite his ass for allowing what they'd done to me.

So that's the guy who attacked you a week ago? I'd forgotten Remi was still in my head listening to my thoughts. *I've seen him before at Hades. He even gave me a business card.* He began rummaging through his armrest.

"He said he worked at a blood lab," I said.

Aha! Remi said as he held up a white card with navy blue letters. *I bet I'll know where to find him.*

Dario winced as he walked over to me, squatted, and looked me over. Then he buried his face in his hands and shook his head. "God. What did y'all do to her?"

"We did what you asked," one guy said.

Dario stretched his hand toward me, but pulled it back like he was scared to touch. "Well, did you at least get what I wanted?"

"Naw, man. She kept saying she didn't know where he was."

Dario rose to his feet in a huff and started cursing. "You fuck-ups aren't getting a dime. Y'all spent all this time getting your dicks wet and still didn't get what I wanted. I ain't giving you shit."

They weren't going to let that ride. No, siree. They expected payment.

Suddenly, the testosterone level rose to a cloud so thick I could have skated on it as they fussed and haggled about money and me.

Nothing good was coming of this.

And just like a bad omen, Little Dick pulled a gun from his pocket and aimed it at me. "If I shoot her right now, you'll never get the info you want, will you?" he said.

Oh, shit! Remi was zooming down the street now, rightfully assuming the worse was about to happen. *You don't have much time. I have to—*

I didn't hear anything else he said because there was a scuffle, no an outright fisticuff. Then just as soon as it had begun, there was a loud bang and I felt a searing pain in my stomach.

Didn't have to look down to know Little Dick mother-fucker had shot me.

CHAPTER 36

Wonderful.

My other wounds hadn't healed yet and I already had a hole in the gut to contend with. At least I'd finally get the trip to La-La Land I'd wanted because I passed out in a matter of seconds.

No more pain. No more conscious thoughts.

My brainwaves went haywire, however. Short-circuiting straight to Remi. Then Max. Then Punch. Franco. Ivan. Saybree. Desperately trying to tap every supernatural connection I had, blood-bonded or not.

Even dreamt of my family. Of happy times with them. Of moments when my mother had blamed herself for giving me the chromosome that carried narcolepsy. Of how my parents had honestly thought everything they'd done was in my best interest. They had fed, clothed, sheltered and given me an education, after all.

Promised God I'd go see them if I survived.

I vaguely got the sense Remi and Punch responded, but it was too much for my brain to process. One of them said, *Stay with us, Willow. Baby, we're on the way*, I think. And I think maybe

Ivan was rubbing my head.

There was no way to tell how long I'd been out when I finally awakened, but I knew it was nightfall. Darkness was calling to me from outside. Night creatures were scavenging for food. Cemeteries were bursting with dead, restless energy. And I was itching to walk barefoot through a recent graveyard, burying myself in the cool, damp earth. Just for a little while.

First thing I saw was Dario because he was checking out my condition. Bastard actually seemed concerned.

Oh, yeah. I was his only link to Max, the maistre vampire who's clan member had killed Dario's family.

Luckily, Dario's bandits had not done their homework. Just like they had no idea the blood they'd been spilling all day would have given them superhuman strength, they didn't know I wouldn't die from a bullet unless it was silver.

So I got the chance to fight another day.

Would have to be later though 'cause I passed out again.

Next time I came to, the scene had changed drastically. There were body parts and shredded clothes all around and a big black werewolf was licking my face.

"Punch?" I said weakly, half expecting him to answer back.

He whined and nuzzled my shoulder as if to tell me to get up.

I tried. Couldn't move.

My mouth was so dry, I gave up trying to talk and hoped he'd hear me telepathically. *Where's Remi?*

The wolf put his head down next to mine and whimpered.

Not a good sign.

I had to get up and look for him, but I still couldn't move. *Punch, I need blood. I can't move.* I'd never taken blood from an animal before, but there was a first time for everything.

He whimpered again, making no move to offer himself.

What is it? Tell me.

His baritone voice came in my head strong and apologetic. *I promised Fire I'd never give you blood again.*

Well, fuck me sideways with a golden dildo. What was I going to do?

I'm sorry, but that was her condition on me coming here to help you.

I understand. Looking around at all the scattered parts, I wondered. *How long have the bodies been torn apart?* There was blood everywhere.

Few minutes before you woke up. Then his wolf head cocked sideways. *You don't think…*

It's worth a try. Drinking blood left in the air too long would be the equivalent of a human drinking spoiled milk. But Punch had said it was only a few minutes ago…

He walked away on all fours and returned with a severed arm. Small enough to fit up to my mouth without me having to move my head, and large enough to have enough blood in it even after a lot had run onto the floor.

The blood was cold and flat like two-week-old soda. And it was gritty from where it had rolled on the dirty floor. I almost spit it out.

Then I felt it start to work. I drank thirstily while Punch pressed the arm with his paw, squeezing the veins until I couldn't get another drop.

It wasn't enough. *More. I need more.*

Punch brought several body parts one after the other until I was finally able to move my head, then my legs and arms. When I was strong enough to sit up, I looked for Remi in the carnage. There was only one body still intact, but it wasn't Remi's.

Crawling over to Dario's body, I inspected him in a detached, science-experiment-y sort of way. He had seen better days. Although he was a bloody mess, I suspected all of it did not belong to him. He had put up a good fight.

As I peeled the bloody blade from his hand, his chest moved up and down, his heart beat faintly. He was alive…but not by much. Using the blade to cut the bullet out of my skin where it had already started sealing, I had half a mind to wait until he woke up to give him a dose of his own medicine. I could jab the blade right through his muscular neck or better yet, slice off three of his fingers.

Then I noticed the teeth marks clawed from the top of his collar bone down to his navel.

"You bit him?!" I asked Punch, who lifted his head up once and back down again. "Fuck. You bit him."

Though they weren't an illegal species, there were laws that governed were-animal interaction with humans. For example, criminal charges for assault with a deadly weapon were brought against any were-animal caught biting a human. Which is why werewolves didn't usually bite humans unless they were intending to eat them up completely or add them to the pack as new recruits.

What in the world was Punch planning?

The wolf whimpered and rolled unto his back where he showed a gaping, bloody hole.

"Oh, no. You've been shot?"

He nodded again, lying still as I inspected his wound.

"Do you want me to cut it out like I did mine? Do you need to go to a pet hospital or something?"

No. Once I nap, I'll heal. The bullet will pop right out. He rolled to his feet and went to lick the side of Dario's face. *This one fought well. He…he may have gotten my blood in his wound.*

Hmmm. Things were getting really interesting, really fast. No witch or ritual was needed for a human to turn in to a were-animal. Just a bite, where the animal's saliva temporarily paralyzed the victim and a dose of the animal's blood at the injury site and…howwwwwl!

You want me to kill him? He was trying to save you when we got here so I left him alive for you to decide. I bit him by mistake.

I thought about that. It was Dario's fault this whole debauchery ever took place. He had tried to save me, sure, but for his own self-interest. Maybe becoming a wolf every full moon and many times in between if he couldn't control it would teach him a lesson. The lesson being, stay away from Sleepy Willow.

Before I could answer, I heard groaning from the hall.

Remi!

I rushed out with no thought for my naked tattered body until I got down next to where he was lying on the floor. The wolf came over with a denim shirt dangling between his teeth. The body it belonged to wouldn't be needing it. I ripped a piece off to tie around my hand where I had missing fingers then balled up the shirt and stuck it under Remi's head to make him more comfortable. I still didn't feel modest enough to put it on. I was only worried about Remi being okay.

The wolf growled. Apparently, my body was distracting him.

"Remi, can you hear me?" I didn't see blood on him anywhere, but he had a lump the size of a boulder on his forehead. It was already turning deep purple. Hopefully, he didn't have a concussion or internal bleeding. Wondered if I should take him to the doctor or just give him more of my blood.

He opened his eyes, looking around wildly. After focusing his attention on me, he said in a small voice, "Who are you and where am I?"

Oh, no, not again. "Let me guess—you're Lil' Aaron?" He nodded, looking fragile, timid. Probably not the best time to offer my wrist. Crossing my arms over my bosom to hide my nakedness, I glanced at the wolf's side-cocked head and knew he was confused. "I'll explain later," I said to Punch. "Okay. Don't worry, I'm going to take care of you," I said to Lil' Aaron. "Just look deep in my eyes."

When he did, I commanded him to return in six months and not one moment beforehand, which meant I shouldn't see him again until June-ish. Like offering a bribe for his cooperation, I promised to take him to the zoo on the night of his return. Couldn't hurt to give him something to look forward to. I didn't know what arrangement he already had with Aaron, but this was the most practical to me. And since I was doing the mental manipulation, I was setting the schedule.

Only time would tell if my captivation worked.

CHAPTER 37

With Punch in wolf form and Remi in no condition to drive, that left me behind the wheel of Punch's truck. We had no other choice. Punch explained he would instantly go in to a deep sleep after transforming to a man in order to heal from his gunshot wound, and Remi had passed out once I'd commanded him to shift. So hopefully, I wouldn't crash the truck and make all our efforts to stay alive futile.

After donning a white lab coat from the closet inside the diagnostic lab where I'd been held captive, we were ready to make our way. Remi would have to return to get his vehicle the following day since apparently, he had driven to my rescue all by his lonesome. I could not believe the story Punch told about arriving moments after Remi had gone in by the seat of his pants to confront my kidnappers.

He'd gotten his ass handed to him, but wow! Talk about big cojones.

Luckily, we made it back to Hades without me falling asleep along the way. Punch intended to spend the night in the basement under Franco's watchful eye since Punch would be in somewhat of a coma. Made me wonder why Punch didn't have a pack since I had always heard sleeping with a pack of were-animals helped them heal faster. Oh, well. Maybe he was banking on Fire joining him once she got off work. Though I wasn't entirely sure she qualified as a were-animal.

Franco took one look at me and said I looked worse for wear so it was good I already had the night off. He also reminded me humans were not allowed in the basement.

No worries. Remi and I had another stop to make.

So Punch allowed another opportunity to test fate by giving permission for me to drive his truck over to Saybree's house. Remi and I needed that amulet ASAP.

As usual, Saybree was not surprised to see me, though she was worried something bad had happened since I hadn't shown up the night before. After her initial greeting, she hardly paid attention to me as she was so engrossed in checking out Remi.

After cutting a small lock of Remi's hair as payment for the amulet, she ushered us to a back bedroom. I laid him down and she handed me some ointment to rub on his head. Then she went back to the kitchen to finish up with another client. I took a long shower then inspected myself fully, wincing at how bad the damage was. Grateful the sons of bitches were all dead.

Except Dario. The ringleader.

Hope I hadn't made a mistake in leaving him behind. He was motivated by something worse than pussy or money, after all. Revenge was a potent elixir of evil. I knew better than to leave an enemy alive when he was that determined to get me. But I just couldn't tell Punch to do it. Lord knows I wasn't going to do it myself. Maybe it was because Dario had suffered a tremendous loss. He had loved his family so much that he had dedicated his life to avenging their deaths. I couldn't relate to that level of devotion, but I wanted to.

Maybe I left him alive because he may share Punch's supernatural essence now. Franco said we supernaturals should stick together. Did that include a newly-made werewolf driven by revenge?

What if Dario was too far gone for Punch's blood to infect him? There was a possibility his injuries were too severe. He could be dead.

Or if Punch's blood had not gotten in Dario's wound at all. Should I have Punch track him down and kill him later if it turned out Dario was no more supernatural than the man in the moon? Was it right to have Punch doing my dirty work?

Or maybe Dario possibly turning had nothing to do with my motivations. Maybe it was because I was attracted to him. Drawn to him by an unidentifiable familiarity. A familiarity that went beyond the drops of his blood I'd tasted when he had first tried to abduct me and had gotten his nose split.

Scary reason to let him live considering my hands were full with Remi and Aaron.

I tightened a towel around myself and went back into the bedroom where Remi was now awake, watching local news. Pausing in the doorway, I looked him over to determine whether he was still Remi.

His metallic blues pinned on me. "It's me," he smirked, "the one who needs a cigarette pretty bad."

Sprinting towards the bed, I wasted no time jumping into his arms, completely forgetting both of our injuries. He grunted. I eased up…after planting a big fat wet one on his lips.

We talked about everything that had happened over the past twenty-four hours and why we were at Saybree's house. I also told him about Lil' Aaron and my plan to keep Aaron off meds and the alternates from shifting randomly.

When he yawned, I thought of everything he had been through to save me. He looked dirty and tired…and totally irresistible. I was thinking sex therapy…

When I heard a familiar voice on television. It had gotten both of our attentions. Apparently, a well-known athlete was coming out of the closet, admitting he was attracted to men, had been dating one awhile and was ready to freely be himself. He asked his fans for understanding, saying even though it would be a shock, he was still the same footballer they knew and loved.

Looking at Remi, I expected to see shock on his face and it was there. But only because he was a fan of the athlete. There was no other recognition on his face.

Well, duh. Remi hadn't been there when I'd taken the blackmail photos. Aaron had.

I shook my head disgustedly. After everything Aaron and I had gone through that night, it had all been in vain. Despite my best efforts, Cin had just lost her leverage with Rafe and I was sure it was coming back to bite me on the ass.

CHAPTER 38

Hadn't seen that one coming. Best to be cool until Cin approached me pissed off 'cause Rafe had reneged on the deal. She wouldn't know his coming out had anything to do with it.

Once I heard Saybree's client leave, I figured she would get to us soon. She did.

Walking in with an icepack, she motioned for me to apply it to Remi's head, then walked back out. A moment later, she handed me a folded t-shirt and cut-off shorts and walked out again. I was grateful for the hospitality, but I wanted Remi to have that medallion more than anything.

What's taking so long? I wondered as I changed in to the clothes. I hadn't expected us to be here for the rest of the night. Once Remi and I rested a little more, I'd take some of his blood, give him some of mine…and you can imagine the rest. We needed the privacy of his place for all that.

When she came back in with a tray of food for Remi, I'd had it. I grabbed her arm and asked where the amulet was. She wasn't fazed. Said she was still working on it and left.

Huh? It was supposed to be ready last night.

Something wasn't right.

Or maybe I just needed to chill. Magic took time and patience. And Remi seemed to appreciate the steak and potatoes.

I decided to call Dr. Floyd and let him know I was okay. Since I had never missed a support group meeting until tonight, I knew he'd worry. I would leave a message if he was still wrapping things up with the group. Aaron would have to give his own excuse to Dr. Floyd later.

Picking up the phone on the nightstand, I nearly pressed the first digit until I was stopped by the sound of Saybree's voice on the other end. Covering the receiver with my palm, I listened in.

"No! I told you there's nothing I can do for you now," she said.

"But Mom! There has to be a spell or ritual. It hasn't been very long," said a familiar masculine voice.

"Your chest is already healing, correct?"

"Yeah, but—"

"You're hungry for flesh, correct?"

"Yes, but I'm surrounded by drained body parts. I haven't eaten anyone yet."

She sighed. "Not yet. But it's only a matter of time."

"Don't say that," he said softly.

"Listen, Dario. I'm sorry this happened to you. I really am. But you knew the risks when you decided to go after her. I warned you. Now you must live with the consequences of your vengeance."

There was silence on both ends while I digested the conversation. Contained my fury. Kept from going ballistic. Accepted Saybree's betrayal.

"So I'm really turning in to a werewolf?" said Dario.

"There's nothing I can do. No spell. No ritual. Nothing. Once you're bitten, your body locks up. That's only temporary, but when their blood gets in your system, you're infected. Permanently. The infection lays dormant until your first victim—"

"So as long as I don't eat anybody I won't turn?"

"The hunger will be too strong. I've never known anyone to fight it and win." She paused. "It'll be better for you to find a pack to help with your first transition before the next full moon. I can make some calls."

Gently laying the phone back on the receiver, I sat still and contemplated my next move.

Never felt rage like this before. Not when Ivan had cheated. Not when my parents had sold my pet rabbit. Not when Dario's bandits had tortured me for info they were never going to get.

I was so infuriated, I began trembling.

Remi looked concerned. I wasn't sure whether he was reading my body language or my thoughts. Either way, he knew not to speak…not to even blink his thick, curly lashes at the moment.

First thing first—I needed that amulet. After all, that's why we were here. Was she delaying us so Dario could come finish what he had started? Then again, she probably hadn't prepared it yet because she hadn't expected me to survive. Second thing—Did I pretend I had no idea what she'd done or did I confront her?

An undeterminable amount of time had passed before Remi finally reached his hand out to me. He touched my shoulder timidly at first, then pulled me to his chest for a hug once he encountered no rejection.

"I'm sorry, Willow. I can see how much you trusted her," he said.

I didn't realize just how much until tears rolled down my cheeks. I was really hurt.

"I can't believe she did this to me," I cried. Then I had another thought. If I had trusted her and this was the result, I couldn't trust anyone.

I pulled away from Remi, but he wouldn't let go. "I swear

on my life, I'd never betray you. You can count on me forever," he said.

Too vulnerable to analyze or reject what he was saying, I decided to accept it for the time being. So far, he had proven his loyalty. Had to trust him until shown otherwise. "You realize that sounds an awful lot like marriage," I teased.

"If you weren't already married, it could be."

We laughed…and as we did, the double-crossing witch bitch walked in with a protection medallion.

"I'm glad you kiddos are feeling better," she said as if she really meant it. "Young man, you must keep this on at all times. When you shower, when you sleep, when you jog, always wear it," she said while snapping it around his neck.

And no sooner had she finished, than I was on her like urine on snow, both hands around her neck, tightening until her eyes popped like a black moor goldfish.

She deserved to die. Tonight.

"O spiritus mortuorum audite me—" she began to chant.

"Speak another Latin word and I'll snap your neck in two pieces," I said, squeezing even more to emphasize my point. She could be strangled or she could be decapitated. Her choice.

"Wait! Wait! Please don't kill me!"

I loosened my grip a bit so she could talk. Part of me wanted a good explanation. The other part wanted her to feel psychological pain like I did by her betrayal. Make her think I would be empathetic then kill her anyway. She should feel physical pain too, like when I was tortured by Dario and his best buds.

"Are you the same witch whose son's name is Dario?" I started.

"Yes, but—"

"And you told him where to find me, right?"

"I was between a rock and a hard place, Willow. He's my son. His family was murdered. He was grieving."

Save the drama for your mama, Saybree. "So that's it. I've meant nothing more to you than that." She had nothing better to say for herself than don't kill her because she had helped her son? Poo!

I looked over at Remi who was watching me with excited eyes. "Do it," he whispered.

"You know what, my boyfriend here's gonna fuck your skull once you're dead. And I'm gonna send your rotted body parts to your son's blood lab each of the twelve days of Christmas."

"Please don't. He doesn't need to lose another family member."

"Like I give a shit!" I squeezed again, taking pleasure in her pain.

"What about the Ten Commandments? You can't kill me."

"We all sin and fall short." How dare she throw that up in my face. "You wanna know what Dario did to me?" I held up my maimed hand. "Wanna know what he allowed to happen to me?" I pulled up the borrowed t-shirt to show her my nipple-less breast. "Save the sermon for your son!"

"I'm sorry. That was not supposed to happen. It was supposed to happen quickly," she said.

Remi stood behind me, pressing his groin against my back, his erection straining for release. As sick as it was, his reaction to my violence was a turn-on. Our own twisted foreplay.

"I know…I was wrong and…you have no…reason…to trust me, but if…you let me live, I'll give you something…you want," she was having trouble talking, but I heard everything just fine.

"What do you have that I could possibly want?"

"I know…how you can break…the bond…with Max."

CHAPTER 39

I threw her on the bed like she was a bristling porcupine. "You what?"

She started rubbing her neck and coughing like she was going to lose a lung. I impatiently tapped my foot.

Once her coloring had returned to normal, I said, "What the hell do you know about breaking a maistre vampire bond? It can't be done."

Cough, cough. Yada yada. "It can be done. I can tell you how if you let me live."

"You don't even know how to reverse a werewolf infection, how could you or *would* you help me break free of Max?"

"I betrayed you, yes, but I have never lied to you. Everything I have ever told you has been the truth. That's why you still trust that medallion to work, no?"

"You've been telling me my bond with Max is eternal. That it can't be broken. You *have* lied!"

She didn't miss a beat. "I only recently discovered the loophole. Had I known before, I would have told you."

I didn't believe her. How could I? "How can I trust

anything you say?"

"I have proof." She stood, raising her hands in the air to show she was making no suspicious moves. "Come."

I followed her to her bedroom…where I got stuck at the door. My feet could not breach the threshold. "What's going on?" I said, feeling like a sap for following her…probably straight to a trap.

"There's a mixture of garlic, silver, lemon juice and human blood at the door that keeps anyone who isn't human out," she said as she walked inside to a locked trunk at the foot of her bed. "Don't worry. It's not a trick. I mean you no harm."

Humph. Made myself a mental note to never bring her human blood again.

Remi walked up behind me as she took an old spell and magic book from the trunk and brought it into the hallway.

"I don't know how to keep my boy from howling at the next full moon, but I do know how you can be rid of Max." She coughed up blood then continued, "It's just not going to be something you're going to want to do."

"I'll do anything for freedom. Tell me what it is."

"Promise you'll let me live."

I studied her long dark hair, large dark eyes, tanned skin, petite frame. Didn't know why I hadn't noticed the relation sooner. She and Dario looked just alike.

Their biology was of no importance now. Important thing was that if she could prove there really was a way to break my bond with Max, I needed her around. Whether I believed she didn't know about it until recently was of little consequence.

"Can you promise your son won't come after me again?" I said.

She shook her head. "He won't rest until he feels his family's deaths are avenged. But if you're no longer under Max's bloodline, you can help Dario find him and kill him. You'll survive it."

"So all you have to offer is your life in exchange for bond-breaking info?"

"Isn't that enough?"

I paced the floor, thinking. "Okay. But your info is good for one save. I let you live after your heinous betrayal *one* time. I catch you slipping again, you sure as hell better have something else to bargain with. Letting you live is not a perpetual deal. Got it?"

She nodded and opened the huge book to a withered page near the back.

Remi sighed like he was disappointed he wouldn't witness Saybree's murder. Not yet anyway.

I folded my arms across my chest, and said, "I'm waiting."

Saybree took a deep breath and pointed to the smeared Latin words. "If you no longer want Max to be your maistre vampire, you have to become a maistress yourself."

I looked at her like she had said I was Jesus's sister. I couldn't read a lick of Latin but I read diagrams just fine. There were plenty illustrating the language, showing she wasn't making it up. "I just want to be free of Maximilian. I don't want to be a maistress. Besides, I'm not old enough."

"That is the only way to be free of him. You have to become strong enough to animate yourself. You have to accumulate power. How long you've been a vampire won't matter then."

"How do I do that?"

She pointed to the page. "You first have to get your heart back. Whoever possesses it, rules you. You possess it, you rule yourself."

I almost burst out laughing. There was no way Max was going to give me back my heart. "What else?"

"Then you have to drain a virgin."

"You mean kill."

"Yes. You drink every drop of the virgin's blood and you will be purified of Max's blood for a short while."

I did laugh that time. "You know how hard it is to find a

virgin these days?" I'd waited until I was eighteen but that was because I couldn't date until I was out of my parents' house. Then I had to meet a guy who was okay with my disability.

"I didn't say the virgin had to be an adult," she said matter-of-factly.

I stared at her, horrified. She was telling me to kill a child if I had to. "Unbelievable."

"I told you you wouldn't want to do it. But that's not all. After that, you must turn six willing humans to vampires within the following six full moons. And it must be done at six o'clock. Morning or night."

The 666 pattern had not gone unnoticed. It made me cringe. It raised the hair on the back of my neck. I should have been used to that whenever black magic was involved, but I wasn't. "You mean kill a child for its innocent blood then kill and take the souls of six men and bind them to me forever...the way Max bound me to him?" This bitch had lost her mind and this book was full of Satan.

"I don't make the rules, Willow. They've been around for millenniums. I'm just the messenger...and a witch who can help you complete the rituals."

"Yeah, yeah, yeah."

"You would be maistress of your own clan, powerful enough to animate and protect them. Powerful enough to govern them with love and understanding instead of cruelty if you so choose. You will grow in strength with each soul you take...like your demon boss, so it would be advantageous to keep adding to your clan even after you obtain your freedom."

"What do you know about Franco?"

"Lots. But unlike Franco, who will never die, you will gain supernatural abilities that will make it harder for you to die the final death. No one knows what those abilities will be, just like you don't know the extent of Max's gifts. He can do a lot more than turn to mist, I assure you. 'Course you know your clan will die with you...should the time come."

This was too much to comprehend. "Let's say I manage to steal my heart back, won't Max discover it's missing and kill me before I emancipate myself?"

"No. He will not be able to kill you without control over your heart. He will still be connected to you psychically. There's no way around that. It will not be easy to keep him from your mind and dreams, but your day companion can help keep Max at bay."

"How?"

"By invading your mind and dreams himself. As a regular blood donor and receiver, he would have a strong connection to you. His psychic influence would interfere with Max's."

I looked at Remi who looked at me and shrugged. His involvement would be a commitment for himself, Aaron, and all the others. I couldn't ask that.

"Where in the hell would I find six willing humans within six months after I killed a virgin?" I said.

"Max found you didn't he?"

"Actually, I found him. With your help. And vampirism didn't become illegal until a month after I'd turned. Those were different times. I can't exactly post a want ad on *Craigslist*, can I."

"You're at Hades. You know people are still willing to go against the grain. People still want what you have. They just have to be smarter about getting it."

I shook my head. I'd be condemning others to soullessness. Leading others astray. For the sake of my independence from Max. "I can't condemn others to my fate. And you're wrong about Hades's clientele. Just because they're different doesn't mean they want this curse. Remi doesn't even want it."

She glanced at him then back at me. "But the ones who do—you'd be doing them a favor, Willow. They will know the risks and still want it…just like you did."

"What about the risk of exposing myself? I've got VET

agents on my ass already. Word gets out that I'm recruiting vampires and they'll shut down Hades, arrest Franco and all the employees, and add me to Denny's breakfast menu as toast."

"You're smart. You're creative. You'll figure out how to be discreet."

"Maybe the laws could be changed first," Remi said, adding to the conversation for the first time.

"What do you mean?" I said.

"Well, that guy that's in Hades all the time…the politician always bragging about how he's been helping to pass anti-vamp laws?"

He was talking about Mr. Cash. "Yeah, what about him?"

"Why don't you use your powers of persuasion to get him to vacate the vampire order of extermination? Make him a sympathizer. Once people are no longer afraid of being punished for associating with vampires, it should be easier to find willing folks to turn."

Weird way of handling vampire-human politics. Wasn't even sure it would work, especially since my captivations could damage Mr. Cash's brain. Buuuut…it wasn't an impossible plan. Maybe by the time I'd figured out how to steal my heart and worked up the nerve to drain a virgin, legislature would be on my side.

Since it took time for things to change in the legal arena, I'd better get started on that right away.

Tomorrow at work, I'd have a little chat with Mr. Cash about reversing the laws that had killed off so many of my kind. Then I'd think about how to get my heart back from Max.

CHAPTER 40

Felt like it had been ages since I had been onstage, and it felt good.

After we left Saybree's house in a somber I-just-found-out-the-witch-I-trusted-told-her-vampire-hunting-son-where-to-find-me mood, I took Remi home. He did the driving since he was feeling a little better after Saybree's salve. He felt a lot better once I fed him my blood in exchange for a dose of his and fucked him one good time. We would have kept going if it had not been for the damn sunrise.

I literally fell into a coma once I returned to Hades and laid down to sleep for the day. Woke up an hour after I was scheduled to work. So I dressed in a hurry and went upstairs. Franco was surprised. He hadn't expected me to work and suggested I take the night off like Punch. No need in me doing that. Punch had Fire to look after him. I had no one.

Plus, I had business to tend to.

So, I was onstage. Dancing with the skeleton I'd borrowed from Dr. Floyd several months ago. I twirled around in my black full-body leotard as Lita Ford's "Kiss Me Deadly" rocked the house. Skele-T, as I called him, was the only one nude tonight, but that didn't seem to bother my audience who sat wide-eyed with rapidly beating hearts. 'Course my wild 80's hair and bright red lipstick that I planted all over Skele-T's bones helped.

Decided not to let my fans see any of my still-healing injuries. They probably would have protested if they had known the black leather gloves hid my maimed hand. That I was robbing them of the gruesomeness they longed for.

I was a vampire, dammit, not a ghoul.

One fan in particular was more excited than others when my performance concluded because he'd gotten a personal invite from moi. Though he was more in to Valentina's dominatrix scene than mine, I had told him I was dedicating the set to him. Hopefully, flattery would get me everywhere.

Since Mr. Cash didn't usually come to Hades on Tuesday nights, I had pleaded with Franco to give me the patron's number. Violate club policy again. Of course, I had to divulge my plan to Franco, which turned out to be a good thing. Once he realized I intended to persuade Mr. Cash to advocate for vampire rights, he gave me Cash's cell, fax, and office numbers as well as an email address and website. Thankfully, it didn't take all that. Just one call to Cash's cell, and he was meeting me at the club.

Sitting in the VIP area grinning like he was running for President. He had that politician mug down pat.

I passed Valentina on my way offstage. It was her turn to perform and she was pulling dog leashes attached to the necks of three of her slaves. They were clad in black leather, showing nothing but their mouths. She gave me treats to reward them while they were on their knees panting and wagging their boodies. I gave each a pet on the head for good measure. Sure, I played along. Why not? If they liked it, I loved it.

After hanging Skele-T up in the prop closet, I went to the dressing room where Cin was sitting on parchment paper, her naked body covered in honey and walnuts. She was waiting for me.

Rolling my eyes, I prepared for what was coming. Prepared for her to threaten me again because Rafe had—

"Rafe gave me full custody…and the house," she said.

My surprise showed. "Wow. Rafe is full of surprises."

"Tell me about it. He's moving in with his…his *boy*friend."

I didn't know what to say. She should be happy right? Was I supposed to comfort or congratulate her? "Uh…you okay?"

She sighed. "Not really. He said he never wants to see me or his daughter again. Ever."

"Why?" Instinct told me I wouldn't like the answer.

"He said he was remembering things. Something about you and a guy visiting him and he was scared for his life." *Uh oh.* "He'll pay child support, but he doesn't want to be in Lucia's life. He said he'd…"

"He'd what?"

"Go to the cops with what he knew if I ever tried to contact him again."

I started pacing. She sat still. "Do you want me to talk to him again?" I wouldn't be so nice this time. He'd have to write a note to the cops after I cut out his tongue.

"Didn't you just hear what I said? He'll go to the cops, Willow. It's not just you. He'll implicate me in your extortion blackmail scheme. I would still end up losing my daughter."

She looked like she was close to crying so I tried to think of something comforting. "Well, at least you get to keep Lucia and the house as long as you stay away from him. You didn't want to be with him anymore, right? Besides, he's g—"

"You don't get it do you?" She had the hand gestures to go with her incredulousness. "My daughter cannot have a relationship with her father now. I just wanted us to co-parent. She needs both of us. I didn't want things to end like this."

Credit to her for holding the tears in, but she lost points for blaming her problems with that cocksucker on me. "I'm sorry. I wanted to make things better. Guess I made them worse."

She looked at me with sad eyes and said, "It's not your fault." She blinked multiple times to keep unshed tears from falling. "We were already getting divorced. He was being an ass and you tried to help. I'm upset with him, not you. If he doesn't want to be in her life, that's his loss."

Glad she came up with that on her own, but Rafe remembering things was a complication I could do without. "Do you think he'll keep his word? I mean, about going to the cops *if* you contact him?"

She thought for a moment. "Yes. But if I catch wind that he considers doing anything different, I'll let you know so you can kill his ass."

I was shocked…and touched. She had all but begged me not to kill him before. "You'd do that for me?"

She smiled. "You bet your sweet ass, I'd do that for you. You looked out for me. I'll do the same for you. I got your back."

After the mess I'd just uncovered about Saybree, Cinnabuns's firm declaration of friendship was welcomed.

Uncharacteristic of me, I gave her a friendly hug then went to find Republican Congressman Kennedy P. McNair, also known as Mr. Cash. I was intending to do one of the things humans hated us for—use my powers to influence the judicial system.

I'd be sure to go after the right politician though.

CHAPTER 41

I exhaled dramatically, hoping he'd catch the hint.

The Congressman was losing the nickname Mr. Cash and becoming Mr. Motor Mouth of the South quickly. He had been going on and on and on about his world-changing policies, his devoted wife, his over-achieving children…and grandchildren. *Shut the fuck up!* was what I really wanted to say. I smiled and nodded instead.

Good thing I was full from Remi's blood because I would have bit Mr. Cash out of boredom or irritation by now.

I'd been trying to ease into planting pro-vampirism seeds in his psyche, but there was no slow way to do it. Either he was going to talk me to insanity or I was going to have to jump in his brain full steam ahead.

I hadn't noticed how many drinks he ordered from the bar. Or the heavy bags under his eyes. Or the sunken, patchy skin. Or his significant weight loss. Only thing different about him to me was his thick gray hair becoming the buzz haircut he now sported. He had to point the other changes out to me.

Right before he mentioned he was undergoing chemotherapy for brain cancer.

Whoa!

I really felt like a douche. Knew it affected everyone differently, but damn. Covering up my routine blood withdrawals with brain captivation had done a number on him. Had affected him even worse than it had Aaron.

Good thing I didn't have to captivate Mr. Cash or Aaron for blood anymore. Remi was more than willing to donate.

But how much was too much? Could I still get away with putting the alternates on a schedule without harming Aaron further?

There was a chance that Mr. Cash's brain cancer had nothing to do with me, but it didn't take a rocket scientist to figure out it was a likely correlation, considering his symptoms started around the time I had started captivating his memories regularly.

"I'm so sorry, Mr. Ca— McNair." Good thing I caught myself before saying his nickname. He didn't know Valentina and I called him that. And I really was sorry.

To make matters worse, he was terminal. Specialists had done all they could do.

Well, there was no way I was going to mess with his brain anymore. Too guilty to do that.

Then again, if there was nothing more they could do for him, why not? He may as well die *after* doing something positive for what was left of the vampire community since he'd been so instrumental in ruining it.

I was about to manipulate his brain again, this time to plant political ideas instead of altering his memories, when he said something shocking.

"I could really use a vampire right about now to turn me so I can be cured. That's the irony of it all. I've worked to put them all to rest in their graves instead of co-existing with us and now that I need one, I can't find one." He took a long gulp and motioned for another double. "Even if I started hunting for a vampire now, I may be dead by the time I found one who didn't recognize me as the hard-ass who fought against them. They'd never trust me. They'd never let me in the clan."

Total shock.

Total truth.

And it totally gave me an idea. Just like how I let the Ten Commandments govern my existence, my sense of right and wrong, I'd adopt a creed for turning humans.

My number one principle for siring vampires was giving full disclosure. That included an explanation of supernatural powers, cautionary tales of our weaknesses, theories on soullessness, and expectations of our blood bond. My next principle would be to only turn those looking for a cure, like me. Those who would have nothing to lose. Those who would feel the risks were worth taking. Who would sell their soul to exist in this world a little longer without whatever ailed them when they were human.

With any luck, being turned would actually cure them.

As far as Mr. Cash was concerned? He was right. He couldn't be trusted. Let's say I wanted to give him hope so I confided in him tonight about being a vampire. If he was miraculously healed tomorrow or there was a medical breakthrough, he'd turn against me.

That was okay for now because I wasn't ready to turn him. I'd leave his mind alone and who knows. Maybe he'd still be alive when I was ready. Alive and desperate for what I had to offer. Like Saybree said, I'd be doing him a favor.

By the time I procured my heart, at least I'd know who to proposition first about eternal damnation.

CHAPTER 42

"So, Willow, how about Belvedere tonight? I'd still like to buy you that drink," said Ming while I was packing up my duffel bag to go down to the basement.

Onyx, who was putting finishing touches on her costume since she performed onstage next, paused in the middle of pulling up her white ankle socks. She popped her gum loudly and stared, anxiously waiting for my answer to Ming.

I really would rather see Remi tonight, but I didn't want to seem too clingy. Maybe I could call Aaron since I hadn't seen him in a while. Just to talk. I needed to have a heart-to-hollow chest convo with him anyway about who I was and what that meant for him. Remi and I had agreed that I should be the one to fill Aaron in on everything, so I would. He had a right to know.

"Thanks, but I'm going to take a rain check on that. I'm tired."

"Aw, c'mon. I've been trying hard here. What if I promise to catch you if you fall asleep?" Ming said as she teasingly poked me with her elbow.

"You might as well go, Willow. Ming's been jocking you

since she first got here. What— you playing hard to get or somethin'?" Onyx said.

Ming was persistent. I'd give her that. Oh, what was the worst that could happen? "All right."

She beamed from ear-to-ear and hurried out saying she was going to pull her car around back. She wasn't fooling anyone. She was hurrying before I changed my mind. Fine. Using the phone in the dressing room, I called Aaron and asked if he'd meet me there. It was all about multitasking. I could finally have a sensitive conversation with Aaron…after a pity date with Ming.

Perfect.

Since I hadn't expected to go anywhere but my room after work, I wore a faded sweat suit with New Balance sneakers. As far as I knew, no one was aware I was staying in the basement except Franco, Punch, and Fire. It was important to keep it that way to avoid questions. Which meant I had to wear whatever I had in my duffel bag.

Ming didn't seem to mind. As she drove with one hand on the wheel, she eyed me like I was a piece of meat. A gazelle to her lioness.

I checked her out too, noticing her hair pinned with a set of diamond chopsticks in her customary tight bun. She wore a white turtleneck with gray leggings and white stiletto ankle boots. Her sense of style was always sharp, but now that I was satiated, she didn't seem as tempting as she had before. Her itty-bitty eyes were not calling to me the way Aaron and Remi's did and that's why I would not be able to enjoy her company tonight. Her being a woman had nothing to do with it.

"Where's your duffel bag?" she said. "I can drop you off at your home when we leave here. Where do you live?"

"I left it in the dressing room." Getting blood from Remi meant I didn't carry my phlebotomy kit anymore so I wasn't afraid someone would snoop and discover it. "I'll get my own ride home."

Some time passed before she spoke again. "This is the first time we've been alone," she said.

I nodded. Hoped she didn't have high expectations. "I don't want to be out too late."

"Thought you were a night owl."

I shrugged. "I just have some things I need to do before morning."

"It closes at two anyway. That gives us about an hour there."

I could do an hour. Especially since Aaron was going to meet me. Maybe I should prepare her for his arrival. "Okay. I hope you don't mind—"

Didn't finish my statement because I fell asleep.

When I awakened, we were parked in a large nearly-empty lot and she was digging in her designer purse. She jumped when I sat up as if I had startled her.

She held her hand over her heart. "Whew, girl you scared me."

"What's that?" I inquired about the trinket in her hand.

"This? Oh, this is my cross." She hooked the gigantic silver necklace around her neck like she was preparing to ward off an army of evil.

"Uh. That's a little odd to wear inside a bar isn't it?" My left eye started twitching so I averted my gaze elsewhere.

"I always wear it when I go out. You never know what's out there," she said, laughing nervously. Opening the door, she got out and waved for me to follow her.

Red flags were going off in my head like crazy. What was this trick smoking? *Please hurry, Aaron.*

I followed her inside and sat next to her at the bar. Looking around, I noticed (like most bars) it wasn't very busy on a Tuesday night. Good thing too, because this swanky bar wouldn't have normally allowed me in wearing sneakers.

She ordered two gin and tonics after I mentioned I didn't

have a drink preference. I picked the glass up a couple of times and pretended to drink. By the time she noticed my glass hadn't changed, hopefully Aaron would here. I'd pretend I was shocked to see him, excuse myself, and leave with him.

She began talking about her family, her college days, and her future plans. Why did everyone assume I wanted to know so much about them?

She seemed surprised when I mentioned I got a bachelor's in fine arts. Like I had no business working at Hades with a college degree. I tried not to take it personally.

"Did you finish up in Germany?" she said.

That really got my attention.

Yes, I did complete my final year of undergrad while I was in Germany with Max. After I had turned and stayed with the clan, it just seemed the most sensible thing to do. Night school had been awesome, in fact. Problem was—I had never told anyone I had been to Germany. My own parents had no clue.

There was one person who knew, however. The one who had set me up with Max in the first place. Had Ming talked to Saybree? If so, this qualified as a second betrayal from the back-stabbing witch as far as I was concerned. Also reminded me I needed to tell Ming to stop babbling about me to Monroe.

But Saybree was Dario's mother. What was her connection to Queen Ming? Dario had been trying to get revenge for the deaths of his wife and son. What was Ming's motivation?

Ming was staring at me, waiting for an answer. "Yes. I finished in Germany."

"What was that like?"

"I enjoyed it." Best to answer only what was asked, but not to lie since she obviously had insider info. She caught me in a lie, red flags may go off for her as well.

She proceeded to tell me about her stint in France.

Whatever.

Looking over her head, I saw Aaron walk in the doorway.

I immediately felt relieved. His blues looked more silver than usual because he was wearing a blue long-sleeved dress shirt with silver stripes and black slacks. His hair was slicked back, of course, and he glanced down at the floor once he spotted me.

Too bad he wasn't great with eye contact because I really wanted to send him a message. Fine. I knew how.

I stretched my psychic waves out to him so forcefully, he misstepped. The gentleman he made waste beer was not pleased. Easing up, I retracted some of my power so Aaron could focus on me. Fully alert. Fully shocked.

Please don't come over just yet. I'm going to excuse myself then—

My psychic message to him was cut short when Ming rubbed me on the shoulder and excused herself to the bathroom. If she was trying to flirt, she was doing a terrible job because her touch had made my skin crawl. Matter of fact, it had given me the sudden urge to flee.

I smiled at Aaron, who stood frozen near the door, to ease his anxiety. It would have been better for him to have had an idea of our bond before I pulled that hocus-pocus, but sometimes you have to ask for forgiveness instead of permission.

He sat in a corner lounge chair and ordered a coke from a waitress.

After several minutes had passed without Ming returning, I decided to go let her know I was leaving with another ride. Sending the message to Aaron as I walked away, I went to the glass stalls in search of her…to ditch her properly.

"Yeah, Monroe. She's at the bar. You want me to kill her now or wait for backup?"

I stood in the doorway a safe distance from her back as she listened then hung up. She put the phone back in her purse and lithely pulled the chopsticks from her hair. The ends of the sticks were so sharp, I was surprised she hadn't bled her scalp. Guess, she was prepared to stake me with them. And I'd bet two million dollars there was also a lighter in her purse to burn me right afterwards.

She hadn't turned around yet, but I knew she knew I was there.

"So, did Monroe tell you to wait so he could see my beautiful face again?" I said.

She unhooked the shoulder straps of her purse, slid it to the floor, then turned to face me. Holding the straps, she began peeling the covering from them, revealing solid, thick silver chains. After hooking her cross necklace to the silver chains, she tugged both ends apart to demonstrate how sturdy her weapon was. I was no weapon expert, but after watching a few samurai movies, I figured the thing looked like a manriki.

And only professionals used those.

Her usually flirty tone was replaced with assassin-like coldness. "Nope. After the money they're paying me to work undercover this long, he told me to drop your ass right here then meet him to collect my bonus." She moved into an offensive posture. "And that's exactly what I'm going to do."

CHAPTER 43

"You're a smug twit and he's a presumptuous dickhead," I said.

She laughed. Loud and haunting. "I know you were ready to make lesbo love to me, but I have different orders."

No time to set her straight on that one.

Too busy ducking and dodging her assault as she rushed me fast, with skill and determination. Chains were swinging from all directions as I bobbed and weaved. Speed was my greatest asset since my lack of skill was a liability. I was too quick for the silver to make contact…until she popped the cap off her cross and tossed garlic extract in my face.

The smell was so strong. Too poignant for my delicate senses. It landed on my skin, seeping into it, causing me to bleed from my eyes, my ears, my nose. It cost me speed. Cost me some standing.

Then she stabbed me with the cross, pushing forward as hard as she could until my back was against the wall. I yelped as the silver began to burn. Grabbing at the end of the cross to pull it from my chest didn't help much because my hands burned as I touched it. But I was tenacious. I kept pulling.

When I saw the sharp points of her heels coming towards me, I managed to protect my face this time. Thankfully, her kicks with the pointy stilettos, punctured holes in my forearms rather than my forehead. But her purpose was not frustrated. She rolled to the floor and bounced to her feet before I could say *karate* and came at me again, chopsticks in hand, swinging with all her might. Grunting as she did so.

I left the cross alone. Let it burn. I had to worry about her other tactics.

Every instinct told me to move fast, get out her way. Dip. Weave. Block. Roll. Repeat. But I was slower. And in pain. Nevertheless, I couldn't let her catch me again. Just as I was about to make an offensive move to end the battle, she faked like she was aiming for my gut, twirled around instead and landed a power kick to the side of my head.

Fucking bitch.

While I staggered and struggled for balance, she jumped and kicked the other side of my head.

I vaguely saw a woman come in the bathroom and quickly rush back out. She'd either gone to get help or she was getting the hell out while she still could. She knew like I did, this fight was going to demolish the bathroom.

Looking at the doorway a split second too long had cost me. It gave Ming the opportunity to stab me twice in the chest with her lethal sticks. One second I was on my feet about to land a blow to her nose, the next minute I was flat on my back. That had been three stabs too many.

Why did the one Asian woman I know happen to be an undercover VET agent AND be skilled in martial arts? If there was a time to avoid the stereotype, this would have been it. But noooo. Not with my luck.

My ass was getting kicked now, but if I survived this, I'd enroll in somebody's tae kwon do class ASAP.

"Get up, Willow. Don't make it so easy on me. Even Ivan put up a bigger fight than this."

I froze. "What do you mean?"

"I'm talking about that golden-tongue mustang who used to fuck you, babe. Shame, what happened to him."

I leaped to my feet, moving in a blur. Punching her face, her chest, her stomach so hard, I hoped to drive a hole through 'til I touched the wall. She grunted this time from the force of my strikes. Intending to pound her into wishing she had never met me, I brought my fist back far and wide—something I was certain was probably a bad move, but realized too late. She dropped to the floor at the last second and I punched through the wall. It gave way as pain racked through my hand, up my elbow, to my chin. Was I rattled to the core? Yes. But I was angry more than anything. Ming had killed Ivan, dammit!

And she'd fucking called me *babe*!

She laughed again. "That's much better. So you vamps do have hearts." She wiped blood from her nose and mouth then spit out a few teeth. "You should have seen your face when I mentioned Ivan. It's not the first time I've seen fangs, but yours got looong. And your eyes…ooooo, man!"

Holding on to my arm, I asked, "Why? Why did you do it?"

She lightly touched the side of her jaw to test how bad it was. She'd need ibuprofen before bed tonight. "I planted a GPS tracker in your bag."

"The night you asked for a tampon?"

"Yes. I couldn't believe I got away with it." She shook her head, pleased with herself. "Anyway, the night I was planning to pay you a visit, Monroe and I had met in Hades's parking lot. Ivan eavesdropped on our conversation. When I went to your hotel room, he followed. And since I can't do that nifty memory-erasing trick you can, I had to kill—"

My arm and stab wounds and burning flesh be damned! Lurching towards her with super speed, I upward kicked her groin like she had balls, then grabbed her head and angled it. I sank my fangs in her neck and sucked. Intending to drain her dry. Making sure she would never speak another word about Ivan.

I didn't need her blood. Didn't want it either. But I didn't want her to have it anymore.

Several gulps in, I realized she tasted funny. Was she anemic? Was she pregnant? Was she on steroids? Max had mentioned you could tell certain things from the taste of blood, but I wouldn't know what to look for.

Suddenly, my stomach literally grumbled. It roared. Loud enough to hear.

I threw her from me and dropped to my knees, holding my gut like it was going to detach itself and run away. After recently experiencing food poisoning, I knew that was not what this was. It was something worse. Something supernatural. Something about her blood was drawing my energy from the outside in. Making my body suck itself dry. There was no heat, no burning. Just coolness. It overtook me like the coolness I'd experienced at my human death. Then it progressed to ice coldness. Frigidity. Constricting and shriveling me up as if from frostbite. From subzero freezer burn.

I looked down at my flesh tightening, wrinkling, shrinking. At this rate, I'd be a prune within minutes. I had five, ten minutes tops to do something about this. To reverse the effects of her toxic blood.

But I couldn't move. Couldn't do anything as my gut continued to protest, my body continued withering.

I stared at her with wild red eyes as whatever voodoo she'd put on me did me in. She took out a lighter and waited. Grinning.

"What are you?" I asked, surprised my lips could still move.

"Human. That is all."

"What's wrong with your blood then?" I said in a small

voice. Pretty soon, I wouldn't have a voice box.

"I've been hunting bloodsuckers for five years. That's longer than you've been a vampire. I'm not new to the game. You learn tricks of the trade. Keeps you alive longer." She stood slowly and walked closer to me. "I've been drinking holy water every day since my first vampire bite a couple years ago."

Awesome.

Not.

Where in the hell was everyone getting all this holy water? I'd been in church all my life, and I couldn't come up with a handful of people who could bless their dinner, let alone bless all this H^2O.

Just as she flipped open the igniter that would finally end my existence, Aaron burst through the door. He had tackled Ming and tightened his belt around her neck before I could scream *help*. Then I noticed the cold, calculating, barbaric way he was pulling the ends of the belt. The calm satisfaction in his eyes as he stared at me. One of his legs pinned both of hers down as she struggled to get away. Struggled to breathe.

She had stopped moving, stopped breathing, stopped living before I realized the beautiful Israeli who had saved the night was not Aaron.

Was not Remi.

"Who are you?" I whispered.

"I'm the one who has to do all the fucking clean up," he said in a Russian accent.

"You do all the killing you mean."

"You complaining?" he said as he got up and brushed his slacks off.

After going to the doorway and telling someone who was trying to enter that he had to help a drunk friend, he went to the sink. He stood in front of the mirror and began looping his belt, pulling his shirt cuffs down, straightening his collar, washing his hands. Then he grabbed some paper towels, ran water and soap over them and started cleaning Ming's blood off himself.

"I thought Remi had killed Aaron's kidnapper," I whispered. Barely.

"You thought wrong. I do the killing. He does the fucking."

He had kept Ming from turning me into kindling, but the holy water-blood tonic was still in full effect. Spending eternity as a dried fruit did not appeal to me.

"Thanks for your help, Vlad, but I need another favor. I need blood."

He turned to me and surveyed my condition, paying close attention to my bloody fangs. After pursing his lips like he had resolved an issue, he got down next to me and rolled up his sleeve. He offered his wrist even though I would have preferred the neck or femoral artery.

He held still as I fed. As I stared into the beautiful eyes of a heartless, soulless killer.

Let's just say, I wouldn't be captivating Vlad to put him on a schedule any time soon. Once a year or every six months wasn't good enough for him. We needed him to shift whenever he was good and ready. He was an essential alternate whether Remi and Aaron knew it yet or not. Especially if he was willing to kill to save us.

CHAPTER 44

His blood filled me out like air inflates a balloon. When I was full of his life force, I told him we needed to take Ming to Hades. There was a warm room in the basement that had her name on it.

He lay on the floor with his eyes closed, unmoving. For a moment I thought he had fallen asleep. Until I shook him and he opened his eyes to take in his surroundings.

The way his eyes lit up when he saw the splayed Ming on the floor told me Remi was occupying the body.

And he was getting turned on.

"I did it again?" he said.

I shrugged. If he thought he had killed Ming, maybe it was best for him to continue believing that just like he did about Aaron's kidnapper.

When he crawled over to Ming and began opening his fly, I thought I was going to barf all the blood I'd just had. Didn't think I had the gall to watch him fuck her corpse on the bathroom floor of a public place.

He leaned over and rubbed her blood all over her face like a kid in art class painting the sky.

I turned my head.

Until I heard the stream. That was odd. Not at all what I had expected to hear. So I turned back around and saw a scene I had not expected to see either.

Remi was standing over Ming pissing on her. "I hope you didn't think I was going to fuck the bitch who just tried to kill you," he said.

I smiled. Remi was my man. "If you like doing that so much, I think Franco may have a job for you in the Mozart room with other coprophilia and urolagnia freaks.

"You mean the shit and piss room."

"Exactly."

He shook his dick clean and zipped up his pants. "Naw. My girlfriend's a corpse. That's all I need."

We shared a warm, intimate smile, then planned our exit.

Remi carried her out like she was passed out drunk. He drove to Hades then waited in the lot as I took her body in the back door. After explaining Ming's connection with VET and Agent Monroe to Franco, I emptied the contents of my duffel bag until I found Ming's device as proof. Franco gladly tossed her body in the incinerator. No amount of holy water in her system kept her from turning to ash. Just the way Ivan had.

Very fitting, if you asked me.

Remi and I went back to his man cave and discussed our future. The one Saybree had mentioned. The one involving a formal ritual that would make Remi my day companion. We'd be bound 'til death, he as my protector, me as his. If I died the final death, he would too. If he died, I had an opportunity to turn him within three days of his death, though Remi was adamant he did not want to exercise that benefit.

As my compagnon de jour, he would still be human, subject to diseases and illnesses. Except with regular consumption of my blood, he'd heal faster, enjoy superhuman abilities, have a psychic bond with me, and age much slower. Eventually, we'd have to move because people would notice we didn't age at a normal rate.

These were all things he had to consider.

Which he did…and still wanted the position.

But the decision wasn't just up to him.

So in another attempt to talk to Aaron, I shifted him in during sex with Remi. I slowly revealed my fangs, my eyes. Gradually explained our bond, our physical and mental connection. Quickly ran through events of the previous few days and nights…and I did all this while I rode him like a pro. Right as he was coming, I explained what Remi wanted to commit to and asked what Aaron thought. "Yes! Yes! Yessss!" was the only answer he gave.

Great. That was the only one I wanted to hear.

As we lay in post-coital bliss, Aaron finally talked about his kidnapping. He had been vacationing in Mexico with his parents when all hell had broken loose. He, his ten-year-old sister, and mother had been left in the car with the windows rolled down while his dad had gotten out to ask for directions. His mother had been held at gunpoint and he and his sister were blindfolded and forced into the trunk of a car. They had been captured by pornographers who specialized in underage children.

It wasn't long before they were told to do the unthinkable. The unimaginable. Together. On camera. If they didn't they would be raped brutally by the kidnappers. Aaron just couldn't do it. Not to save himself or his sister. She had begged him to kill her. She knew the bad guys had planned to kill them both anyway since they hadn't worn masks. There was no way she and Aaron would get away with a description of the perpetrators.

At least, Aaron would be gentle, she reasoned. At least she would not be violated.

Aaron loved her so much, he couldn't do that either.

So he witnessed things done to her that he could not even repeat to me all these years later.

I didn't need details.

The last thing he remembered was holding her while she screamed for him to kill her, to take her out of her misery, to show kindness by delivering death. He had blanked out. When he came to, she was dead, in his arms, eyes frozen wide. He remembered the look of peace on her face, of gratefulness.

Their kidnappers, on the other hand, were outraged. He remembered a dull knife being held over his genitalia and them threatening to cut it off unless he had sex with his sister's corpse. He passed out again. This time, when he awakened he lay next to her on the cot with evidence that he had performed, with no memory of it.

Unfortunately, it had all been recorded.

The kidnappers had only intended to sell the tape on the black market to other perverts, until they saw Aaron's mother and father on the news pleading for their children's lives and safe returns. Being the opportunists they were, the kidnappers sent a copy of the video to Aaron's father demanding ransom in exchange for the footage not being released to the media.

Aaron had blanked out shortly after discovering the kidnappers' new and improved plan. He later learned from Remi's diary recount that Remi had stolen the same knife Aaron had been threatened with and stabbed one of the kidnappers one hundred, eleven times. He managed to escape and was reunited with his parents, who could not face him after seeing the video.

Interesting how Remi kept waking up after the killings thinking he had done them.

Sadly, Aaron's mother ended up in an asylum, where she died a year later. They never found his sister's body. Never gave her a proper burial.

It was the saddest tale I had ever heard. Due to no fault of his own—the day Aaron had been kidnapped, was the day he had lost his whole family. Lost his family and his grip on reality.

No wonder he was so mixed up.

Well, he had me. I accepted each sordid part of him. From the little boy stuck inside him who never made it out of that shithole to the necrophiliac who fucked the blowup doll in the closet because he couldn't find a steady, understanding girlfriend.

Until now.

So Aaron, Remi, Saybree, and I had a date. Next full moon, which was in two weeks, we'd have ourselves a vampire-human ritual.

CHAPTER 45

It was one week ago that I had fought Ming and watched her take a dirt nap at Vlad's hands...uh, belt. One week ago that I had fucked Remi and made love to Aaron. Learned Aaron's secrets and divulged mine. Made a pact with Aaron and Remi that involved an upcoming ritual that meant more to me than when I was turned by Max.

Oh, yeah—and it had been one week ago that I had moved in with them.

Until Franco eased up on his no-humans-allowed-in-Hades's-basement rule, I had to move out. Had to leave the safety of his sanctuary. No sense in bringing up the fact Cin had been in the basement. If I was to protect them and they were to protect me, and if we needed to share blood often, Remi, Aaron, and I needed to live closer to each other anyway. Plus, their place was niiice. They had even gotten a coffin though I had yet to use it. Since they had also installed wooden window shutters that operated by voice command, I slept in the bed with them.

Aaron had agreed to my plan to put all his alternates on a schedule, so I did. Except Remi and Vlad. Remi shifted randomly and I got the feeling I wouldn't see Vlad again until an execution was in order. Between Remi and Aaron shifting unpredictably, there was never a dull moment. Especially since Remi was trying to quit smoking. That made him extra twitchy.

Turns out, Franco, who appeared to know most everything, had not discerned Ming's true thoughts and purpose because as Saybree had said, there was a protective shield around the foot queen. She was not a supernatural being, but the holy water insulated her, blocking her spirit from supernatural interference. The force was with her, so to speak.

Good thing Aaron had been there. And good thing he had a personality more than capable of getting down and dirty because I wouldn't have been able to kill Ming. I would have wanted to, but only another human could. Aaron's human involvement was exactly what was necessary to break past the holy shield and send Ming back to her maker. Or wherever she was destined.

When Monroe had come in to question us about Ming's disappearance, he got no further than the front door. Franco and I had induced the help of Mr. Cash, in his official capacity as Congressman McNair, to get a restraining order against Monroe. His continuous harassment after we had disproved his theory that I was a vampire was illegal. According to the judge's injunction, Monroe would be arrested and subject to civil penalties if he came within five hundred feet of me.

There were no laws to protect vampires, but there were plenty to protect humans. Even humans who had been accused of being vampires. As long as the evidence proved otherwise. And since vampires could be tried, convicted, and executed out of court, when someone proved he or she was homo sapiens, no court order was necessary to cease a VET investigation. Case closed.

For now.

As long as security kept cameras out of Hades and I didn't stab myself again onstage, all should be well.

I had also gotten by to see my parents as I'd promised God while I was between consciousness, lying on the floor of the blood lab. I had gone alone, walked up to the house, and chickened out at the last minute. Peeping through the bay window into the well-lit dining room, I saw them all sitting at the table eating. My mom, dad, brothers, nieces, and nephews. They looked happy. So much so that I didn't want to intrude. Didn't feel like having one of those prodigal-daughter-returns-home-after-school-special moments. So I left.

At least I had fulfilled my promise. I had *seen* them.

What else?

Well, Punch and Fire got engaged and started planning a destination wedding. Hawaii, I think.

Guess who was not invited.

I just wished the best for them. Hope they lived happily ever after, blah, blah, blah. They better had considering how his being with her precluded him from being with a pack because wolves did not typically interrelate with dragons. He wouldn't even be able to have children unless he mated with another wolf. He was throwing it all away for her. Romantic…or stupid? Time would tell.

Thankfully, I'd gotten around to making my purchase from Amazon. I'd bought something that was going to teach Fire I was not her bitch the next time she got jealous and attacked me. I'd known for a while I was going to need an extinguisher for her, and if the internet had been working in the basement that day, our little spat would have had different results. But the past was the past…and I'd be ready next time. Hoped Punch would understand.

Speaking of werewolves…

Dario's blood lab was on the news. The break-in was being investigated. Not because anything was stolen, but because Dario had gone missing. Apparently, remnants of blood were found on the ceiling, though no body parts were reported. Made me wonder if Dario had eaten them and left to

283

grow body hair and long canines.

So much had happened within the past few weeks that I had been the first one to show up for Dr. Floyd's support group meeting. As usual, I did no talking, but it felt good listening to everyone else's sleep disorder issues. Reminder that it could always be worse.

After the meeting, Dr. Floyd had spoken to me about my blood results again. In his smart British accent, he told me my blood was ancient, dating back to old Germany. And just as I thought he was about to tell me he had reported me to VET, he said he would help me find a cure for narcolepsy…and vampirism, if I wanted.

Something to think about, I guess.

I had also seen Ivan a few times. We went for long walks through the cemetery and he watched me perform at Hades a few times. I wanted him to get whatever closure he needed in order to pass on to the other side. It just didn't seem to be working.

When I asked Franco about it, he said it may take time, but not to worry. Once I died the final death, Ivan would move on to his version of the final death too.

Ha ha.

So now I was meandering around Hades's Graveyard room, chatting with patrons, encouraging them to spend more money on booze and aphrodisiacs…and prophylactics. Suddenly, I started choking, gagging. Not wanting to gross anyone out, I ran to the bathroom and took a long look at myself in the mirror. I was no longer gagging and nothing seemed amiss. Making my way out again, I stopped halfway to the door. My body was buzzing, vibrating low and then more intensely until I was trembling like Hades was in the middle of a California earthquake. What the…

My vision blurred. My mouth went dry.

Then I smelled sweet vanilla.

No way.

I took off fast…down the hall, out the back door, out into the lot, into the trees…

But there was no outrunning it.

No outrunning him. I just needed to get him away from Hades. Away from humans. Away from my friends.

I finally dropped to my knees and rolled around in the damp earth.

"No, no, no. Go away!" I said in the darkness.

I came for you Willow, he said from inside my head.

It was just a whisper, but it made my whole body tremble as if he was right next to me. And then I knew he was.

Buzz, buzz, buzz. The buzzing of mosquitoes got louder as he formed on the earth next to me. In the flesh. Mercedez formed next to him.

I could see nothing but her eyes and teeth as she grinned. Maximilian the Great on the other hand, I could see clearly since his Celtic skin glowed in the moonlight. Even the twinkling stars kissed his blond hair.

"Aren't you glad to see me?" he whispered.

"Not really."

"Is that any way to greet your maistre after I've come from such a long way to see you?"

"No. I guess not. If you would have given notice, I could have been more prepared."

His laughter rumbled through the woods. Then in his most menacing Max way, he said, "Well, I'm here now. And don't worry. I won't be leaving without you."

Chilled me to the core.

I didn't know what I was going to do about Remi and Aaron. Didn't know how I was going to continue working at Hades. Didn't know how I would keep Max away from everyone I cared about, including myself.

How in the hell could I keep him happy enough to not punish me while I strategized how to get my heart from him?

'Cause as ominous as it was to have Max here in the flesh,

it would be much easier to figure out how to find the first thing I needed to gain my freedom. I could find it, steal it, and finally release myself from this unwanted bond.

In that regard, Max had come to visit right in the nick of time.

~~~~v—v~~~~

Thank you for reading SLEEPY WILLOW'S BONDED SOUL (The Narcoleptic Vampire Series Vol. 1). Consider writing an honest review, telling your friends, and checking out more of Dicey Grenor's books. They are for readers who do not offend easily and enjoy reading unpredictable plots with unique, diverse characters.

www.diceygrenorbooks.com

Books by Dicey Grenor

The Narcoleptic Vampire Series reading order:

Sleepy Willow's Bonded Soul (Vol. 1)
Sleepy Willow's Heartless Soul (Vol. 2)
Sleepy Willow's Loosed Soul (Vol. 3)
Zeek's Loving Thorn (Vol. 3.1)
Wolf's Fire (Vol. 3.2)
Along Came a Killer (Vol. 3.3 or standalone)
Sleepy Willow's Redeemed Soul (Vol. 4) **coming 2016**

How to Have a Perfect Marriage (Dark Comedy Novelette)

Shameful (Taboo Erotic Romance)

Best Friends, Fantasy Lovers (Rock-n-Roll Erotic Romance)

SLEEPY WILLOW'S HEARTLESS SOUL

The Narcoleptic Vampire Series Vol. 2

DICEY GRENOR

Chapter 1

Buzz, buzz, buzz. Mosquitoes flew from everywhere with their irritating noises and bloodsucking proboscises. Very fitting in a way, since Maximilian the great maistre vampire was controlling them. Guiding them. In my direction.

He was pissed and he had every right to be, considering he'd been demanding I return to the clan. He'd also forbidden me to give my blood to Remi, but I hadn't listened to that either. I'd been feeding Remi my blood and feeding from his and fucking him every chance I got. Bonding myself to a human. So I deserved whatever punishment my maistre was here to dole out.

Buuuuuzzzzzz.

But those damn insects were the worst.

Saybree had been right about Max being able to do more than change his form to mist. I'd seen him do pretty disgusting things with leeches. Now, I was beginning to wonder if he could control all bloodsucking creatures. Scary thought. Although after over two thousand years of existence, he should have a few more tricks than say…me, someone who'd only been turned a few years.

"Willow, you are coming back with me right now," Max said in his authoritative I-dare-you-to-fuck-with-me voice.

Mosquitoes rushed me in swarms, entering my nose, eyes, ears, and mouth. Filling my stomach and chest cavity. They were everywhere at once. Lifting me upwards from the inside out. Steering my body towards Max as he lay on cemetery dirt next to me. He rose as I rose, his arms extended like we were long-time loves finally reuniting.

I wanted to barf, but I couldn't move. Not of my own volition.

Mercedez, the vampire clan human ~~whore~~ willing blood donor, who lay on the other side of him, jumped to her feet to get away from me as I slammed into Max. Into the arms I'd been avoiding for the past couple of years.

Max grinned, his eyes changing from emerald to glowing neon green, as he wrapped his Celtic arms around me like I was a prize he'd won.

"It is so good to finally have you back, my love. This time, I will never let you go," he said as we continued to levitate. As the mosquitoes continued buzzing. As the last of my freedom was snatched from me.

Mercedez walked towards us as a large green and black swirling wormhole opened a few feet away. It was Max's preferred mode of transportation. And it was here to transport us back to the clan house. Back to where all the vampires in Max's bloodline lived. Where hundreds of his brides were. Away from my friends, my job, my lovers…my independence.

Buzz. Buzz. Buuuuuuuzzzzzzzz.

Knowing it was no use didn't stop me from fighting back against Max. The closer we got to the hole, the more I

289

struggled in his grasp. First, it was only in my mind. Particularly since the mosquitoes had taken over my body. But I was too strong-willed. Too focused on resisting. My body had no choice but to respond. Then I tried kicking him where it counted and missed. I tried head-butting him and missed. None of it was any use because he could read my mind. Knowing what I was going to do before I did it gave him the advantage.

Mercedez stood next to us, her feet firmly planted on the ground while Max and I were floating in the air. Getting nearer to the hole. "Stop fighting, Willow. Don't make him hurt you," she said.

I would have yelled for help if not for the mouthful of insects. Or maybe told her to shut the fuck up. Or to take her ass on through the hole. Or moisturize her damn 'fro. But there was no sense taking my anger out on her. She'd only been looking out for me, and she'd be the first to offer her blood once we made it back to the house.

Just as we were about to go through the hole that would separate me from all that was important in my undead existence, time stood still. Literally. The three of us froze. All movement and sounds ceased, even buzzing from the mosquitoes. Remembering one other moment when the atmosphere had been manipulated in the same way, I felt great joy. Help was here.

"Evening, Maximilian," said Franco in his sexy Spanish accent, as he leaned against a tree directly behind Mercedez.

I felt relieved. He wouldn't let Max take me back.

"This has nothing to do with you, demon."

I was shocked Max was able to talk, but it got worse. He was able to move too. In fact, after removing his arms from around me, he effortlessly lowered himself to the ground. Then he turned to face Franco.

Franco didn't seem surprised at all. "Al contrario. You appear to be taking my employee back to your clan, and I still need her to work."

Mercedez and I were still frozen while tension between Franco and my maistre grew.

"Hire someone else," Max said coldly.

Franco shook his head. "Ever since the extermination order, it's hard to find a vampire to blend in *and* please my necrophilia clientele." He stood up straight, his long dark ponytail blowing in the wind. Many indescribable tattoos were visible since he was shirtless, wearing only tight black leather pants and pointy toe boots. "Besides, she agreed to work at Hades until the end of the fiscal year. And I'm afraid she's still under contract."

"You are aware she belongs to me and had no business making any such agreement."

"Nevertheless, I don't agree to release her from it. I know you're a man of your word. You will see to it that she remains a woman of hers."

It felt very 1950ish that these two men were deciding my fate without my input, however, I was grateful to Franco for his interference. He knew how badly I wanted to stay. How badly I wanted my freedom.

"I will buy her out of the contract. Name your price," Max said matter-of-factly, while running a hand through his short blond curls.

Well, this was getting interesting, considering Franco was making this shit up. There was no contract.

Franco clicked his tongue three times and walked closer to Max, until they were face-to-face, eyeball-to-eyeball. "You know I only make deals in exchange for souls. And since you don't have one…" He left the sentence hanging, raising his arms outward, which apparently broke whatever demon magic that had Mercedez and me frozen like popsicles. My insect-infested body fell to the ground as Mercedez turned around to face the two oldest men I'd ever known.

"Perhaps there is something else I can offer…or some*one*

else. You may take another of my brides in her stead. There is one in need of banishment."

Another bride in my place? He couldn't be serious. We were *all* his property. His trophies. What could she have done that was worse than me bonding with Remi and refusing to return? I'd bet anything he was referring to Mayhem. Though not as rebellious as I was, she embodied her name fully, and liked to stir it up.

Franco shook his head again and rubbed his chin. "Not until Willow has satisfied the terms of our agreement. Then you can send whomever you wish."

Suddenly, the mosquitoes disappeared. Tension in the air eased. And as the glow in Max's eyes diminished, I had hope. Franco had a comeback for everything. He had the most sensible response for each of Max's suggestions. At this rate, Max and Mercedez would leave the way they came—as a duo.

"How much longer?" Max said. "I risked a lot to be here."

"Surely, you can wait another few months, my friend. Especially after years of putting up with her insolence."

Hey, wait a minute…

Max nodded. "She has been that. Believe me, she will be punished."

I gulped. At least, Franco had stalled whatever hell Max had waiting for me. With Max gone, I wouldn't have to worry about—

"Perhaps I can offer you sanctuary in the meantime," Franco said. "For as long as you want. Tonight. A week. The duration of her contract…"

What?! Noooo! Though screaming inwardly, I remained silent, trusting Franco to know what he was doing.

Max's eyebrows raised skyward. "Sanctuary?"

"Yes. In the basement of Hades. I've been preparing a safe haven for supernaturals to peaceably coexist. A place for us to band together against humans in preparation for the revolution. We could use your power." He glanced at me.

"Plus, you will be able to watch Willow more closely since she's been staying there."

I couldn't believe it. First, Franco *knew* I'd moved in with Remi and Aaron and had no intention of moving back into the basement. I'd been shielding my thoughts from Max so he wouldn't know. Secondly, why the fuck would Franco encourage Max to stay at Hades to watch me!

Fury turned my eyes to glowing red and elongated my fangs before I even knew it was happening. But just like it was no use fighting Max, there would be no winning against Franco. Then again—forget winning. Once my vampire instincts took over, I had no choice but to react. It was a matter of biology. And my vampire biology, my nature, had me fuming for an opportunity to strike Franco right across his pretty, tanned, dimpled-chinned face.

Franco was supposed to look out for me, which meant sending Max's evil ass away. Not inviting him over for tea. He *knew* the kind of damage Max could inflict on Houston residents, on my lover, on ME while he was here. Why ask him to stay? What the fuck!

Maybe Max would decline. It was too risky, after all. He had been a high-profile celebrity type vampire before the Human Preservation Act made vampirism illegal. If anyone recognized him while he was here, the Vampire Extermination Team (VET) would be on his ass to execute him. Which would kill his whole clan, including me. Surely, he knew staying was not an option.

And like nails scratching down a chalkboard, so were Max's next words. "Well, old friend. Thanks for the invitation. I would be happy to stay a while."

ABOUT DICEY GRENOR

Wife to my best friend and biggest supporter.
Mother of two handfuls.
Attorney in Houston, Texas.
Author of sexy, wild, daring and risky books.

Let's keep in touch:

www.Diceygrenorbooks.com

www.facebook.com/DiceyGrenor

www.diceyblog.wordpress.com

www.goodreads.com/DiceyGrenor

www.google.com/+DiceyGrenor

Twitter @DiceyGrenor

Instagram @DiceyGrenor

Made in the USA
San Bernardino, CA
14 May 2016